Fishing with God

Chris Gordon
Shane Hutchison

Fishing with God
Copyright © 2015 by GoHu Books (GoHu, LLC)

ISBN-10: 0-9971478-1-4
ISBN-13: 978-0-9971478-1-0

Created in USA by GoHu Books (www.GoHuBooks.com)

Dedication

This book is dedicated my sister Christine who has left us early in life leaving behind a legacy of five children. To all of my parents, my family, all those who have befriended me in life to this point and to all whom I have experienced life with and through. To all who seek continually to understand life through challenges, experience, choice, and forgiveness. To all who fish with god whomever their god may be.

-- Shane Hutchison

This book is dedicated to, my brother Salaam, my grandmother, my uncle and aunts, whom, have gone home to be with the lord. To my mother and father, who have given me 48 years of marriage and family, strength and resilience. To my brothers, whom have been the segments of, the body of our family. To my Michelle Gilgan who, with love and care, forgiveness and understanding, guided and supported me through my most poignant period of growth and life to date. To my Willow, who's miracle birth and beautiful life, is the lighthouse that's keeps my ship from wrecking upon the rocky shores of this world and of course all those who are fishing with god.

-- Chris Gordon

Introduction

Fishing with God is a book that is cathartic, it's an alchemist style written book. It delves into the deepest longings of the human soul. To solve pain, anguish and questions beyond our grasp, those questions you try to grasp, but need help in solving, so you get on the bus and move forward to the answers. Ordin's journey speaks to all of us and moves us towards the answers one may not want to hear, but need to for our self-preservation. It's well written and as a reader you will identify with one or two or five of the characters written. Chris Gordon and Shane Hutchison have outdone themselves on writing this spiritual journey.

-- *Darcy Robinson*

CHAPTER ONE
"Other"

He isn't black, he isn't white, not Latino, not Asian. "Other," he thought with a chuckle. "I am an other," he said out loud. "Other than what? Other than black, Asian, Latino, and white or other than human? Other than what?" He sat in the same place he had every Saturday for the last seventeen years. A boat, a pole, drink, some bait, some music, and when he felt like it, silence; no sound, sometimes no thoughts, just silence. To the right, some spruce trees, standing like giant sentries; guards of a private sanctuary for hundreds of years; dark green, brown undertones, limbs like muscular arms. To his left, a weeping willow, not naturally grown in this region, but rather seemingly placed here with the feeling "there is a need for tears here," as if someone thought this place is so beautiful I could cry. Pinks and blue hues decorated the landscape of his lake. "His lake." He liked the sound of that. "Here is the 'other' on his lake."

CHAPTER TWO
Fast Enough

"Fast enough for me," the more decorated of the two bellowed when the speedometer reached seventy-five. "Heck no! This ain't fast enough for me. If I am going to be working on a Saturday, then we're breaking some rules, so go faster," Paul, the rookie trainee thought before saying, "Damn, you're good!" maybe too sarcastically to pass for sincere. "Shit," he thought, "Better not to lose this job on my first assignment. They put me with Bubba, the misplaced redneck. Just play it cool, nab our man, forget about right and wrong, get to next week, change partners and voila, you've made it. Then it's a hop, skip, and a jump to detective, a fifteen-year hop, skip, and jump, but a hop, skip and a jump nonetheless." Paul's lips parted at the corners slightly.

"What the hell are you thinking pup!? I can always tell when a rookie is thinking," Detective Graves said. "Nothing," was what Paul said what he thought was. "Oh, just thinking how you woke me up at six thirty in the morning on a Saturday to take an eighteen-hour drive to catch, or should I say, persecute an innocent man for a twenty-two-year-old crime, so you can glorify your overweight ego. Oh, and how I hate when you call me pup." "Nothing at all sir." "Good! Don't, just drive, rookies who think are dangerous. They believe that they can save the world. They believe in good guys and bad guys. Heck, they even believe in justice. Yeah, thinking pups are dangerous, get a man hurt is what they do, or let a perp get away. Worse, they get a good man killed. Son, there is no justice, just us. Drive faster, but be careful pup."

CHAPTER THREE
Karen

It had been twenty-four hours since Karen put the telephone down after she saw the picture after she had made the decision based on a conclusion she had drawn twenty-four hours before the call as she reported to the man on the other end of the telephone. "Graves was his name," she thought, "J. H. Graves, senior detective San Francisco P.D." She recounted what she said, "Yes, I'm quite sure he is the one I saw on the show. I watch it every week, and I always knew someday I would see one of these "Cold Case Killers," but I never thought one would live so close to me. I mean he seems so quiet and peaceful, but then again, don't they all." She sat there in her stained robe, short of breath as always, coffee cup to her lips, eyes blazing. She felt prettier and more important than she had in years.

Karen Miller was a high school dropout whose only furtherance towards her collegiate career was a weekend on campus that turned out to be the beginning and end of her attempt at higher learning. She was senior prom queen the year before. Before her father had beat her mother so senseless that when he went to work the next day the whole family; mother, two daughters, three brothers and the dog "Crumbs", all left in the family car. The entire family, except for the father of course. Now Karen was a thirty-seven-year-old mother of none. One abortion and two miscarriages had seen to that. She liked to think of herself as a banker, though she was only a teller at the local check cashing franchise. She wore her robe most of the time when she was home and most of the time she was home alone Several boyfriends of hers had found her, shall we say.... abrasive.

Today she sat with her hair done, her best dress on, and even her makeup, which she rarely wore, was applied. Karen Miller sat on the couch pretty as ever, beaming. "Today I'll be on TV. Today fifteen minutes won't be enough." Detective Graves had promised that should her lead "pan out" and they captured their "perp," she kept saying that word, "perp" it sounded so dangerous to her, should they apprehend their "perp" she would be on 'Cold Case Killers.' Karen could hardly wait. Today was the day.

CHAPTER FOUR
Ordin (the "Other")

The pole jerked, the boat rocked. Something was happening, something big. Ordin tensed himself. He put his foot against the port, stuck his arm out for balance and pulled. "Whoa! This has got to be somebody's daddy! He is a tough one alright." Ordin pulled again, this time the pulling jogged his memory. Suddenly, as he was pulling the butt of a long barrel shotgun, there was an uneasy smile on his face. "Gimmie the damn gun, you fool." The nervous sneer on the other side of the gun jerked the barrel and laughed, "It's my gun, and I'll shoot the varmint." The pulling continued. Ordin gave one last tug, a loud boom like thunder filled the air. The tourist with the camera instantly turned as his flash went off, capturing the moment. In time, this moment would cost three men their lives, in three different ways.

A splash of water on his face yanked Ordin back into the present. The sweat was heavy on his brow, not from his struggle with his day's prize, but from the sudden shock of the flashback, of which he had been experiencing a strong re-occurrence after several years for several weeks now. It had him weary in mind and cold in his body. Ordin dropped the pole. Underwater, the fish wiggled from the hook that suspended it on the verge of life and death and swam away.

CHAPTER FIVE
Paul's Daughter

"Daddy! Daddy! Are we going today? You said we were going today."

"Willow, sugarplum, I wanted to rest today, but you're right I told you we were going today. How about this, you get your mother and ask her if she minds if we go down to the river, just the two of us, okay?"

"Oh, thank you daddy, you're the best."

"I love this river daddy, it reminds me of grandpa and how he would tell me stories. Is it true that there's a fish here as big as me, huh?"

"Well, sometimes grandpa stretches the truth… but he just loves to see you smile."

"You know what I heard daddy? I heard that cops are the people who shoot everybody. You said that you were a good guy?"

"Who told you that and who said we were called cops. We're policemen, and we don't shoot everybody. We don't hurt people unless we absolutely have to. I especially don't like hurting people. Now, who's been telling you this stuff?"

"Jimmy Halbert. He said he saw it on TV, the 'Code Cases.' He said it's a show where people in black and white shoot all these bad guys and…"

"Whoa! Whoa! Hold it right there, sprite! I don't know why Jimmy's parents let him watch junk TV like that, but that is not real, sweetie. If you ask me, there is far too much of that stuff on TV these days. There's no way to let you kids watch TV anymore without seeing so much violence and people hurting people. Now enough of that. Let's talk about something nice and enjoy our fishing. This is supposed to be about a quiet appreciation of God's beauty, just like grandpa and I used to do."

"Hey, you know what daddy? Your boss, Mr. Gaves, kind of looks like grandpa did in those pictures, huh?"

"It's Graves honey, and yes I guess. Okay, it's fishing time."

"Dad, can we go to the park tomorrow? It's Saturday tomorrow, and they bring the pony there for rides."

"Okay, sure sugarplum. I have another day off tomorrow so we'll see."

CHAPTER SIX
Karen - "Cuddly and Simple"

"You're fat and stupid!" exclaimed an exasperated man in his 40s.

"I am not, and you're mean, mean, mean!" Sure, Karen could lose some weight, and you could say she was a little less than average when it came to intelligence, but she was far from being "fat and stupid." She was just "cuddly and simple," or at least that's how she thought of herself.

"You never do anything right, and you say the wrong things all the time."

"I do not Ted, I do not. I do a lot of things right. I have never even made a mistake at work."

"You call what you do work? You stand behind a counter and cash checks for people who either don't belong in this country or can't manage their lives well enough to have a bank account." Karen began to cry. "Karen sweetie, listen, I'm sorry I yelled, but I'm having a hard time these days at my own work, and the pressure of this relationship is too much. I just need some time."

With that sentence, Theodore Alphons Eckard was out of the door. It had been more than three months since he'd called and Karen figured he just needed time, just like Mike Allan, Paul Ellerd, Sam Waterford, and even the awful experiment with Cynthia Rudd. Karen Miller fantasized sitting in her robe, her pretty clothes underneath, and her makeup on. All of them would no longer "need more time," she thought as she sat anticipating her call from Detective Graves. Then they would all see her on "Cold Case Killers" and then they would want her, all of them, even Cynthia Rudd. Karen was optimistic.

CHAPTER SEVEN
Karen and Ordin

Karen first met Ordin Arlin Aire after he had been living next to her for three weeks. She assumed he was both French and black (though terribly light skinned) from the way he pronounced his name. Karen had wandered over, feigning interest in the objects Ordin seemed to be placing at the curb for local sanitation pick up. They made fast friends, though Ordin thought the woman was a bit imposing sometimes. Karen had made a habit of inviting herself over for late lunch on the weekends. She would bring the same pumpkin bread, even though Ordin or "Ordy" as she took to calling him... the word reminded her of the word orgy, which reminded her of her college visiting days. (Karen had been the subject of several of these experiences, and she liked to think of herself as experimental. This is how she accounted for the awful experiment with Cynthia Rudd). Ordy had told her several times he was not particularly fond of pumpkin bread. Nevertheless, Karen dutifully stormed Ordy's back porch every Saturday, which is where she first saw the photograph of Ordin with the gun and the man in the air with an expression that was half smile, half puzzlement.

Ordin had laid this particular photograph along with several others he intended to burn on his back porch that Saturday. It was time to move on with his life, not so much flee as to casually walk away from the ghosts of his past.

CHAPTER EIGHT
Ponies and Sassin'

"Tell me again why I had to disappoint my little girl on Saturday? We were supposed to go to the park for pony rides." Paul was impatient.

Detective Graves responded, seemingly unaware of the impatient tone. "Ha, ponies. Pup, ponies are for pansies. You gonna make that little slugger of yours a pansy with junk like that. Ha, ponies. Boy, I remember my daddy tried to take me to some girly pony ride. I kicked like a soccer player on fire. I did. No way, I said, that's for girls is what I tell him."

"Sir…"

"Yep, my momma, God rest her soul, used to say I was a bottle of lighting. And don't call me sir, pup. That's my daddy's title, and I don't want it no sir, I don't. Heh, that's funny. I just told you not to call me sir and there I go calling you sir. See that, Pup? That's instinct. A lot of fellas with less years wouldn't have caught that, but I did. So what was it you were asking me, pup?"

Paul's brain screamed "how the hell did a troglodyte like you ever ascend to a leadership role, or was that a testament to just how desperate the force is for people that you even made the first cut. And damn it stop calling me pup." However, Paul's mouth uttered, "I was asking you to explain more clearly exactly what we are doing on a Saturday morning when I was supposed to be taking my child, which is a girl by the way, to the park for pony rides."

"Don't you sass me pup, with all that New York talk, Pup. I know your kind. You think your smart with your college, but college can't teach you how to hold a man at bay when he's got a

44 mag on your face, and he's all doped up with the PCP and sweating like a pig, can they? Can they?"

"No, I suppose not. I did not infer that college had anything to do with the force. I'd just like to know what's going on."

"I dun told you not to sass me! Anyway, if you must know, we are heading east about 18 hours to meet some crazy cooped up goon who says she has a tip on one of those cold case murders that have been on TV lately. And I'll be damned if that show ain't costing every station around this country a crap load of man hours chasing cold case tipster tips. That's what they done taken to calling those bored housewives and wackos that watch that show. Well, were heading to meet one of 'em. Says she saw this guy on the show and has proof he's the one they're looking for. Don't ask me how she got my name. Apparently, the murder they were showing happened some years back up in San Fran's west side district, so they piped her over to me seeing as how that's my district now and I was in on it back then."

"You mean to tell me we're chasing some ghost of a story from some glory hound with a TV? Do you think that's why the force has the bad rep and all, putting people on the chopping block on a hunch, like some late night TV paperback gun show dick?"

"Now don't strain yourself, pup. I don't make the decisions. I leave that to the brass. I just do what I'm told. Besides, someday I'll be brass and get a shot at making some of those calls myself, so if this hunch as you call it pans out and I get myself this perp, I'll be one step closer to being brass. Then I can leave the grunt work to pups like you. Yes sir, a big office, fat salary, maybe even a new pretty wife. So sit back and enjoy the ride, pup. You can take the little one for donkey rides some other time."

CHAPTER NINE
Ordin – The Cell

"Get in that cell, nigger!" The words hit him like a gunshot. Ordin put his hands to his ears. The sounds of wails cascaded over him as if he was still there, while he rocked back and forth in the boat. How? How could I be here again? They let me go. They understood. They knew it was an accident. How could this be real? That's it, it's not real, it's another daymare. Daymares are what Ordin had begun to call the terrible flashes of memory that hit him almost always at first, but now only every once in a while, when he became troubled or had a bad feeling.

That's all, it's a daymare, and all I have to do is breathe. The air is coming. I'm okay, the air is coming. Ugh! The rap of the guard's nightstick cracked his rib. He could hardly breathe. Ugh! The breaking of his other rib made him feel as if he would suffocate. "The air is coming, the air is coming," Ordin began to say out loud now. Tears mixed with the sweat that was pouring down his face. His body shook so hard the sweat leaped off his face into the water. A fish nibbled at the strange hurt fish remaining still, unmoving in front of it. Suddenly, the wounded fish sprang to life and jerked away out of the water. Ordin stood. His pole fell to the floor of the boat, which was now rocking violently. Ordin could not sit still. "How many times!?" he screamed. And then it happened, just like it had every time before and it was over just as suddenly as it had begun. The rush of fear and fury was gone, the tears were gone, the pain was over. Ordin sat down.

CHAPTER TEN
Karen – Call to Cold Case Tipsters

She had just one glass of wine; Karen was not a heavy drinker. She liked to have a little something now and then. Nevertheless, Karen found that these days there were more nows and thens. In fact, Karen had had a few the day she made the phone call to the "Cold Case Tipsters" hotline. "Just for kicks," she thought. "I need some excitement. Karen Miller is a fun person; I just need to get kick started." She was talking out loud now, and if truth be told, Karen was slurring her speech. It was a night like this when Karen first tuned into 'Cold Case Killers' for the first time. "Wow," she thought, "if I could find one of these creeps, it would be so exciting." Tonight it was just about her and her loneliness. The fact was, she was desperately lonely and didn't like her life all that much.

She had had an unpleasant conversation with her mother earlier on the telephone. That had ended in shouting as it always did, except this time Karen felt empowered. "Well, I don't care what you say because I'm going to be on TV and everyone will respect me. Even you mother, even you will finally see that I'm worth something. I was Senior Prom Queen. I was pretty and smart." Stunned by her sudden burst of exuberance, Karen's mother whispered a sentence that caused Karen to become ghostly white. Karen gently put the telephone down, walked stiff-necked into the kitchen, opened the cabinet, and took down the finest bottle of wine she had (the one she was saving for the night her boyfriend, whoever he would be, proposed to her). She had considered champagne, but the bubbles made her feel like New Year's Eve, and the last New Year's Eve she had spent had been with Cynthia Rudd during the awful experiment. Karen opened the bottle, poured herself a large glass, and drank until she had forgotten the words her mother spat. How could she? Of course, it was not true, how could it be? No one pays the principal to elect someone prom queen. It's not real. Karen was crying now. She had always felt a "farawayness" from her mother, but this, this took the cake. Her mother had gone too far and had hurt her too much. Karen made up her mind that she would write a letter telling her mother why she would never speak to her again. And when she was on TV when everyone could see her, they would ask about her life, and she would say her mother had died an awful death. Then everyone would love her even more. Being on 'Cold Case Killers' would make her famous. There was no other way.

CHAPTER ELEVEN
Cold Case Killers

Paul really didn't understand exactly what was supposed to happen when they got to where they were going. But he was sure the experience would be unforgettable. All he could come up with was that he and Detective Graves were headed eighteen hours out of town to track down a person whom he had received a tip about who had allegedly committed a murder some twenty-two years before, the likes of which had gone unsolved. The idea was that Detective Graves would follow up this tip which came via a tip hotline that was part of a television show called 'Cold Case Killers.' A cold case is a case that had gone unsolved for twenty years, remaining open, if not dormant, with the hope that one day new evidence would turn up and provide law enforcement with the missing pieces to the puzzle enabling them to finally solve the enigma that lingered. Detective Graves had reason to believe he would find his new puzzle pieces eighteen hours away via this tipster from the 'Cold Case Killers' tipster's hotline. However, Paul had his suspicions, both about the program and the tipster's motives, not to mention Detective Grave's motivation for wanting to take this trek with a trainee.

First of all, the tipsters were called "Cold Case Tipsters" and were encouraged to identify people they believed looked like someone that had been profiled on the program. The series ran new episodes on Thursday, but subsequently ran reruns and update specials almost every night. The program also offered a two-tier reward: the first part was being able to be live on the show, and the second was a $10,000 reward. This was the basis of Paul's suspicion that the tipsters were less interested in accurately identifying a potential suspect than they were with dreaming about the potential glory they would obtain from being on the show as well as the cash reward. Paul also speculated that most of the audience was made up of overweight Middle-American women, who lacked a certain sense of adventure in their everyday lives.

Also, Paul felt Detective Graves harbored serious delusions of grandeur about the chief of police. Paul thought it would be a sorry day when a pig-headed redneck was elected chief of police for S.F.P.D., but then again, he knew that people everywhere were the same in at least one respect, be they overweight middle Americans or bi-costal Bohemians. Paul knew that in modern society that perception becomes reality. And if Graves could find a way to be perceived as an ace detective and worthy leader who never gave up, he would be taken as just that. And in San Francisco, voters went for anything that shined clean, sincere, and upright.

CHAPTER TWELVE
Paul

Paul grew up on Long Island, Babylon, New York. His father was a drug and alcohol counselor, his mother a teacher of mentally handicapped children and adults. Paul had known from an early age that he, like his parents, and even some of his brothers, wanted to help people. There was something about the way people responded when they knew or came to an understanding that someone could make it (whatever their respective it's) people are soothed to know someone could make it better. He loved the way their faces changed from contorted masses of self-doubt and worry to natural bright smiles of relief. Still, he had to work to overcome the feeling of embraced humility he felt when those he helped in some way voiced their appreciation. He never liked the gushing or welling up with tears in the eyes. His parents had taught him not to expect credit or reward for doing the ordinary. In fact, they had told him, "We are commanded by God to serve others and help in any way we can, so these things we are supposed to do deserve no special reward. It is when we go up and above the ordinary that we are acting out of even greater nobility. And nobility, they had explained, was not what made you better than anyone else, it is what makes you better than what you were the day before. Paul had become so used to the way his parents treated people that he made the mistake, more than once, of expecting others to behave the way he did in any given situation.

Paul never thought he would join the police force. For the most part, he had always felt about police officers the way most people do: they were all overbearing, corrupt, macho pigs. It was perhaps the worst of Paul's virtues that led him to become a police officer. Paul had always been given to a stubborn ride. When he felt he was right, he was right. During an extended argument with one of his collegiate cohorts, Paul had made the point that there are people like themselves who join the force to help others. Paul's group of friends then challenged him saying, "If that were true, why hadn't anyone in their college including him join?" Paul argued that theoretically, he would join the "force." His friend then challenged him anew, "Then theoretically join, just to take the test." Paul joined "just to take the test." When he scored higher than he had believed he would, Paul reached the conclusion and determined to do some good someplace where a good guy was really needed.

His first week out of the academy Paul was involved in a search and rescue of a teenage biker. His second week he had helped a woman give birth at a park. Paul had found a spot in between the TV super cops and the jaded patrolmen he had come into contact with before his time on the force. It wasn't until Paul had been on the force for two years and looking forward to being a rookie on the detective squad that he began to see the "other" side of the force. It was then that Paul began to understand that there are two forces: the spirit and idea of the force, and the reality of the force.

CHAPTER THIRTEEN
Ordin and Peter – Fishing with God

As he docked his boat and began his walk to his car, Ordin felt a weariness, a world-weary feeling in his legs, his eye, and especially his soul. How long would his daymares persist and what would he have to do to end them? He had made the decision a few weeks ago to throw away all the photographs that reminded him of that painful period, especially the photo of Peter Draingold.

Peter and Ordin had gone hunting in Marigold State Park. Peter had been particularly successful that day and Ordin and he were wrapping up. Remembering a wager they had made, Ordin realized he was one fowl short of his friend. When he spotted a flock, he picked up the shotgun and Peter grabbed it with the notion of keeping himself the winner of the bet. What ensued became more than a nightmare for all involved. For Peter, it took his life in a blaze of light that he never felt. For Ordin, the misunderstanding, the accusations, the incarceration, and the mistreatment, had all sucked what he thought was the last of his soul away. For Laurence Lemn seeing what he saw, thinking what he thought, a strange thing happened, the thing that happens with everyone. There's a moment that time makes when a picture or a thought is burned into your mind, your memory, your perception. It takes a moment to imprint, yet a lifetime to undo, and sometimes we can never undo that moment. For Laurence, that moment was the second, which seemed like an eternity, it took to turn an autobahn society photo hunt into the capturing of death on film.

Ordin couldn't help Peter anymore. He could do little to help Laurence change or erase the perception of what happened. As for himself, he could make a decision to forgive himself and walk away from the time and place of his torment. He could let it go, just let it all go. Moving to this location, finding this lake, and attempting to live with faith was his walking away, and it was almost enough, it was almost like fishing with God.

CHAPTER FOURTEEN
Detective Graves

S.F.P.D. (San Francisco) – 20 years ago.

"Graves! Graves, get your miserable, fat, red, carcass in here!"

"Yes, sir! Right away, sir," stammered a young Graves.

"Graves, what the hell is going on with this Aire case? Did this guy go nuts or what?"

"Well, sir, as far as I see it, some gun nut, or hunter or bird killer, shot another guy. He says the guy was a friend of his. I don't know enough to call it yet, sir."

"Okay. Well, it's been two weeks so what's taking so long? You, uh, you're trying to bump up on this squad right?"

"Right, sir!"

"Well then, understand we don't move people up who don't solve crimes. We promote people who solve crimes, find evidence, get the perp. And I mean find evidence, you get me, Graves. Get me? Huh?"

"Yes, sir. I'll find some evidence."

Ten years on the force and here I am with the biggest case of my life. All I need to do is put this guy away and I'm made. Graves had spent the previous ten years putting people away, finding evidence, cracking skulls, and pounding the pavement. Now he was on the DT squad and trying to move up. He wanted to be in politics but found this as a good route to garner influence in the community, which would then lead to some small office somewhere. He could make the jump to commissioner quite easy. It all starts with this Aire case, some guy who shot "his friend" and says it was an accident. Well, accident or not, I need this one, and I'm going to get it.

CHAPTER FIFTEEN
Karen – Prom Queen

With a quick jolt, she awoke. "Oh, only twenty minutes, that's not too long, I haven't missed them." Karen had to reassure herself that her big moment hadn't passed. This 'event' was to redefine Karen's life, finally legitimize her, and make it something worth living. She would not be just this person existing. Sometimes she felt that people like Theodore were right. She was just fat and stupid. But how? How did she miss it? How did she fail to turn a beautiful young girl into a beautiful, famous adult? Maybe that 'curse' of the prom queens she had always heard of was true. Maybe all prom queens turn out to be fat and stupid. Maybe that was just the price one paid for being beautiful so early in life. Karen cursed her early beauty, and she cursed the prom, even if her mother was telling the truth and paid for her to win her title. She still must have been pretty enough to make it seem legitimate…right?

Karen had a plan, though, a new hope to turn her life around. No longer would it be meaningless. She could just see it: all of her neighbors would say, "Hey, isn't that Karen Miller from down the street? My God she looks so beautiful on TV. Let's go to her house and congratulate her. We must start spending time with Karen Miller. Maybe we should make her president of our neighborhood association. I mean, she's practically a brand new celebrity."

"We'll, I heard she was going to be on a reality show, or maybe it was a soap opera or something, but no matter what, she is important now, and we would be very smart to include our own Karen Miller into our ranks."

"You know I always liked her and wanted to include her. It was just that I thought she would take all the focus away from everyone else, so I wanted to protect everyone."

"Yeah I wanted her all along. I thought all of you would suffer if we had someone as talented as Karen in our group."

Karen decided she would remain magnanimous; she would not make her new friends jealous or ashamed. She would still remind them every now and then that she was the only real celebrity they knew, or would that be too harsh? Karen's buzz was wearing off.

CHAPTER SIXTEEN
Ordin's Experience with the Police

When the police and ambulance showed up, Ordin started to explain, he was looking around for the other man he'd seen about, but he was no longer there. "I... I grabbed his shotgun, we were laughing, I didn't even know which end I had. Is he o.k., is….is he alive, we're friends, we…we...we are friends is he dead? The detective seemed soft-hearted, and ready to listen, but Ordin began to notice the accusatory tone in which the surrounding deputies. This tone appeared to be contagious to the detectives as well. The mood of the questions began to change also. They started to sound like, "Did you have any reason to want to kill Mr. Draingold." They weren't calling him "your friend, Peter."

What happened next was the stuff of nightmares. One deputy came to the car of the chief detective and whispered loudly "someone overheard them arguing before he shot him." Two officers quickly turned him around placed him in handcuffs, drove him to the station, put him in a cell, and beat him about the head and body. Within forty-eight hours he found himself, in front of a judge, and having to possibly spend the next 15 to 30 days in the county jail while the bail demand of $500,000 was processed. The next court date to sort out the evidence was set to 30 days from then.

The second beating was worse. Just after dinner (if you can call it that). In Ordin's cell, there was a bar that held his dinner plate. As the guards pass by after dinner, one is to place his tray on the bar for pick up. On this day as the guard passed, Ordin dropped his tray, which startled the guard. Ordin responded with nervous laughter. The guard called for Ordin's cell to be opened, stepped inside to confront him. Ordin made the mistake of standing at the ready. The guard took this as a defensive maneuver and took out his nightstick and struck Ordin so hard in the rib cage that the air crashed from his lungs. Before Ordin could catch his breath, another blow brought a rush of heat to his head, the sound of his ribs breaking seemed to bounce off the walls, as the air exploded from his frame. It felt as if it took him years to fall to his knees, which he hit with a thud, but only lasted for a moment, because the guard kneed him in his chest sending him sprawling across the concrete floor, of this arena. A trickle of blood slid from the corner of his mouth as the light started to close in on him. Seconds later the knight stick was beating him about the thigh's and shoulders. Ordin struggled to remain conscious, made even harder by the fact that the guard's nightstick was placed against his neck, nearly crushing his windpipe. He heard the voices, felt the vibration of the boots pounding down the hall towards their direction, but could not move, could not take it all in at the same time. "Oh God I'm paralyzed, I...I can't move. I can't move. Now the blood, the breathlessness didn't matter, the pain from ribs on both sides broken, possibly shattered didn't seem to take precedence. The fact that Ordin could not feel or move his legs nor his arms replaced the image of the raging deputy perched over him. Fear, fear...fear...then black.

CHAPTER SEVENTEEN
Mom's Coffee Shop

The coffee stop was called "Mom's", but Paul thought "I don't think anyone's mother would be caught dead in here, let alone eating here." Paul and Detective Graves took a sip of the coffee respectively. Graves eyes spun. Paul's nose wrinkled, they looked at one another and broke into laughter. The waitress came over, peered over the rim of her glasses, and under the bangs of her beehive hair-do (as if she had stepped out of a fifties film) she spoke with a misplaced southern drawl, saying, "You boys like my special brew?" Graves spoke up, "Gal, this here mud reminds me of the stuff my ex used to make," then just turned and affectionately said, "Thanks."

Graves turned to Paul and said "you know pup, I've been on the force for thirty-something years, and I've done seen a lot of things. The good stuff and the not so good stuff and the really, really, bad stuff. What I'm trying to say is that a man gets tired, all the time tired. I'm no fool. I've seen the way you look at me sometimes. Like I'm some sort of red neck, pig-headed fool."

"No, sir. I would nev'."

"Calm down it's all right, I know what I am. I guess I'm saying when you look at me that way I feel the way I used to look at my superiors. I use to feel like this all had some meaning like I personally made some kind of difference, then I relegated myself to the thought that if I can make this what I want it to be, then I've done my part. So I let go. I let go of the notion of justice for all and good and bad guys. I just let go. Don't get me wrong some get justice and some, what they deserve, and it sure as hell ain't justice. There's no such thing as good or bad guys. Just good and bad causes and situations see in a lot of ways we all got both the good guy and the bad guy in us. It's the situation and the cause you're serving that makes the difference. Take for example a man calls "us" the good guys on the phone; say's something going down at his house. We came out, and the situation is his old lady's going all banana splits and what not. You would think its cut and dry. See this is where it gets sticky. The problem is while she was tossing everything 'cept the kitchen sink at him, he manages to scratch her somehow, or let's say in all the excitement she may have even scratched herself, well we have to take him in. She gets the option of pressing charges against him, he gets maybe a year in the slammer. Now, while he's gone she files abandonment charges, sells his house, 'cause it's legal seeing as how he abandoned her and all and since she never worked a day in her life, she claims hardship and gets to sell the house. She then proceeds to find a new beau, and by the time he gets out, he's lost his house, his job, maybe his car and kids, and his gal; if he ever really had her to start. See what I mean? He called us with the pretense that his cause was just, doing the right thing and all, but the situation dictated that he got the raw end of the meat, and we went from good guys to bad guys in another person's eyes, but subsequently we were heroes to the gal. So there ain't really no good guys or bad guys, just good and bad causes and good or bad situations. And it makes you tired after a while, deep down bone weary tired."

Paul responded, "I see" and his day had just gotten longer.

CHAPTER EIGHTEEN
Ordin – In Front of the Judge

As Ordin stood in front of the judge, he looked as if he had been in a boxing match against Mike Tyson in his prime. The most honorable judge Harry Weinstein smiled down at Ordin and said: "Mr. Aire I have some good news for you and by the looks of things you can use some." Ordin attempted to smile, and as he did, he winced from the pain. "Mr. Aire it seems that you were telling the truth about your unfortunate accident, and I offer you my condolences on the loss of your friend. We have gathered eyewitness reports that saw the beginning of the incident and of your long-standing friendship with the victim. Though we cannot entirely rule out the possibility of foul play as of yet, we cannot support a murder charge or conviction at this time. So while I am ordering your immediate release, with my apologies for the incident you suffered during your time in our correctional facility, I will order that your case remains open pending further investigation. Understand that should at any time new evidence surface, you will be remanded back into custody until an investigation of the evidence can be conducted. Have a good day sir."

With that, Ordin left custody and back to what remained of his life. Apparently during his thirty days in jail, his case had made the top story on the daily and evening news. His house had become a circus. His wife and child became media victims, having their every move watched. The N.R.A. held a press conference on his front lawn, supporting Americans right to bear arms and how apparent unfortunate accidents should not have any bearing on that right. To oppose the N.R.A., the National Association of Gun Violence Victims held a rally and conference of their own, touting the dangers of gun violence. When the N.R.A. and the N.A.O.G.V.V. demanded that Ordin take a stand, he took the position that what happened was an accident, and no one should prosper from it. Needless to say, this infuriated both associations, so much so that Ordin and his family became the target of aggressive campaigns by both sides; leaving accusations that Ordin had been paid by the other side to smear their cause. At its worst someone fired a gun through the front window and door of his house.

Because Ordin's case became a national debate, causing a disruptive stir in his life and for his wife and infant child. His wife decided that their already rocky marriage could not stand being on the run forever as his face had been splashed all over nationwide TV. Despite Ordin's pleas for his wife, Sonya, to reconsider, she went her separate way. She also took full custody of their child Blain through an emotionally charged divorce. The divorce court ruled that Ordin could not have any contact with Blain until his 12th birthday when a letter from the court would go out to both Blain and Sonya providing the address of the other. Ordin wound up, as a single man working as a mechanic, in a local garage, living by a lake he liked to call "his lake."

CHAPTER NINETEEN
Graves and Bear

Paul and Graves took the next hour apart to get some air, and as Graves so eloquently put it "get the hell away from each other for a while." Graves went directly to the telephone as if drawn by some force that had a hold over him, which he both loathed and depended on. "Hey Gert" he rumbled into the phone, "how's Bear?" Bear was the name of the Graves' dog, a British Bulldog. Bear had been stricken with canine leukemia several weeks prior, and the Graves had taken him to a vet. The cost was in the thousands and rising.

Gertrude Graves was a smallish woman, now like her husband in her mid-fifties, had never really regretted not having children herself, or at least that is what she told James Harold, her somewhat loving husband. After all, they did adopt a boy named Winslow and raised him from eight to eighteen. However, Winslow promptly left the state for college after high school but not without first letting J.H. know exactly what he thought of him and had not called since it had been 7 years now.

James Harold called the episode with Winslow a mistake that was set up by Gertrude's biological clock. So J. H. and Gert bought Bear, they both felt that Bear would bring into the household what was so obviously missing, a neutral loving presence with no way to disapprove or walk away. The rising cost of Bear's treatment seemed expensive, but worth it. Graves no longer had to speak to Gert almost at all anymore. For the Graves, Bear had become a sounding board. While James Harold was gone at work Gert would tell Bear how she wished he wouldn't ignore her so much. She could understand a little ignorance of her presence; Gert knew she was no beauty anymore, nor was there ever much of a passionate sex life with James Harold. Gert told herself her hips were too big for a lithe woman who had never had children, her breath was bad sometimes, and her deteriorating eyesight had forced her to wear glasses. Sometimes she wondered how those women on TV stayed attractive and youthful looking, relative to their age of course. She figured it had a lot to do with their being rich and being able to lavish themselves with all sorts of expensive facial, and beauty products. Gert always thought of herself as way too practical and frugal to be so vain. She also figured that what her mother told her about men was just true: that at some certain age men just needed their own space and went their own way.

For James Harold, Bear provided a companion for those times when what he called his "natural stubborn streak" needed agreeing with. Bear always agreed and never talked back. Bear also agreed that J. H. Graves should have made captain years ago; he felt James Harold was way too intelligent to be stuck in the suburb he lived in, and should move to the city. Bear almost never got temperamental when James Harold was too busy, to give him a hug. Bear did not have a bunch of what James Harold called "cackling chicken heads" over twice a week to ruin his good mood with tea, biscuits and groaning about their husband's collective failure to make all their domestic dreams come true. For James Harold Graves, Bear's mounting medical bills were cost nearly the same as some "chicken head, or U.S.M." (ultra-sensitive male) marriage counselor would, and Bear would actually choose his point of view, not like those intellects, who never even tried to understand him. Yes, Bear was definitely worth it. So much so that James Harold feared with great dread the day when Bear would die, and leave him alone with Gert. Sometimes he thought they should buy a new dog now. Even though Bear didn't actually walk, or bark anymore, he was still the best thing he had going.

CHAPTER TWENTY
Karen – Phi Alpha Alpha

Karen was beginning to stretch her imagination and her confidence. She thought this would be a perfect time to go over to Ordy's house or even better to go Sabrina Marshall's of the Oregon Marshall's. Karen always hated when she said that, this would be the perfect time to march right down to Sabrina's house, open the front door, and invite herself in, during their neighborhood woman's meeting.

Karen never really had the best luck when it came to groups she seemed to always get in uncomfortable, compromising situations. Like that time after she had dropped out of high school and decided to go to a college campus visiting week. Karen had barged into a Phi Alpha Alpha Sorority meeting, after having a little, well a lot of wine. She felt like she deserves to have just as much fun as any of them, after all, Karen was a prom queen and wasn't it the right of all prom queens to join sororities, even if she was only a senior prom queen?

At first the girls welcomed Karen in, their smiles seemed harmless enough even if they were a bit sly looking. The girls told Karen that they had been wrong to overlook her and that she was welcomed to join if she passed a few typical tests. Karen was game, she felt so accepted. Tiffiny Mulberry, then head phi, led Karen upstairs along with two frightened doe-eyed freshmen.

The room was pitch-black. Karen began to feel hands on her back and shoulders. Tiffiny's voice came like a crack of light in a brick of darkness. "Okay, future Phi's, all you got to do is survive one hour in the room of delights and you have made the first step." The hands grew more and more exploratory, soon they were tugging at her blouse and skirt, voices were laughing in the background, betting on who'd leave first. Karen was determined, this was the crowd she belonged to, and she would be damned if a few cheap thrills were going to keep her out, Karen Miller prom queen can do this she thought. Several hands slid her skirt over her head and were beginning to draw her panties down. She stiffened, but her will helped her to calm down, she thought, "Mother always said I was stubborn, well I'll just be stubborn now, they won't force me out. As her thoughts returned, her panties were around her ankles, and she felt warm air crossing over the hair of her vagina, then a hand reached over her shoulder and firmly grasped her breast. The heat of hands on her skin gave Karen a shiver that started in her toes, went up through her thighs and ended in the tip of her nipple; Karen was being forced to her knees.

Karen realized she had been holding her breath. She opened her mouth to gasp, and someone filled her mouth with themselves. Karen was so startled she almost bit down, but instead she did not move a muscle. She could feel the person gyrating in front of her, and sounds of laughing and moaning, and even faint animal like whimpers and barks were all around the room. The person in front of her grabbed her hair, not hard enough to hurt, but hard enough so she knew who was in control. I'm still in control Karen thought. I can leave anytime I want, but that's what they expect me to do. The hands were now all over her grabbing and prodding, exploring everywhere, thick fingers inserted themselves into her, she spasmed on reflex, the wiggling and thrusting of the digits made her stomach cramp, she was on her hands and knees now. Before her mind could decide what to do, someone else placed themselves in her mouth, and the fingers exploring her insides were replaced by a man's unit. What felt like fear to Karen gave way to confusion. She could not tell if it was the wine or the powerlessness, but she had gotten herself into a situation. Now the pulsing of the unit inside of her became a hard pounding. Kare could hear herself grunting deep guttural barks, though her mouth was still filled with someone else. Then a digit explored and quickly slipped into her anus, then was joined by two more, when they rescinded, Karen thought she could endure only a little more when she felt what could not be mistaken, a person was inserting themselves into her anus. Now the movements were going at a fever pace, she heard the two other girls whimpering and moaning, one girl gave up and cried out "let me out, stop!"

The movements did not stop for Karen. Just when she thought she was going to throw up from disgust, she felt her insides begin to spasm, and her head felt as light as a feather. Karen was orgasming and more and harder than she ever had. By the time the lights came on, Karen had gone from fear to shame to resolution and back to shame. Her fear became shame because she came so hard, from blind passion; however, she Karen was resolute that nothing was going to deter her. Karen was further ashamed when she noticed that there were no men in the room at all, only Tiffany Mulberry and the other phi's each with a rubber phallus in hand and adorned with a strap-on The embarrassment Karen felt made her eyes flood with tears. The Phi's left her in the room after assuring her Karen had passed the first test, and if she wanted to tell on them, no one would believe her because rubber doesn't leave D.N.A, and they were all wearing gloves. Karen decided right then and there she did not want to be a Phi.

After recalling the memory, Karen thought twice about barging into Sabrina Marshall, of the Oregon Marshall's house. They would just have to wait until she was on TV and famous, to have the privilege of inviting her to join their little group. "Maybe," she thought, "I should go over to Ordy's, after all, he was going to help make me famous, and he seemed safe enough."

CHAPTER TWENTY-ONE
Paul – Heroism Backfires

Paul sipped a few more times, shuddered, and then placed a dollar on the table. As he pushed the front door open, he heard a voice say "Hey that guy is trying to run out on his bill stop him!" Paul pushed out of the door to look for the man who was skipping out on his bill. Paul thought, no doubt, that the terrible coffee had driven some poor sap crazy, and he had probably just forgotten to pay his bill. One of the chefs, a husky Latino man, burst through the kitchen doors, jumped the counter, and sprinted towards the front door.

Paul turned to walk back into the shop to ask for a description of the guy and pay the bill himself, if it was not too much, when the chef rushed up to Paul's chest, startling Paul. "Where the hell do you think you are going, pinche gringo"?

"What the hell are you talking about"?

"You trying to leave, you didn't pay," said the chef to Paul's response of "my partner paid, and if I were you, I would get out of my face." "I don't want to hear about your domestic situation, you eat and drink, you must pay the money." and with that, the chef now backed by two bus boys and some locals, grabbed Paul's wrist and reached into his pockets.

Paul pushed the chef saying, "Back off I'm a policeman," but in the excitement of the shove, no one heard him. The bus boys rushed Paul. No doubt this had happened before. Seems that in these podunk towns there's not very much listening to reason, people react or shoot first then ask questions. The first of the two bus boys swung at Paul's face, connecting flush on his right cheek. Good thing that Paul was about four inches taller, being six foot one, he also outweighed the pugilistic bus boy by about fifty pounds, his lean two hundred and ten-pound frame was all muscle. In spite of this, the hit did shock Paul. In the background he could hear the waitress saying "we better get to calling Jimmy down at the station, tell' em there's trouble." Paul backed up again trying in vain to identify himself as a policeman, but the overzealous busboy would not relent, so Paul, who was quickly losing his hold on restraint, shoved the bus boy onto the ground.

Graves' head nodded waking him up from dozing off in his car after his phone call to Gert. Shook himself further awake, then decided, for what he calls shits and giggles, to monitor the local police scans. The first dispatch he heard was a description of a Caucasian male approximately six foot to six foot two, brown hair, brown eyes, wearing a dark gray jacket, no tie, and blue slacks. Graves immediately burst into laughter at the dispatchers prompt for available deputies to head for Mom's Diner for a possible two eleven in progress. "Can't leave those damn pups alone for a minute less they go messing with folks and causing a ruckus. Guess I better head on back in there and straighten this mess out."

Paul was spitting mad and showing it. He had knocked down the busboy and the chef, and by the time the local sheriff arrived, the placed called 'Mom's Diner' looked more like a cross between a music video and the sight of the recent wrestle mania. Graves arrival on the scene was met by Paul hogtied on the ground. Ten officers, which represents the town's entire police force, standing guns at the ready. Graves took his time explaining the situation. Yes he had paid, he was with Paul, and they are both policemen from S.F.P.D. Yes, he would take custody of Paul. Yes, he would authorize a check for S.F.P.D. to pay for the damages. Yes, Paul was sorry, and he would definitely apologize to the chef. Yes, he would call the chef's wife and explain how her husband got a black eye and bruised ribs. Yes, he would see to it that Paul paid a week's salary for the bus boy who most certainly could not come to work with a broken nose, dislocated wrist and wounded pride, and finally, yes they would get the hell out of their town.

All ten cops holstered their guns. Some were sighing, some quietly cursing to each other, and with the situation diffused somewhat, Graves led Paul to the car, motioning him to take the driver seat. As Paul began to speak, Graves shushed him and said: "Ya see pup this is why thinking pups is bad for folks, less thinking, more driving." Paul began to say something, changed his mind and just sighed then pulled off.

CHAPTER TWENTY-TWO
Karen and Ordin's Story

I'll just drop in for a minute or two, I'm sure he won't mind, thought Karen. Ordin's house seemed warm and inviting, despite the chill he felt from the emptiness of losing his family of wife and child; he hid it well.

The knock on the door gave Ordin a start. After the experience at "his lake" earlier this morning, he was still somewhat shaken. While he had composed himself, and the nervousness that the daymare brought on had subsided, he still felt a tinge of strangeness coursing through him. He sometimes attributed it to the residual effects of not having someone there to deflect some of the pain of this isolation, which he found choked him sometimes with sadness.

Ordin got out of his chair and headed for the door, but before he got there, he heard Karen Miller's voice cackle "Oh for heaven's sake already Ordy it's me." Ordin froze in his tracks; he knew dealing with his neurotic neighbor could possibly push him over the edge. He slowly turned and was trying to tiptoe to the back door when Karen opened the door and in a huff stated, "Ordy are you trying to hide from me?" Karen had a knack for recognizing the obvious. The skin on Ordin's back began to crawl, he wondered if she could see it through his sweat soaked shirt.

"Karen, you really should not just walk in, I could be naked or something."

"No you couldn't," she said. "You're not that type of guy." "Although once on Cold Case Killers they had this guy, he was some sort of sex offender or something perverted like that." "There was a bunch of people."

"Mostly women, right?" Ordin interjected.

"Of course who else is brave enough to stand up to these people and drive them out of our communities and keep our children safe."

"But Karen you don't even have kids."

"That's beside the point. Anyways, there was a bunch of people marching and protesting outside of his house, then he just up and shot one of them. Just like that, and he started screaming that they had ruined his life! Then he took off and disappeared. They say he went down to Mexico. You know those people let anyone in. You know, I went there once and…"

"Karen, what's your point?"

"The point is I would have done the same thing as those brave women, I mean except get shot, you know."

Ordin snickered, not because he thought that what she said was funny. He snickered because he found himself entertaining the thought "maybe someone should shoot you, and put you out of your suburban misery." Ordin rarely thought such black thoughts, but hey, sometimes you had to stretch yourself.

The look on Karen's face was one of puzzlement; then again she had seen that look before. Most of the men in her life had given her the same look at some point, and it usually meant that not only would she no longer see that look again from them for she would most likely, no longer be seeing that particular gentleman anymore.

Ordin's voice broke her blank stare, "Karen you can't just put people in some category and run them out of town. There are times when 'people' do the most harm to people when they give up on them. Have you ever stopped to think that this 'sex' offender may not have done what he was accused of, that he may have just acquiesced to the road that was laid out for him?"

"Well if they aren't guilty then why would anyone who loved them give up on them?"

"Let me tell you a story, where the main character is not guilty, and loses everything." "The guy has an accident, and it seems like there has been a crime." "He's dragged into court, beaten in jail, and then made into the spokesman and scapegoat for everything that's wrong with our country. His wife and only son are demonized, scandalized, and drug through the mud until they reach a point of no return. They abandon him, Karen, rather than face life being associated with the man whom they 'love' as a killer of his best friend; they turn away and walk into a life he doesn't have the privilege to." "So he makes a decision to start over, just throw it all away, he can't let go." "Everything in him wants to, needs to but the ghost of what his life was won't let him let go."

The look of distant pain and longing on his face confused Karen. She could see that there was a feeling he was trying to convey and at the same time a distance he was struggling to maintain from his own words. Ordin seemed to only half say the words and half sprout them from some deep secret place.

Karen attached herself to those words. She had felt that way before as a matter of fact, she felt them rather recently; when the words, "You did not pay for me to be prom queen" sprang from her mouth, at her mother.

Karen softened the expression on her face, reached for Ordin's hand and squeezed as she said "I think I understand, but where does the guy in the story go now? I mean, what happens to him?"

Ordin smiled a faint smile, took his hand from Karen's and placed it on her opposing shoulder, "I don't know, I don't know."

CHAPTER TWENTY-THREE
Karen – Feeling Shame

Karen's face flushed, and she was hit with a sudden feeling of shame. Shame that she now realized that the man in the story was him. And that at this very moment, at her prompting, two detectives were barreling down some highway toward her town. Their arrival would write an ending to the story she had just heard and that had affected her so much; an ending that left Ordin more than just broken and his life stolen, but completely destroyed and placed behind a stone wall and a caged ceiling where even the sky wasn't free for him. She also realized that if this came to pass it would be what got her fifteen minutes of fame and the chance to stretch that fifteen minutes into an hour or maybe into the life that always seemed to belong to everybody else, anyone but her. The question was, could she trade that fame in, could she live with not having her moment and could Karen look at this man; who suddenly seemed more fragile and human than she had ever known any man to be? Could she look at him and know she would play a significant part in ending his story?

Ordin sensing he had gotten through to Karen reached out and put his hands on her shoulders. Karen felt a rush and at the same time, she felt smaller. It was the type of feeling she would get when she stood in front of her father, as he tried to make one of the few lessons he ever taught her stick. The feeling that she knew had led to the submissive yet grating posture she took with the men in her life. Why this happened, she did not know. Was it the way her father's eye would search her face for recognition of his point? Or the way his hands trembled with the importance of his meaning? She did know, yet Ordin's touch brought back these same feelings for her.

She wasn't sure if she was feeling vulnerable or turned on. It was this same confusion that had countless times landed her in bed with an older gentleman or a man that just happened to exude that same "power" over her. Her reaction to the men that looked or treated her that way endeared her to them at first, but quickly lost its "deer in headlights" appeal. Her relationships usually ended in men asking for, then taking "a little time for themselves," after they had verbally berated her and/or used her body for experimenting with facets of their sexuality that they had never explored. Karen would endure everything from mild beatings with sexual overtones to painful episodes of Sado-Masochism. She had heard herself called everything from "bitch to stupid whore" sometimes these rantings were during sex play, at times they were directly related to something she had done or said that exposed the fact that she was less than a genius. Karen would go first off into denial, then she would soothe herself with drugs, wine, or pointless promiscuity.

Pulling herself out of her journey into her past, Karen dropped her eyes from Ordin, but felt herself giving away to his grip and wanting to be led; led out of her life, led out of this new vulnerable feeling, led out of this situation. Karen now felt wholly responsible for Ordin's upcoming plight.

"Do you see how dangerous it is to blindly lash out with popular opinion?" His words had a new value to Karen, and something new, something different happened to her; she understood, she got it, it made sense. What had usually turned out as a cold lecture and even more icy stare, transformed into a fire of understanding. She had judged him, and wrongly at that. Ordin let go of her shoulders and walked toward the door; this episode brought back a deep pain that had been continually growing over the past few weeks.

"Karen, I'm sorry I'm feeling terrible suddenly, can we continue this conversation some other time"?

"Oh sure" is what Karen's mouth said, but what her heart screamed out was" Run, please run from this place, I've done something rash and terrible, and I don't have the courage to try and call it off." Ordin opened the door, but Karen couldn't move. She had changed her opinion of him and wanted to say so, but she slowly trudged to the door, and as the door closed, Karen stood on the other side and felt "why didn't I say something? Can I really let this happen"?

Ordin walked back into his living room, slumped into his easy chair, put his head in his hands and cried.

CHAPTER TWENTY-FOUR
Simplicity as per Detective Graves

"What the hell were you thinking pup"? "Yehaw, ha-ha, they 'bout kicked your ass up onto your shoulders didn't they? Pup, ya gotta learn to be subtle when you're 'round townsfolk. Ya gotta have certain genes for dealing with 'em. See pup the thing is; you have these people ya see, who don't know too much more than what they was raised to believe. See, most of 'em never went to some fancy college like you, or even learn to read and do math proper like. Most of them folk don't care to go any further in life than they already are, but you still gotta treat them with respect. In the game we play down here on earth, it's delicate like a dance."

"I know what you're thinking, you're thinking how can some pig head, stubborn son-of-a-bitch redneck like me know anything about being subtle? That's what you were thinking, wasn't it pup. Don't answer that. Just, just listen up."

"You take that guy who you punched in the eye, the chef or cook or whatever. You take a guy like that; comes into work every day 'round four in the morning to start cooking, leaves around eight at night, goes home to a heavy set woman; not that there's anything wrong with that, it's just not my cup of tea you know. Well, this guy goes home to his woman and maybe two, three kids, he rents his place, makes payments on his car, has a big screen TV that's his pride and joy. But he has a brother-in-law who hounds him for a job as if he's got any pull and a mother-in-law who's a widower and threatening to move in any day now. Now this here is your average guy. In your eyes, he's a real schmo, but the truth is, he's not so different than you and me."

"Me, I may own my home. You? You may have gone to college, but are you any happier than he is, and if so, why? My gut tells me that you're not and neither am I. The same things that motivate you and I are the same things that motivate a guy like that. You want to know what those things are? Simplicity and simplicity. We all want the same things. A simple life, the accomplishment of some goals and dreams and to know we stood for something and that we tried. Does that make sense to you, pup? Wait, don't answer that, of course, it does. Under that Ivy league tie of yours, you're real meat and potatoes just like me."

CHAPTER TWENTY-FIVE
Ordin and Sonya

As Ordin sat in his chair weeping, he called out to no one, "how much pain? How much?" It was a question he had become accustomed to asking himself, never expecting to get an answer, but this time, he thought he heard something, someone.

"You choose this pain; You put us here."

Ordin's head popped up. "What? Who's there?" Inside he knew, there was no one really there. It was the voice he had heard countless times before, it was a voice he had come to expect in times of stress, sorrow; soft, penetrating, with a tone of conviction and deep hurt, and longing. At first, he thought it was the voice of God; coming to him as a comforter. Then slowly he made the connection and attained recognition. It was the voice of his wife.

"Sonya" he cried, half weeping, half whispering. "Sonya, I never wanted this, I never wanted you and Blain to suffer. He is my only son. How could I have wanted you and him to be alone, to have to start over? No, I know I never wanted this, the same way I never wanted my father to leave! Seven years, seven long years without him, without me. I cried almost daily. I remember the feeling of being rejected, of not knowing where I belonged, not knowing who I would or could become. Sonya, when the deepest part of me was bathing in darkness, he couldn't rescue me. I couldn't hear God. I was numb, lost whole chunks of my memory. How could I want that for my own son, for our son, for Blain? Sonya, what I want for him is the miracle that happened for me."

"You see Sonya, when I'd almost given up on everything, even myself, even God, something wonderful happened. He... my dad came back. He came through the door, an ordinary man, who left his reasons for leaving wherever it was he needed to go, and he picked up his life with us, with me. And in that way, an ordinary man, the most common man I knew became a hero, my hero. He became with one act everything I wanted him to be and everything I knew I would be to my own children one day. That's why Sonya, that's why I left. Why I gave you a choice instead of making it for you, for him, I wanted to come back, to do what was done for me."

"They say we travel the same roads; fathers and sons. I wanted to be for Blain what my father was for me. Someone who filled in the blanks, someone who took away the pain. A hero Sonya, his hero, and in that way I could fulfill my own legacy, be my father's hero too. There's one difference Sonya between him and me; you see my father had her, my mother, and in her own way she was the stronger one, she was the one with the unbreakable will. She took him back Sonya, she let him back in. Not because she needed him, but because I needed him."

"You talk about pain Sonya, you call me weak, say I caused this, that I wanted this, but I believe you wanted this, you're the weak one. You choose to bathe in pain then crucify me for your drowning. Why couldn't you take me back, give Blain what he needed, what I needed? So you see Sonya it was not I. True, I chose to give you the option to stand up with me or walk away, but the decision was yours, but did you know your choice is breaking me?"

Ordin tumbled from his chair; lay on the ground and wept, and when the tears obstructed his vision, he blinked twice, closed his eyes and let go…again.

CHAPTER TWENTY-SIX
Karen "Waiting"

It's the waiting that kills you, I mean kills you like drop dead. Yeah, it's definitely the waiting that kills you. Karen sauntered down the street. Here I am waiting to become famous, and he is over there waiting for his life to change. I mean what a story and if it's true then…my God that poor man. Maybe it was me, but I felt like he was going to kiss me right there. I don't know why I attract such desperate men. I guess once a prom queen always a prom queen.

When Karen reached her home, she called it a house she hadn't felt like it was a home, not since her divorce. It wasn't so much that there were ghosts there, the house just lacked a certain warmth. What gives a house warmth? In Karen's view, it is as if the feeling that someone was waiting for you, that someone gave a damn whether you showed up or not. There hadn't been anyone waiting for Karen in a long time, no one seemed to give a damn.

Subtlety, suddenly, Karen felt drained. She couldn't quite put her finger on where she felt tired; in her soul, her body, her heart, or her mind. When she got to the door of her house, she nearly fell into the living room. The mailman had been there and slipped a letter through the slot. Karen picked the letter up and read the address. She had gotten her mail mixed up before, with a Karen Milner, who lived somewhere on her mailman's route. She looked, not so out of concern for Mrs. Milner's privacy, but more so in vain hope thinking someone had written her a letter.

Karen beamed, the letter was for her, "it's for me" she gushed out loud, then with a dint of a smile she let her eyes go to the return address; there was none. "Humph," she sputtered "I guess they forgot. Just in a hurry to get it out," Karen never even gave thought to the notion that maybe whomever it was that had written her, did not want her to know where they lived, and really didn't want her to write them back. What this said about her, that she didn't even grasp the notion of why the writer wouldn't have left a return address, spoke fathoms. She went to the drawer, pranced over really, and recovered her letter opener, sliced the seal and carefully removed the letter from it an envelope.

Karen thought about that for a few seconds: how a letter comes in an envelope, something that covers and protects it, something that announces it, and represents it, holding it almost jealously inside. How Karen longed to be enveloped by someone or anything, the thought now warmed her. She would soon be surrounded by the chance of fame. This wasn't as personal a thought as being enveloped by a great love or lover who yearned for her, but that would come too. Karen gleefully unfolded the letter and began reading the first few lines.

The letter was from an agency that had gotten the delinquent accounts of several of Karen's creditors. Although Karen liked to think of herself as a financier, she was in all actuality little more than a clerk at a local check casher, and she had screw-up her finances terrible. A rush of blood ran to Karen's head as she read the agency was offering to either consolidate all other loans, and her mortgage for a nominal fee or they would hire a lawyer to litigate against her and have the local authorities systematically began removing all the items from her home.

Panic set in Karen's face at the reading of the last few lines, and as she placed the letter on the top of her television, the words of her latest boyfriends' tirade of belittlement came raging back at her. She wasn't stupid and fat as he had said and she would prove it. Karen now knew how she could turn in the man whom she's just learned was a real and affected human being. She would go through with her plan to help the detectives get Ordin, and when she was on "Cold Case Killers" Karen would be famous, and she'd have all the money she needed. Not that she had any real doubt what she would do all along, but now Karen was thoroughly convinced.

CHAPTER TWENTY-SEVEN
A Moment of Life

There's a moment in every human life that leaves an indelible impression. That moment when one realizes all that a man achieves and all that he fails to achieve is the direct result of his own thought. In a justly ordered universe, where loss of equipoise would mean total destruction, individual responsibility must be absolute. A man's weakness and strength, purity and impurity, are his own and not another man's. They are brought about by himself, never by another, and they can only be altered by himself, never by another.

His condition is also his own and not another man's. His suffering and his happiness are evolved from within, as he thinks, so he is, as he continues to think, so he remains. A strong man cannot help a weaker man unless that weaker man is willing to be helped, and even then the weak man must, by his own effort, develop the strength which he admires in another. No one but himself can alter his condition.

A man can only rise, conquer and achieve by lifting up his thoughts. Before a man can achieve anything, even worldly things, he must lift his thoughts above slavish animal indulgence. He may not, in order to succeed, give up all animalism and selfishness, by any means, but a portion of it must be sacrificed. A man whose first thought is of bestial indulgence can neither think clearly nor plan methodically. He cannot find and develop his talent or resources, and would fail in any undertaking. Not knowing how fully to control his thoughts, he is not in a position to control affairs and to adopt any serious responsibilities. He is not fit to act independently and stand-alone. But he is limited only by the thoughts, which he chooses.

When he learns this, he becomes aware that thought and character are one, and character can only manifest and discover itself through environment and circumstance. The outer conditions of a man's life will always be found to be harmoniously related to his inner state. Men imagine that thought can be kept secret, but it cannot. It rapidly crystallizes into habit and habit solidifies into circumstance. The saying, "as a man thinketh he is", rings true.

CHAPTER TWENTY-EIGHT
Paul and Graves

As they sped up their pace, Paul gave thought to Grave's comments and found himself pained, hurt by the thoughts of the commonality between not only of Grave's description of what the men in the diner really wanted out of their lives but also between them all as men. It was those thoughts which prompted Paul to reach out a little further to Graves and ask him "detective what role does God play in all of this for you?" It was hard for Paul to tell what the expression on Graves' face meant, was it shock at such a personal and connected question or was his expression one of dissatisfaction? Paul did not know.

However he felt about Paul's question, Graves stared blankly at first, then just replied "I don't really know Pup, I kinda never really think, or thought about it. You tell me what God means in your view in all this."

"Paul's face relaxed into a mask of peace. "I think God comes into your life to rule and reign, bringing a sense of right and wrong into your heart through the in-dwelling of the Holy Spirit. I think he reaches up trying to affect us for the good of not only our lives but the lives of those around us. For me translating this feeling into the work that we do in particular is of the utmost importance. To tell the truth, I really don't know anymore how much or how many people who do what we do have any connection at all. I've been having second thoughts about being on the force. I guess what I really need to say is, I don't see God anywhere in our force and it disturbs me greatly, and I was wondering if you felt God in your life at all. I mean here we are going halfway across the country to investigate and possibly apprehend a man, who obviously has been through hell, based on a tip from a popular trash TV show."

"Ah shit pup, there you go again with your hollering that high-fluting bullshit. Boy, I don't know too much about God and feelings and that kind of thing. I try to do the best job I can, I think I have a decent sense of right and wrong and hell no, I don't feel sorry that we ain't singing hallelujah at the morning roll call. Get that pup."

"I thought you might feel that way, as do most of the members of the force. What bothers me most is whether this is how most officers feel, and if so, then how can we profess to be keepers of that same law that comes from the same God we hardly believe in? There's too much hypocrisy in that."

"First, I don't make 'em I just keep 'em" Graves replied. "Second, the police force has no connection to any God, only the law as decided by the governments and courts of man. Pup, I'm a simple man. I keep it simple for me, and for God's sake, change the subject."

Paul sat quietly for a moment thinking yes detective for God's sake indeed.

CHAPTER TWENTY-NINE
Ordin and Sonya

"Tell me about your wife." Calvin was his name. He spoke with a serious tone, with a voice that had weight to it. Somehow you could tell the weight came not from his being a baritone, as much as it came from years of suffering.

"My wife," Ordin responded. He looked around, he was back in his cell, it was his first week, and reality was setting in. He was 'here' and 'here' was a level on the spiral to hell he was walking. "Ok, ok. Her name was…is Sonya. She talks to me softly as if I can hear her better when she's gentle. We get along…I mean as much as any couple can. I love her... I... I don't know how to talk about her. What do you want me to say? I mean, what do you want to know?"

"I don't know man, just trying to start a conversation. I mean you've been here a week, and you haven't so much as blinked, or said a word man. Something has got to be going on."

"I miss my wife. I can't believe what's happening to me. One moment I'm hunting with my friend, the next thing I know I'm here, and scared to death…damn, that's so fucking cliché, but it's how I feel…"

"Sonya, huh?"

"Yeah, well…"

"…Sonya's got a knack for being there to tell me how I must feel in any given situation… I mean she's a good woman, shit I don't know man… I guess I never thought about what the truth about us is. We lie to each other almost all the time now. I don't know why we do it. I guess we do it because the other option is, to tell the truth, and how could we ever stay together if we did that?"

"You know I could tell her. She isn't a remarkable woman as far as strength goes. I could tell her we don't see eye to eye on anything. You beat me, you anger me and call me a loser and an asshole when you're angry at me. When I make up my mind, you tell me I haven't thought things through enough, and when I'm pensive, you say a man makes decisions and sticks by them. You emasculate me in public and castrate me in our bedroom. Who am I to you and what the hell are you doing married to me? You don't even like me, and the worst part of it all is I love you, and I can't stand it."

"I would tell her I'm not so strong and that I can't do more than I have, and I don't want to do more. And that it's you Sonya who never understood that there's a difference between a person who is being and a person who is becoming."

"Sonya just was. She wasn't becoming anything other than what she'd been for years, and Sonya wanted to change through me; figuring that if she could change me, then somehow she could change, without all the pain that comes from looking at yourself in the soul and telling the truth. The fact is that taking responsibility is a fear of the very truth that we proclaim to want. Responsibility for the things in our lives that we are, the raw, ugly, dark things that come out when our guard is lowered, the things that exist in the middle of our souls."

"Sonya and I lie almost all the time now, but were getting better; we're moving closer to lying to each other all the time. We don't want to, but it's the only thing that is keeping us together."

At that, Ordin closed his eyes lightly, banged his head on his bunk repeatedly and didn't say another word for a week or so more.

CHAPTER THIRTY
Paul – Doubts About the Force

A little more than halfway into their trek, Paul was having serious doubt about the Force and his chances to bring light to such a dark thing. The Force had always been a battle for Paul. Already his reasons for joining had run thin. The ugliness that invaded Paul's image of the Force had crept into his marriage, his relationship with his daughter, his home, and his friendships. The ugliness had crept all the way into his life and deeply rooted itself. Paul could not see any way to dig the ugliness up and out of his life except to bring light to the force and flood the darkness with so much light that it could turn, slowly, but it could turn.

Paul thought about his daughter, Willow, and the world she would grow up in. He thought about how she made the comment that her friend at school said that the police were the bad guys, and that they hurt people's lives, as well as how on impulse he answered that they were not.

Paul knew that on its deepest level, if he told the truth to himself that truth would be that somehow, someway, over some arc of time when no one was watching or paying attention, they had become the bad guys, and they did hurt people's lives. Paul wondered if he could do that anymore if he could be a part of the darkness that the force had become.

Paul began to understand why people would try and handle their disputes themselves instead of calling for help. This was because he had started to realize that his job had ceased to be about helping others, it had become about "getting your man," and getting more arrests, all to show the tax paying public that their jobs and salaries were necessary.

Paul could see the new mentality of the force: to use fear to motivate, to use fear to push the public into leaning on them and their "whatever means necessary" methods of "serving and protecting." Now Paul began to understand that he didn't want to ruin lives and that if he could not figure out a way to serve and actually protect, that he might have to not serve at all.

Paul turned slightly in his seat and looked at his partner J.H. Graves, and he saw all that was wrong with the force. He turned back, closed his eyes, and made a decision.

CHAPTER THIRTY-ONE
Ordin – Letter from His Son

Ordin had become so preoccupied with his daymares that he hadn't noticed that his hand was resting on a stack of mail. He picked up the stack and began sorting through it. He tossed aside some bills, and he threw away some advertisements. He picked through some mortgage refinancing papers and then he looked down. What he had in his hand made him turn whiter than the last series of daymares had. Ordin looked at the name and address on the letter and put it down, then turned it over and tried to get up. Half way out of his chair his knees went weak and betrayed his attempt to stand. He fell back into his chair and put his hand on the letter. He turned it over and again the name on the front of the envelope made his blood run cold.

It was a name he had thought about a thousand times since he ran from the place he once called home. It was the name of his son, a son that echoed his now ex-wife's name, a son that life had taken from him. It was taken not by death, but then again wasn't he dead to him? Wasn't there more than just one kind of death, something besides the passing of the body? Wasn't there also the death of the mind, death of one's freedom, the death of one's sanity, and even death of one's soul?

Ordin had seen plenty of people who had lost marbles over one situation or another. Ordin had experienced that death. And wasn't there also the death of one's relationships? Hadn't he killed or let die his relationship with his son, his only child? And now that son was in his hands in the form of a letter, but in his hands nonetheless.

Ordin slowly opened the letter as if he were afraid that if he opened too fast that it and his son would disappear again and this time it would be forever. He began to read it aloud hoping to hear his son's voice in his own, "Dad how are you? It has been some time hasn't it?"

Ordin's eye twitched as he thought, "Look at this opening. You would think he thought I was just on vacation." He read on, "Dad, I need to talk to you, and if not in person, then this will have to do. Dad, so many things have happened in my life over these past twenty years."

Ordin read the word "dad" and felt a shudder of guilt run through him. It had been so long since he had heard that word "Dad." The reading became difficult. Ordin felt tears well up, but he wiped them somberly and kept reading.

"Things were really tough, and there were times when I thought I wouldn't make it and times when I didn't want to make it. There were times when mom's anger with you seemed to control our lives. I grew up believing that you wanted to break our family, to break me. I didn't know what I had done, but now I think that it wasn't me you were running from, that maybe it was you running from yourself. There were bright spots, too, like graduating college early and winning sports awards. But it seems like just when I get it all together, something comes in to steal away my joy. Like now. I have this girlfriend, and that's part of the problem. You see, dad, my girlfriend is pregnant, and we just found out that we are having a son."

Ordin dropped the letter and wept openly. The thought of his son being a father and needing the advice of his father when he had been missing from him for so long overwhelmed him. Once Ordin composed himself as best he could, he read on.

"Dad, I don't know what to do. We were only going out for five months before she got pregnant. And I don't know how to tell mom, or if I even should. By the way, mom's fine. Dad, I don't know what to do. I do know that I need you and your advice. I mean, I can barely remember you, but I know you're my dad, and I need my dad. I want my son to know his grandfather. I don't think I could forgive myself if I took that away from him, just because of what was done to me."

Ordin thought for a moment about how that made him feel. His son, the son he walked away from years ago, felt abandoned, just like he felt abandoned by his father. Could he now do what he felt was done for him? His son was giving him a chance to make things right and all he had to do was make the choice. But Ordin had learned that the choices that one makes last more than a lifetime, they translate into others' lives, others lifetimes, and had the power to ruin them both. Ordin could ruin no more lives. He turned his eyes back to the letter.

"Dad, would you write back or think about coming to see me? There has been an emptiness lately. I can't explain it. I can only feel it. I know a few things, though. I know that love fills the emptiness, I know that love creates hope and that if anything can, love can heal, even the old pains. I have found out in my twenty-two years that some men can move mountains, and some can move and control the sky itself, but some men, the men who have love, can move the world, no, the whole universe and space and even time. They can make it stand still and then it wouldn't matter how long they have been gone. They can still be the root and the bringer of love, just like God. Dad, they can bring love just like God. I am smart enough, and I have learned enough to know that. Dad, it has been too long. I need your love. I need you to bring your love, just like God, and I know it is overdue. Thank you. Your son, Blain."

Ordin stood up walked across the room. He stopped at his cabinet, opened the drawer, took out a piece of paper, and then sat down and wrote the first words he had written in years. Those words began with "My son."

CHAPTER THIRTY-TWO
Bored Karen

"Oh, crap, would they just come on! La, la, la, la, I'm so freaking bored, I can't stand it. I just can't." Karen's patience was running thin. Maybe it was the wine. Maybe it was her life that was running thin, and Karen was becoming real, and real people feel the thinness of their lives. The past few years for this woman had been disappointing. She felt it in every smile she faked. The sadness and wanting had taken the place of a real personality and what it created was an open wound that didn't hurt as much as it just itched. Itched and chaffed her skin against her. Sometimes the irritation the injury caused pushed her into different decisions. It distracted her just long enough for her to mistakenly stumble into uncomfortable situations.

"Funny how life turns on situations," she would say. It was her one intellectual thing to say. She used it at parties and gatherings, not that she got invited to many, but the few she had been too she used it. And she used it very carefully and very sparingly so as not to spread it too thinly. And people who she had been talking to earlier heard her saying it to someone she would be currently talking too and knew that she wasn't very intelligent and really didn't have much to say. Karen relied on what had become a fact, and that was that everyone who she used her "nugget" on, had a comment about it, and it would usually stir up or stimulate some conversation. However, this was where Karen dropped the ball because she never really could hold her own once the conversation got started. She usually backed away, or slowly turned her back on whoever was talking, as if she had something much more important to do. What Karen didn't notice was that people always saw that she was shying away from the conversation and that she floated from group to group, only staying for a few seconds, then chortling, then floating away. In a lot of ways, it was good that Karen never noticed the obvious. Her obliviousness kept her from getting her feelings too hurt when someone she was talking to give her very clear and somewhat rude signs that they were ready for the conversation to end.

Unbeknownst to Karen, her obliviousness was part of why her life was in the state it was in. Karen had not moved one step closer to what they call "getting a clue" in years, but she didn't know that either. All she knew at this very moment was that if "they" would hurry up and get here she would not be bored. "Boredom was very bad for the skin," Karen thought. And God forbid Karen Miller had bad skin when the cameras got here! This was her moment in the sun, and she would not have it ruined by the bad skin. Karen frowned, and a little line appeared on her forehead.

CHAPTER THIRTY-THREE
Graves Biting Inner Lip

"You know, Pup, all a sudden I don't feel so good. I think I got a bit of the adgida, you know one of them I-talion indigestion things."

"Do you mean angina, Detective Graves? Are you okay?"

"God dammit, Pup, I just told you I got sumpin' in my chest or gut, or maybe even deeper inside. Must have been one of them belly busters I had back at the diner. Damn woman of mine keeps telling me that junk'll be the end of me, and dang if she ain't right."

"Detective, do you want me to pull over? You don't look so good, and you're as white as a ghost." (Paul also thought "and the redness around your neck makes it stand out even more.")

"I don't think so. I got me a perp to catch and I ain't gonna let no damn upset stomach stop me. No, no you just keep on going."

"Okay, you're the boss, but I'm telling you if you start to look any worse, or I see the slightest hint of sweat on your brow, okay?"

"Yeah. Yeah, sure, Pup. Graves laughed., Look pup.. heh heh heh, look at you, starting to act like old Gert, and will you make me eat my veggies too?"

"No, but I will call a paramedic and have them haul your ass off to the nearest hospital, and old Gert will have to come pick you up."

The thought hit detective Graves like a fist to the chest and all of a sudden he felt his chest tighten all the more. "Gert..." thought Detective Graves, "I can't be with Gert. I haven't even replaced Bear yet. What the hell would I do with Gert? Hell, she wouldn't know what to do with me either, no, no I can't be with Gert. All those problems and issues that woman has, from being adopted in infancy to the physical and psychological abuse, to all those years of disillusionment, to the barren womb. She has way too much going on inside that little head of hers and all them fancy head-shrinkers ain't done a damn thing to fix her. Got me stuck with a broken, crazy woman that what they did. Just went ahead and made her more insane.

I had her all sewn up, had all those things in her head all pressed down and almost forgotten. Years of trying to convince her that all that stuff didn't really matter and that it might not have even happened, that it might all have been just her crazy head dreaming it all up. And them head doctors was supposed to fix the last pieces of her. Instead, they went ahead and let it all out, encouraged her to let it all out, and told her it did all happen and that she needed to embrace them, own them, then forgive it all. Forgive her parents, who weren't responsible or man and woman enough to think before fucking and bringing a child into this world, a child those bastards didn't even want or have courage sufficient to stand up and tough it out for. Forgive the angry mixed up people who took her and promised they would love her and give her a family, but rather gave her fear and bruises. Forgive all the lying men and the bullshit women who feigned friendship to get close only to fuck with her screwed up head. Those doctors didn't know what the hell they were doing. "Yep, if I had my way, I'd shoot them all."

"Stop traveling and be with Gert? No way Jose. I think I'll take my chances in the hospital or in the damn desert."

Detective Graves bit his inner lip and took the pain. He didn't wince when his chest thumped and felt like it was caving in. Instead, he just smiled thinned lipped and smacked Paul on the arm. "Drive on the boy and stop all that sassin'. It ain't good for a pup to sass his superior. Builds bad habits and I'm here to teach you about life as a detective." With that Paul sped up, pulled to the middle of the road and drove closer to Ordin, closer to Karen, closer to going home to be with his little girl, closer to freeing himself. He just didn't know it yet.

CHAPTER THIRTY-FOUR
Karen – At Odds with Herself

"It's his own damn fault, and I will not feel bad, as this is my moment. I don't care how nice he is. I don't, I don't, I don't. I want this. I need this. Why are you trying to take it away from me, stupid brain?"

Karen sometimes thought out loud. It was a habit that caused people to believe she was a bit immature and maybe even a little "bothered." The truth was that Karen was starting to feel a bit guilty about what she was about to bring down on a man she knew, she admired, and maybe even felt an attraction for. Karen Miller did things like this a lot. She would make a decision based on some burning desire she had, without thinking it through, of course, and then she would feel a little pang of guilt or doubt. This would inevitably sink her further into the self-loathing state than she usually existed in. Immediately following would be the overwhelming urge to do something, or say something, which would lead her to wind up with her foot in her mouth or some other very uncomfortable and usually embarrassing situation. This was the cycle of Karen's conscience. Today it was about to get a thorough work out.

Karen had already made the call to 'Cold case Killers' and she had already had her first tiny bout of guilt. She had even almost told Ordin. It was only her deep desire to break out of the life she had now and into the life, she thought she should have that kept her from telling Ordin to run. However, Karen was now starting to get that anxious feeling deep down, and she knew from experience that it would only be a few hours before she was doing or saying something crazy again. Not that she wanted to do or say stupid things. After all, Karen thought of herself as quite sane; she just always wound up in that place. First in her gut, then in her head, then in her mouth, then with her whole body, as was most notably exemplified in the awful experiment with Cynthia Rudd. Nonetheless, Karen was determined that she would not mess this up.

And still, something inside of her wanted to protect Ordin from the people coming to get him, protect him from the bad things that people would say about him, especially the girls from the neighborhood association. Karen wanted to protect Ordin from her herself. Karen wrestled with that notion for a second, but how could she protect Ordin and still have her big debut? How could she find a way to turn him in and still keep him safe? "What would I do," she thought, "if he was killed in jail, or worse if he put up a fight when the cops tried to take him? What if there was a huge standoff and he even took me as a hostage?"

Karen was working herself up into a regular tizzy. "The possibilities... and what if I wound up on the national news? I would have to tell my story of how I survived the harrowing experience. Of course, I know how I would survive it. I would just let him have me and manhandle me any way he wanted to and then I would talk to him very softly and tell him how much he had to live for, and why letting me go would be for the best. I would use every bit of love in me to get him to understand that I would never let people forget him or his sacrifice for me. I would go on the talk show circuit... I mean, except for Maury. I don't like him much, and his shows are always so boring. I mean, there is always about some poor sap wanting to know who the father of her child is and oh whatever, and I would even write a book to keep his memory alive."

Karen was thoroughly gone by now. Her next thought was typical of her and indicative of why her life never quite turned out the way she wanted it to. Where once she thought about warning Ordin, or Ordy as she called him, she now thought, "Wow, with all the possibilities, maybe I should just keep my mouth shut, or maybe I can even arrange to be close to him or the house when they try to take him and conveniently place myself where he can't ignore me." That will surely get him thinking about some hostage taking." Karen felt a spark of what she confused as happiness hit her, this truly was her day. At least for now.

CHAPTER THIRTY-FIVE
Ordin's Letter to Blain

When Ordin finished writing the letter, he felt totally and utterly exhausted. He was tired in his mind, wearied in his soul, burdened in his heart. He was exhausted. He sat back down in his chair and begin to read the letter back for the fifth time, not the entire letter this time, but bits and pieces he wasn't sure about.

"Blain, one of the most important things is to touch your girlfriend, as there is nothing like the human touch." He wanted to sound wise and close like it had not been so long since they had spoken, but his words felt hollow. They felt like replacement words for what he really wanted to say. Ordin wasn't sure how much he should say, or if he really even had the right. Lord knows he didn't feel like he had the right to tell his son, the son he had abandoned, that the human touch is essential, especially when he hadn't been there to touch his own son for so many years. Nevertheless, Ordin let himself feel good for a moment. For a moment he let himself just be a father giving advice, just be a friend trying to say the right thing, just be a man trying to be soft and human… and hard all at once.

The mirror across the room showed Ordin how his short cropped hair had new patches of gray in it. "Hmm, I don't remember being so gray." His bones ached for a second as if to say, "Yes, you are that gray and we're here too. You are getting old, Ordin, and too much time has passed since you looked into the mirror. Ordin turned his eyes away from the mirror, shifted his weight in the chair, and continued looking over the letter.

"My son, it feels good to read your words, and it hurts at the same time. There are so many things to say to you, so many ways to say I'm sorry, but I think I'll start by saying I've been a coward.

I've been a coward in my life, a coward in my relationships, a coward in my career, a coward to my family and a coward to my God. I don't know how you recover from that, or if a simple apology is enough. My father once said, 'Son, never apologize, because it does no good to the person you hurt. It only makes you feel better that you said something, but the hurting is already out there, and sorry does not make it hurt less. It only means you know you hurt them.' Sometimes I agree with him, but sometimes I think that he was wrong. He never knew that saying you're sorry was not the end, but the beginning and that you have to back it up with actions. Words can never fix what actions broke. Actions have to be the glue to repair the damage done, but words accompanied with actions are powerful, and intend to back up my words with actions now in life."

"I don't know how to give you advice, it feels like a ghost trying to tell the living how to live. I do also remember something my mother said, and I think it might help. She said, 'The difference between a man and a boy is that a boy from the time he wakes until the time he goes to sleep is consumed with his own selfish needs, doing anything and everything to fulfill those needs regardless of who he hurts along the way. On the other hand, a man is consumed from the time he wakes until the time he goes to sleep. Consumed with fulfilling the needs of the ones he loves, doing whatever it takes regardless of how much he has to sacrifice himself, and being wholly mindful of any he may have damaged in the process.' Take these words to mean that I love you, and I know you will stand up for your new family, and do better than I did." Ordin reread that part over again, just to make sure the words were right and he felt his heart say, "Yes he will understand."

Ordin took the letter, folded it into thirds, opened it again, and then folded it into thirds once more, put it in the envelope, but didn't seal it, just in case he had more to say later in the day after he ate and had his evening tea. He shifted his weight again, looked up into the mirror anew, and this time, the gray didn't look so gray, his bones didn't ache so much, and he didn't feel so far away from his son. Ordin smiled a slightly pained half-smile, put his hand on the letter and for a moment he was home. The accident had never happened, the two extremist groups had never decided to make his life and his home and family their battleground. He never had run away, Sonya had never left, and Blain his son, his only child, was still just a boy, who like any other boy needed his "father" and his "father" delivered. Ordin's half smile blossomed into a full grin. Ordin felt hope.

CHAPTER THIRTY-SIX
Gertrude

"Hey, Val, I'm back, so you don't say, uh-huh, no, yes. Anyhow, I have to go, but let's decide between the brown gravy and the white for the main sauce, okay? Gotta go. Love ya."

Gertrude put down the phone, walked past the humming TV, and looked out at the garden, then to her cottage cheese and pitas she prepared for lunch, thought about it and grabbed the chips next to the counter. "Oh well, back to my diet tomorrow then."

The loud ding told her that a load of laundry was finished washing and was ready to go into the dryer. Gertrude always used All with fabric softener, because J.H. claimed that other detergents made his clothes stink and itch, and also they always seemed to be coming up with a new and improved version. She did this without ever thinking that, if it was new, how could they be improving it and if it needed improving what was wrong with it before and should they just wait till they get it right before they release it?

"Errrr, she huffed, with every fold of the laundry, Gert thought of a couple things that frustrated her about J.H; like his inability to see that if he would just put his darn toothbrush away, it wouldn't leave those spots on the counter which he squeals he hates so much. And how he leaves those smelly black police shoes at the door, which causes him to blame Bear for the constant smell of flatulence that ruins his appetite as he says, which ruins the food that I spent all day making. Because if it weren't prepared, he would make me feel incompetent, with comments like, "Damn, Bear, what does that damn woman do all day?" There's no food, the place stinks like a fart, and there're spots all over the bathroom mirror."

Sometimes Gert felt as if she could just murder him, then she might have a bit of peace for a while. Then sometimes she giggled a little and thought, that fool man of mine. Because after all, at least in Gert's mind, it was better to have a man to take you for granted then to be like Val going from man to man, hiding it from their father, whom Val still lived with at age 49. Masking the fact that Val could never move on from our parent's divorce when we were eleven and five and having to live with several relatives from both sides of our estranged broken family.

Gertrude knew that this was one of the primary reasons that she as well as Val always felt a dark void that hung around like a friend you met in kindergarten that starts to cling and annoy is sweet and innocent but also eats paste. This very thing is what created the difference between Gertrude's not being able to separate from anyone or anything she in any way held dear and her sister's inability to put faith into holding on to anyone.

So Gert folded the laundry, cooked the food, gardened a little on Tuesdays, has a mint julep around three, not to get crazy, but just to take the edge off as she starts preparing dinner. She goes to the farmers' market on Thursdays to check on the freshest produce of the week, because God knows J.H. just will not shop with her on Saturday, which is his day off. She visits Clara Burton on Wednesdays, a quadriplegic woman, whose aid she gives a well needed three-hour break once a week, and hosts the Monday bridge game with the ladies from her Rotary club, whom all see the game as the perfect way to end a weekend of dealing with their husbands. "Nothing like a little gossip and a mint julep to energize your week and start it with a bang," Lanette always says. Mostly, Gertrude thought about how she was going to make her life better, make it feel better, make herself look better, make her do something better with her life, just be better.

CHAPTER THIRTY-SEVEN
Kristine and Willow, Paul's Wife and Daughter

"Oh boy, oh boy, what time will Daddy be back? We're going to ride ponies today you know."

"Daddy may not make it back in time, honey," Paul's wife Kristine said

"Why not? What do you mean?"

"Well, sometimes daddy's make promises they can't keep."

Kristine Johnson was more than Paul Johnson's wife. She was also vying for head of pediatrics and a seat on the hospital board. Most of the others practitioners saw Kristine as ambitious, gregarious, astute and sure of what she wanted.

Right now what Kristine wanted was a call from her husband, to say that he was done with this little tryst with the police force and that he would return to finish his doctorate in anthropology. True, Kristine always knew Paul had a lofty desire to change the world. She just did not know it would be one seedy criminal at a time. Kristine also could not shake the revulsion she felt for the modern police force and the effect it was having on Paul. She saw him changing before her eyes and felt powerless to stop the changes she felt and saw in him.

Once upon a time, Paul would respond to a story on the news concerning a domestic violence situation with a concerned diatribe about how low self-esteem leads to opening the self, to relationships where they are either abused or the abuser. Now he would respond to the same story with an explicative laden rant about how those idiots are still choosing this life and choosing each other when they should either blow each other's heads off or walk away from the relationship. Changes like this were beginning to concern Kristine about the effect on their relationship and what affect his growing negativity and cynicism were having on their daughter, Willow.

Kristine's pause and blank stare caused Willow to tug at her sleeve and look up wide-eyed at her seemingly dazed mom. "Mommy, Mommy, when is daddy coming home then?"

"He will be here when he gets done." Kristine knew that this was the best explanation she could give Willow for when her dad would be home. She had learned in Paul's first year on the force that just because he said he was done at 2 p.m. did not mean Paul would be finished, and it especially did not mean he could just leave and come home. Kristine had far too many experiences where Paul said he had a "situation" that was going to keep him "here." She also learned this could mean "here" at the station or "here" on the streets chasing down some ne'er do well, who was either trying to kill him or get away.

"But I really wanted to go ride ponies today," squeaked Willow." But Willow knew that when she hears 'he'll come home when he's done,' most likely it meant that daddy would not be home until it's too late. So Willow went up to her room, took out her stuffed rabbit, Mr. Floppy, put one of her dad's police hats on his head, sat him down at the table, crossed her arms, thrust her hips to one side (a posture she had no doubt seen her mother take), and began to admonish Mr. Floppy about his unreliability, though she was only repeating words she heard her mom say, that is, when she wasn't supposed to be listening. Willow was clearly upset with Mr. Floppy.

CHAPTER THIRTY-EIGHT
Blain – Breathing

... 6 days earlier

"Breathe, breathe. Take a deep breath, lean back. Okay, husbands, this is where you come in. Support the back, hold the neck and the hand, look her in the eyes and tell her how painless and easy this is going to be."

Blain was growing tired of the droning voice of the Lamaze instructor, who seemed to be a throwback to the seventies, replete with tie-dye shirt, (with that really weird green and funky brown) frizzy white girl half fro and large feather earrings. Why did she keep saying husbands? Did she just assume that we were all married, or did she know that some of us were not married? Did she know that some of us were scared as hell at the mere thought of being married and that this whole child thing was a bit overwhelming? Why did she keep using words like, support and courage and be there?

Why did she feel the need to lie to these women, about it being easy for them, when there was nothing easy about forcing a six to 10-pound thing out of your body? Maybe she knew that relative to the whole situation that the women actually did have it easy and that it was the fathers that were in for eighteen years of child support prison. If so, then yes, he could just hold her hand and say it's all going to be easy.

Blain had spent the last six months thinking about what it was like to grow up without a dad and what exactly that made him. Was he some statistic or was he just a product of a bad situation? He could not help but ask himself, whether his father ever really even wanted him? Or did he just run away? Was he also feeling the same sense of being overwhelmed that he was feeling now? It was thoughts like these that prompted Blain to sit down and write a letter to his father, though he was not the letter writing type. Nor did he know what to expect or even hope from it.

Blain only knew he needed something more than he had now, some sort of connection with the man that gave him life. He did not want to be buddies or romanticize about some tear-filled reunion where his father would apologize for all the years away, somehow knowing exactly what each day without him felt like. Blain did not expect his father to understand what it felt like to be one of the only kids that could not participate in the father-son pictures at the end of the school year. He wondered whether his father felt the same incomplete, empty feeling whenever he saw some professional ball player make some tearful speech after Blain had won whatever championship it was that he had competed for, professing how he owed everything to his dad. No, Blain only wanted a connection and some sense of assurance that he was good enough, that he was man enough to pull this off. He wanted that thing that sons want from their dads, that intangible sense of protection, something like the feeling that if it all became too much, you could just let it go, and your father would step in, step up and take over. Kind of like his pastor had explained what it was like to know and depend on God. Blain needed his dad. He wondered had his letter been enough if it alone could move a mountain of time and produce a man out of thin air.

CHAPTER THIRTY-NINE
Eleanor, Karen's Mom

When the contestant said, she thought the showcase item price was worth $4,000, Eleanor, Karen's mom, nearly jumped out of her skin, yelling at the TV, "You stupid shit! You just lost an Italian vacation!" Eleanor usually lost her cool when she watched the Price is Right, especially when they reached the showcase showdown. To Eleanor, this was what separated the women from the girls. Any good shopper or person with any semblance of intelligence whatsoever would know the price of an Italian vacation, she thought. She also thought, "This is just the kind of mistake that her daughter Karen would make."

Eleanor always cared for her kids, some more than others, but she liked to think that she hid her favoritism well. Eleanor knew that Karen always felt she was her least favorite. The fact that she never made it to any of Karen's recitals or even a single parent teacher conference likely spoke volumes to Karen about her place in the family pecking order. Eleanor had felt somewhat responsible for the state of her middle child, although traditional psychology would say that most middle children do not receive the attention that they need, which leads to a lack of nurture which often manifests itself in various forms of acting out.

Eleanor recalled one specific episode of Karen's which affected her so much that it alone shaped the arc of their current relationship, though it had happened years ago during Karen's senior year in High school. This was a few weeks before the start of what was to be Karen's senior year and her run to take what she thought was her rightful place as senior prom queen and Bronson High royalty. Karen's principal, Mr. Macky, had called Eleanor to ask her to come up to the school for an emergency conference. It seems Karen had behaved in a manner so unbecoming of a prom queen that Mr. Macky intended to indicate that Karen was no longer welcome to complete her senior year at Bronson High.

It seemed that Mr. Macky and the Bronson High faculty did not approve of Karen's assertion of her rights of royalty. Her assertion evidenced by her putting several of her loyal subjects up to painting "Hail to Queen Karen" in both end zones of Bronson High's new 750-thousand-dollar stadium, in preparation for the first football scrimmage. To Karen, the football field seemed like an obvious choice to remind the student body whom "they "elected their queen the previous year. To Karen's "loyal subjects," this incident had less to do with the fact that they saw Karen Miller as a beautiful, strong, deserving debutante that anyone would do anything for. The incident was their recognizing an opportunity to get a girl whom most of her fellow students saw as arrogant, mildly attractive, a self-pious fraud, and whom they realized that no one voted for, kicked out of school.

Not only did Mr. Macky insist that Eleanor pay for the expensive astroturf to be replaced, but he also considered pressing criminal charges of vandalism as well as having her paying for the counseling of the poor misguided students that Karen had talked into doing her dirty work. It was at this point that Eleanor stopped feeling guilty for moving the family half way across the state and taking the kids away from their father, which she had up to this point overcompensated for by being less restrictive and punitive towards her children regarding their undesirable behaviors. This particular behavior however took the cake, and Eleanor was both embarrassed and livid. In her mind, it was hard enough being the often talked about the single mother of five, but to also have to foot the bill for Karen's display was where the line needed to be drawn.

Karen had become less of a victim of her father's abuse and more of a burden to a family struggling to hang on emotionally and financially. The confrontation that ensued between Karen, Eleanor and her younger brother and sister, not only brought several neighbors out of their sleepy homes, but it also brought two patrolmen that had been called by a neighbor reporting a possible homicide on the Millers front lawn. Needless to say, the ostracism of the Millers became a neighborhood sport and forced Eleanor to uproot her three children remaining home and move to yet another town almost at the edge of the state.

Eleanor never forgave Karen for her antics, nor did her siblings who felt that Karen had caused them to lose their friends and any chance that they had for a normal life. In fact, they weren't so sure that it wasn't some of Karen's famous behavior that caused the fight between her mother and father that ended in a bloody tirade, which lead them on this journey, to begin with. Now several years removed from that time, whenever Eleanor became agitated she found that her thoughts returned to that one significant incident and sparked a now deep seeded angst towards Karen. This feeling was also echoed in her siblings' aloof attitudes when it came to the subject of why they never spoke to or about their sister.

"You dumb asses could have been soaking in Italy near the Mediterranean Sea, but no, now you'll go home with a lovely sunbeam toaster and a year's supply of Rice-a-Roni. Yep, just like my Karen, destined to be a loser no matter what is given to you." Eleanor picked up the remote, changed the channel, grabbed her TV guide and began to read.

CHAPTER FORTY
Emergency Response Lights

The scene is always the same on these roads, Graves thought. Evergreens now filled the landscape, you could feel the change in population. A few cars here and there passed, mostly going from community to community to get their daily chores done. This was one part of the job that Graves did not mind. In fact, he actually liked being on the road. For one it got him away from the desk and away from Gert. Also, he always felt a sense of adventure, and truth be told, Detective Graves was given to fanciful thoughts of adventure. He liked to believe that if he had been born in another time, he would have been a sheriff in the old west on horseback, or perhaps a captain in the British Royal Navy, chasing pirates across the seven seas.

"Detective?" Paul had repeated himself several times now and was growing annoyed with Graves and felt a bit nervous about the detective's condition. He had never seen Graves so listless and sweaty. As they passed the 150-mile marker of the I-80, they begin to see signs for Lake Tahoe, colorful signs of happy people with big smiles either enjoying their day or on their way to enjoy some outdoor leisure activity. Paul slightly bemused himself, thinking of the local population which is made up of sleepy retirees, who would rather play bingo than a softball and would cherish the thought of a hot cup of tea over a hot night of dancing.

Paul was jerked back to attention by the sound of a heavy grunt. He looked over and saw, or rather felt, Detective Graves curl up in his seat. He saw his hand clench into a tight fist and beads of sweat pour down his brow. "Detective!" Paul shouted, "Are you okay? What the hell is going on with you, detective?"

"Russ dive on't ass up hart," Graves slurred, upon hearing this, Paul made the decision to pull the car over.

"Detective, you are not alright, and we need to get you to a hospital now." Paul pulled his coat from the back seat throwing it on Graves and considered whether or not to get the silver blanket from the emergency kit from the trunk. Instead, he decided to get back on the road and head to the nearest hospital.

Not only was Grave's color disturbing, but also the fact that he had not opened his big fat mouth to chime out some red neck jargon was the most telling fact about his condition. His complexion had gone from a reddish-white to a pallid gray. Paul knew two things about this color change. One that it meant the person was either having a stroke or a heart attack. And two, that they immediately need some extra warmth, so Paul also turned the heater on low, hoping this along with his coat could provide Graves the warmth he needed until he could get Graves to the next town with a hospital. Paul got on his radio to reach the local dispatch as well as to determine the nearest medical center, which he found out was ten miles or roughly fifteen minutes away. Paul also switched on his emergency response lights and pressed hard on the gas pedal.

For Paul, the trained automatic response to an emergency kicked in, yet this felt different. Next to him was his partner, who at this point had not even contested having Paul's coat draped over him as if he were a small child. Usually, an emergency response dealt with someone you did not know, someone who you were there to serve, but had no personal connection with. Graves had been Paul's partner for only two weeks now, but Paul had been familiar with Graves during his five years in the precinct. As dysfunctional a family could be, the police force was neither close as one is close to a brother or sister, nor was it distant. There existed a bond that was robust and unbreakable, a bond in purpose and experiences. It was this bond that sharpened Paul's focus and heightened his intensity as he went from merely pressing the gas pedal to full out flooring the sedan, with both hands tightly and alertly on the wheel. Paul needed a hospital, and he needed one now. As much as Graves was a loud-mouthed, pig-headed, red neck to him, Paul was determined not to let Graves die on his watch.

CHAPTER FORTY-ONE
Ordin's Going into Town

Had it been an hour that he had slept or just a few minutes? Ordin raised himself up from the chair, stretched a little, and looked at the clock. "Good, only twenty minutes," he thought, "still, time to get to Howard's Garden Supply and Hardware." Ordin's love of cooking kept him a slave to the care of his garden, and it was the time he started the process of prepping the garden to be turned over and put to bed for the winter. The process consisted of tilling under the old plants back into the ground, adding soil nutrient supplements, spreading the frost tarp, and securing it to the ground with stakes.

It was for this purpose that Ordin was headed to town. He grabbed his key chain, with the pocket Leatherman attached, his Kangol cap, and the letter. Ordin took a few steps, became mindful of the letter in his hand, and turned to place it back on the counter. Then he thought again and clutched it a little tighter and turned back towards the door. His mind told him that he wanted to wait to send the letter until he reviewed it after dinner, but his soul told him that it was time. No more waiting, it said to him, no more time going by, no more second guessing. It was time to start the process of recreating his relationship with his son and this time he would write the story with his own hands. He would not let a judge or jury write it. He would not let the NRA, or the N.A.O.G.V.V. put their spin on what was to happen to his life. He would not let an accident determine who he was, nor would he let situations beyond his control steal away the potential his life had. Ordin would not let the past determine his future. The letter was coming with him, and he would open the mailbox at the post office, place the letter inside, watch it slide down the chute, turn and walk away and not look back. This time, when he walked away, he would actually be moving forward.

As he started the car, his hands shook a bit, but then again they always shook these days, whether it was the result of his aging body or the daymares that kept his nerves frayed and on edge. Ordin's hands were never really steady and probably would never be again. He turned on the radio as he pulled out of the driveway. It was on his favorite station these days, a political talk show that featured news and viewpoints from both perspectives of the political landscape. Pundits would come on air and expound about the latest hot issue in Washington that they were certain was a game changing the decision that would shake up the country. The country had changed so much since Ordin was a young lad. Gone were the Dan Rathers and Walter Cronkites, who came on the few television stations that carried extended news coverage and gave us the "plain truth, raw and uncensored." There were no twenty-four-hour news channels back then, neither were there stations sponsored and controlled by a political party and a corporation's that fit them in their pockets.

Ordin liked this show for its 'old time appeal' and Alan Taylor was old school. Today he was talking about gay marriage, a topic that was on fire in Washington, with both sides claiming that the core of the issue was family, what it meant to the idea of the tradition of family, and what it could mean to the future of that tradition. For Ordin, the idea of family was painted by the events of his past and the circumstances of his childhood. He rarely thought of himself as having a position on the issue, but he knew that family was the one most important thing a person had these days. He was finally in the process of giving his, or rather what was left of his family, the attention it deserved. He could only hope that the actions he was taking today would eventually yield the fruit he desired. Ordin turned the radio up and made a left out of the driveway, a right at the corner, and headed straight onto Highway 34 into town. Allan Taylor continued to mock the pundit's positions. How they were saying the same thing, about the importance of family, while accusing the other side of destroying it. Ordin chuckled to himself, put his left blinker on and changed lanes, just as he hoped he was doing with his life.

CHAPTER FORTY-TWO
"The" Call

He went down the hall, around the corner, into the waiting room, and onto a couch in the Intensive Care Unit. Paul had been in many ICU's before for various reasons: to question a suspect, to identify a victim, even with his own mother-in-law who had died of a heart attack several years before. Paul was never very close to his mother-in-law, ever since he chose to join the police force early on in his marriage. It was his mother-in-law's opinion that it was a waste of his potential and definitely something she could not see her daughter marrying into. She felt it was beneath both him and her daughter to do something that would expose them and her granddaughter to the dregs of society.

Maybe she watched too much TV. Maybe she was too conservative. But her feelings about the police force and the officers that served on it was solid and unchanging, even after Paul had done such noble things early in his career as helping a mother give birth, and finding a teenage runaway returning her home safely. This, Paul thought, would undoubtedly have altered her opinion of officers as egomaniacal brutes and corrupt thugs. Unfortunately, all this did was give his mother-in-law something to wave off as a kind of anomaly that was destined to be tainted.

This trip to the ICU for Paul was different as this trip involved a partner who there was definitely an emotional closeness, a closeness that was hard to be as objective as is required when Paul is in the ICU as a police officer for other victims. It was these thoughts that troubled Paul, as the idea that he would have to call Graves wife began to crystallize. This was a woman whom Paul was only familiar with through occasionally overhearing Graves' side of the conversation.

Paul's perception of Gert was that she was like most wives of policemen who actually stuck it out. They were in a relationship of servitude and solitude, each of them waiting for that call or the knock on the door that ushered in the feeling of utter sadness or relief if not both. Most of these women lived in a suspended state of life, where life insurance and health insurance were their primary source of solace. As the phone rang, Paul took a deep breath, while attempting to frame his thoughts of how to deliver the news. Would he give his standard speech to families of victims, or would he take a more personal approach?

The voice on the other side sounded tired, but content. Paul's voice cracked, "Mrs. Graves, uh, Gert, or is it, Ms. Graves?" Gert answered apprehensively as this sounded already too much like 'that call.' The call that she always dreaded but knew had to come. There was also something else in her voice, something Paul unexpectedly recognized as a hint of relief that the call was finally here, no longer to be dreaded in anticipation. This troubled Paul as he realized that his own wife had to be building if not already feeling this anticipation as well, and what this really meant about their relationship. The thought that there would be freedom on the other side of the phone call for his wife deeply pained him. Paul also felt that this was sadness that each officer lives with and accepts as part of the cross to be burdened with that comes with the territory of being a police officer. But being on the force was always a choice, a choice that Paul made as well as any other officer. Choice is what life is made of.

"Uh, who is this?" Gert replied.

"Oh, sorry, this is Officer Paul Johnson of the San Francisco police department. I am Detective Graves new partner. We have not met yet. Uhm, ma'am, please do not be alarmed, but there has been an incident involving your husband..."

"Okay, just get to it. Tell me what is going on," Gert interrupted, "what is the incident?"

"Mrs. Graves…"

"Please call me Gert."

"Okay, thank you. Gert, your husband, seems to have suffered a heart attack. We do not know the severity yet. It may be mild, or it may be more severe. Does your husband have a history of heart problems or any member of his family that you know of?"

"J.H. has not had any issues that I know of. Come to think of it, I do not know anything really about his family's medical history or otherwise, that is something we have never talked about. I know that may sound incredible, but it is part of being a police officer's wife. I am sure your own wife would not know of such things off-hand." Paul paused and thought, "Does she? How would Kristine respond to this situation if it were me lying in the ICU?"

"That's okay, ma'am. We were in the middle of an investigation. You may have to actually come over to Carson City, Nevada for the duration of his care here. There are procedural protocols that only a spouse or family member is authorized to handle. My best guess is that he will have to leave the investigation and take some time to recover at home under your care."

Gert responded back after a pregnant silence that Paul mistook as a shock, and with a stutter, in her voice, she asked, "Where do I need to go?"

Inside Gert's head was a confusion of thoughts that had both the long rehearsed necessarily unemotional response of action and the realization of her fears of "this is the moment." But this "moment" was actually worse, for JH was not mildly injured or dead. Mild injuries did not need her to come to the hospital, and dead she had rehearsed for, but this was something she had not rehearsed or planned for. Gert's response betrayed that she did not

90

know exactly what to do. She realized that she would be driving to the hospital to pick up JH, but what was she to do afterward?

In all their years of marriage, Gert and JH had become accustomed to a shell of communication to each other first through their son Winslow, and later with Bear when Winslow left home seven years ago. With Bear likely not going to be alive much longer, Winslow long out of the house, and unfortunately seemingly out of their lives, Gert would have to talk directly with JH. What would this feel like? How would they do it? What would they talk about?

Gert had accepted the distance in communication that existed between her and JH, for this is how it was, and it helped her to build up a defense against "the call." This realization and the accompanying fear of a lack of knowing built up inside of her like a lump that had lodged itself deep in her heart. And yet it was now ready to be painfully excised.

Gert packed swiftly and lightly with only one change of clothes for J.H., a bottle of water, and a can of trail mix. As she grabbed her jacket and keys, and her hand pressed upon the doorknob to turn it, something else happened within her. Within the lump, there was a small light that came on, something that bore a strange semblance to a feeling she had some thirty-odd years ago when a young girl said to a young man, "I do." That faint light was a surprising shimmer of hope.

CHAPTER FORTY-THREE
The Awful Experiment with Cynthia Rudd

All there was for Karen to do now was to wait, sit and wait. "I wonder what is on?" I really do not watch the trash that is on during this time of day, but I have nothing else to do while I wait, so why not? And if they show up, I can always say I was doing research for when I am to be on talk shows." Karen grabbed the remote and sat down on her favorite spot on the couch. As usual, that spot was to the left of the sofa where a TV tray stand stood conveniently for any snack she would want while she flipped through the channels.

Karen generally looked for TV shows that both titillated and fascinated her. For Karen, this was not a hard effort to achieve. If the show included any form of sensationalism or drama where one person ended up in one compromising position or another, or if the show illustrated how one person got a lot of credit or glory, Karen was hooked. Of course, being a megalomaniac, Karen could easily put herself in the role of either character, preferably the one with the grander position.

Today the first show that popped up was the Jerry Springer show. It was a classic episode titled, "My Awkward Lesbian Love Affair."." In this episode, Jerry would have the unsuspecting protagonist on stage under the false pretense of being reunited with a long-lost crush, when from backstage would march the antagonist, who ended up being a participant in some past awful lesbian experience. Next, the two would start yelling at each other, as they blamed each other for how the experiment went bad. And this would be followed by the two going directly at each other like cats in a fight, attempting to rip each other to shreds in front of a jeering audience, usually chanting in rhythm, "Kill, kill, kill, kill…"

For some reason, this form of entertainment had become the escapism of choice for prime daytime TV. This said as much about Karen as it did about modern society and what we allow to entertain us. It would seem that Augustus Caesar's idea of entertaining the masses with blood and a fight for one's life has never actually left our collective psyche, as humanity has claimed to have evolved into an enlightened state. Seemingly the only true difference is that we do not allow someone to actually get killed in reality, but certainly something akin to it.

Karen felt a slight shudder as the topic and the very title of today's Springer's episode was uncomfortably related to her previous affair with a lesbian, the lesbian by the name of Cynthia Rudd. It was long ago, or maybe not that long ago for Karen could not be "that old." Not long after her experience with pledging the Phi sorority, when one would think that type of experience would dissuade anyone from pursuing anything like it, and after a three very short-lived dating relationships with, what shall we say, men that seemed less-than-enthusiastic about Karen as a girlfriend and more as an easy lay. Karen found herself perusing the shelves of a local bookstore in the same-sex relationships section.

Karen remembered what happened. She was looking at a book on how to date a woman when a somewhat stout woman of about 5'6" or 5'7" introduced herself as a fireman. At the time, Karen did not notice that Cynthia had presented herself in the masculine term "fireman" rather than simply as a firefighter. The irony of this missed nuance would serve as foreshadowing for what was to come. It was not long after the introduction that Karen's naivety came to the surface when she gingerly accepted Cynthia's invitation to her house for a light snack. Not more twenty minutes had passed when Karen found herself in one of those

93

compromising positions she commonly wound up in. Cynthia had Karen strip from breast to toenail, with a can of whip cream in one hand and a piñata in the other. Needless to say, when Karen left that evening, she was slightly sore, confused, and perplexed.

One would think that this was a scenario or situation that one would not repeat. Nonetheless, not five days later, Karen found herself accepting a second invitation from Cynthia. This time, it was to be at Karen's house on New Year's Eve. Again, Karen's naively thought that since it was at her own house that it would be safer for her and that she would be more in control. Alas, this was not to be the reality. To Karen's surprise, Cynthia showed up not alone, but rather accompanied by two other persons whom we shall call "ladies only" for the sake of politeness. In all reality, they were what are referred to as "bulldykes," Bonnie and Pauline, who were sisters from Abilene, Texas. After making themselves comfortable on the couch and Bonnie opening up the duffle bag she walked in with and removing what looked like a forearm with a rubber-cased fist attached, Karen knew at this point that there was to be no safety to be had.

What was safety for Karen? It was the feeling that somehow she had made a good decision, and someone had recognized that decision and had acknowledged her for it. That someone had opened their mouth and said something, and the words would make Karen feel warm, and in that warmth, Karen could find a small space for herself, where protection was an afterthought, and she could float carelessly in her thoughts. This was safety to Karen.

Bonnie removed what seemed like a vat of lubricant with the label reading "Jam It," personal self-lubricant, but it didn't seem as if this would be the kind of adventure where Karen would be self-lubricating. It looked like the sisters were bent on lubing and jamming Karen themselves. It struck her as odd that Cynthia, whom Karen thought was really into her, would just stand idly by and let the girls have their way with her. "This can't be what lesbians usually did," Karen thought.

The girls were heavy handed and were rushing through all the parts she thought should be slow. They were holding her down and jamming what seemed like everything in the house into her, regardless of the fact that she must have looked like she was miles away and was not making a sound. Or maybe this was just the way lesbians made love, and that was the reason that they always seemed so angry. No, there was no safety here, and it was somewhere between the third round going into the not too soon final round and before the saddle, but after the ball gag that the experience earned its name, "The awful experiment with Cynthia Rudd."

With this memory swimming on the surface of Karen's consciousness and a slight feeling of unease, Karen decided that watching Jerry Springer was maybe not the best thing to do to prepare for her upcoming stint on the TV talk show circuit. Perhaps a talk show like Stephen Colbert or maybe something between the edgy Springer and the conservative Michael Savage, something like Conan O'Brien would be best. And with this, Karen took a bite out of her bag of pork rinds, took a sip from her diet cola, and again began to flip through the channels.

CHAPTER FORTY-FOUR
Graves - Come Hell or High Water

Graves was sitting on the hill of a park watching his son Winslow tossing a Frisbee with Alan, his son's closest childhood friend. Winslow was only 12 in this dream. The day was warm with a slight breeze and some clouds billowing above. It seemed like today, yet it was so long ago. What had happened to those days? Why could he not have his son back to the way things were when he was 12 before the teenage years hit? It had been 13 years since Winslow was 12 and 7 long years since Graves even spoke to Winslow.

It had taken Graves the first eight years of Winslow's life to actually begin to feel like Winslow was his son, and not just an adopted child that pacified Gert's maternal instinct providing a means to compensate for God's cruel humor on the simple woman in not giving her the ability to have her own child. During Winslow's final days at home, Graves somehow had drawn the line too hard, thinking only what he thought was best, what he thought was right. And by not accepting Winslow for who he was and wanted, Graves had lost a son.

At this point, Graves knew he was in a dream. As he woke, he found his head cloudy, not the relaxing clouds of his dream, but one with the lack of ability to focus, an aching, groggy, disoriented feeling. He did not know immediately where he was, but the surroundings looked hazily like a hospital room. As Graves became more awake, he noticed his side ached like he had been kidney punched by "Iron Mike Tyson." The last thing Detective James Harold Graves remembered was being in the car and listening to his smart-ass trainee blab about ideals.

Now Graves was steadily becoming angry because he knew enough to know that he was in a hospital, and that meant he was in some kind of trouble. The type of trouble that would have Gertrude Graves not far behind with insufferable prodding about eating healthy shit like he was some damn rabbit or perhaps one of those new metro-sexual man-girls that ran around on TV these days. Graves could hear Paul's voice in the hallway, and it sounded like he was having a serious conversation with someone. Then it hit him. Paul was talking to Gert. He had sold him out, turned him into the enemy. He had become Benedict Arnold, or maybe he saw the opportunity to pin him down and collar the perp on his own to grab the publicity that belonged to Graves.

Of course, this was all in Graves' mind, because Paul did what any good officer would do when someone was experiencing a heart attack, that is, get them to the nearest hospital and call the nearest relative, which in this case was Graves' wife, Gertrude. Paul had no idea that to Graves this was akin to committing some cardinal sin, or like igniting the long fuse with its ominous slow-burning that will inevitably and unnervingly head towards the final explosion of the powder keg. In this case, Graves' powder keg was the home life that he created with years of taking for granted and emotionally abusing his wife, and running off his only son. Regardless, even if Paul had known all this, he still would have done his duty first, which was exactly what he did.

Disregarding his present strength, Graves out of anger and fear called out to Paul with what energy he could muster, "Pup! Pup!"

"Okay, Gert, Graves is calling me, so I will see you here tomorrow. If you are still here, I wish it was under better circumstances that we could talk and meet." Paul hung up the phone and entered through the door of Graves' room. "I see you are awake now. That's a good sign. How are you feeling?"

97

"Cut this shit, Pup. That better not have been my old lady you were talking to. Do you know what kind of mess you would cause if she knew I was laid up in a hospital? Before you know it, Gert would be here doting all over me, while meddling with my affairs, like some middle-aged Florence Nightingale."

"I am sorry to hear of that, but I did what I was supposed to do. One minute you were grabbing your chest in pain, incoherent, and the next I am driving you to the hospital and calling your next of kin. Your wife seems like a very sweet, caring and loving person whom you should be lucky to have in your life. Not for nothing, but you are a hard-ass sometimes, so it is almost surprising that you would have a wife who would unquestionably stop everything and come here to help you. Not everyone who we have to take to the hospital has such a person in their lives."

"You have no idea what you are talking about, Pup. Maybe that's how it works up in the upper crust neighborhoods, but where I grew up, a man takes care of himself. He doesn't drag his old lady up every time he has a mere bump on the head or a hiccup of a heart murmur."

"I'm all for a man taking care of himself; however, this is no mere bump on the head or a hiccup of the heart."

"Listen, you do not need to be putting your hands into my business, or getting Gert mixed up with this. You have no idea what you do not know what you are doing. You do not know what Gert is like. She is like the brow-beating moth to a lamp that just will not leave. The last thing I want or need is to have to be under her constant care or her constant scrutiny, and have to deal with that woman on a daily basis with no break."

"She is always going on about all those wild and fancy ideas from Dr. Bill or Phil or Wilbert, or whatever his name is, you know, that guy from the show with that self-important black woman, - about how couples should communicate. As if it was their business how I communicate with my wife. The only communication I need to know is that Gert is not going anywhere, and neither am I. She does her well-enough cooking, and I bring home the money, that is communication enough."

"Our life is fine the way it is. We have a good rhythm or good thing going. Pup, it's like climbing a hill. Your life is a good 'B' where you are. If at the top of the hill was the possibility of an 'A', and you climb the hill, and only still have the "B," did it do you any good to climb the hill? Did you get anything but a lot of waste of effort and time? So let's do this, let's let you keep your life and your house and I will keep my life and my house. Not crossing the lines into each other's personal affairs. Enough said."

With that, Paul turned and begin to leave the room, turning back to Graves as he was exiting the door, "Uh, just one last thing, Detective. You ever stopped to think Gert believes in the "A", and that is why she is willing to drive a half a day's drive to pick your sorry, ungrateful ass up?"

Detective Graves rolled over on his side, winced a bit from the pain, pulled the cover over his shoulder, and murmured something under his breath.

CHAPTER FORTY-FIVE
Paul - Finishing the Task

Paul put down his cell phone, realizing that his reception was no good until he left the parking structure. Besides, he had no idea who he wanted to call or what he wanted to say. The very act of picking up his cell phone was a combination of habit and of not knowing what to do next. He just knew he had to make a move and keep moving. Paul realized that he really didn't know what to do or where he was going, or even why he chose to say yes to this task rather than spending the day with his little girl at the park riding ponies as he had promised.

He gathered his thoughts, leaned forward to reach into his pocket and grabbed his parking ticket. There always seemed to be some issue when you leave a parking structure of a building you don't work in Paul thought. Either you did not get your ticket validated, or the validation is not quite long enough to cover the full price that the attendant, who coincidentally seemed to be in on the scam, always pretended like he had no idea what companies were even in the building.

"I jus' do my job, sir, esir I jus' take the ticket, eplease pay, sir."

Paul could see it coming and was in no mood for it after his slight blow up with Detective Graves. He just wanted to get out of there and to get back on the road to wherever it was he would decide he was going; to do whatever it was he was going to do.

To tell the truth, Paul was relieved he was rid of Graves. He felt he needed his own space at this time. Paul did not wish ill will on the man, and certainly felt sympathy for Graves and what he was about to go through. It seemed like he had a very constrained relationship with his wife and even looked frightened a bit by the prospect of his wife having to come get him and be in charge of his care. Paul wondered how a marriage got to that point, and then he thought of his own marriage. He mused about the strain being on the force was putting on it. Paul could dimly see how one could get to a place where the very idea of being around your wife would cause one to lash out at any and all things. The anxiety and guilt of putting his wife, family, and loved ones in that situation. Like in Graves case, closed down behind a wall to protect yourself and the ones you love from your life as a police officer.

Nevertheless, that was Grave's life and his problem, and like it or not, Paul had a job to do, and he had to push on and get it done. But first, he had to figure out just what that job actually entailed. And surprisingly, Paul thought, if he even had the heart to do it.

Paul had been feeling very agitated about his place on the force. Questions were swirling around his head. Questions like: "Though I'm on the force, do I really belong or want to be a part of it;" and "What, was my real reason for joining the police force in the first place and what was I hoping to accomplish;" and "What has the force become?" Paul did not have answers to these questions, though a part of him knew he would get these answers on this trip. What he could not reconcile with was what he would do with his life once he got those answers.

Paul was pleasantly surprised when the parking attendant took his ticket, lifted the gate and smiled politely as she said, "esir have a nice day." Paul grinned and drove onto the street and onto the main throughway, thinking sometimes you get people wrong by assuming they are what you've already experienced from others.

Paul pulled to the gas station curb, took out his file on the case and began to look it over. What he found seemed like some set up for a reality show or a typical C.S.I episode. It seemed as if his earlier rant at Graves was almost spot on. They were to drive to a small town where a man, who had been living in solitude away from the noise and label of being a murderer of his best friend, and a man who lost his love and his child for the past twenty something years, had secluded himself too. Reach out to what amounted to a nosey neighbor with way too much time on her hands and a remote that seemed to find the programs which illustrated that the lowest common denominator usually finds its own level, even on TV. Gather what was supposed to be new evidence of a crime which was loosely still ruled as an accident, though not a closed case, and confront the gentleman with it. He was to try to pressure him into making a confession and take him back to San Francisco, thusly destroying what must have been the remainder of a broken life.

Paul began to get a sick feeling in his gut. This was not what he wanted to be the catalyst that heralded him into the next step in his career of becoming a senior detective. Though this was weighing on Paul's conscience, the more pressing matter was what was going on in his own marriage and what being on the force had done to it, as well as how or if being a police officer or even a senior detective was fulfilling his original intent and desire for his life. And frighteningly enough, if his current career was not fulfilling his original intent and was taking too much away from his wife and daughter, his family, what would be his alternative?

Paul took a quick inventory of his life. He was thirty-six years old. Paul had a wife whom he had been married to for over fifteen years but did not know if they would make it to sixteen. He had a beautiful daughter whom he loved and cherished and was neglecting for his job. He was in a career that he had spent ten years in, that he had initially taken as a challenge to his sense of civil obligation and was now in complete doubt about. He had a partner whom he could not figure out, and against his sensibilities was now feeling rather relieved that he was going to be out of his hair. Finally, he was now on the road by himself about to destroy one man's life completely which in and of itself was in opposition to everything he thought of himself as, and he was going to do this while bringing glory to some thoughtless, selfish busy-body.

All this cycled through Paul's head, and it seemed the situation would only get worse before it got better if he continued on this path. Paul had some choices to make, and wasn't that what courage was - making hard choices even though you know the outcome is going to bring you some pain as well as a resolution?

Paul pulled out of the gas station and onto the highway, checked his navigation, saw he had slightly over twelve hours left before he even reached the destination, and let out a heavy sigh, things were about to change, and Paul knew he would be the one changing.

CHAPTER FORTY-SIX
Blain - Seven Days Earlier

He turned over the letter again and again as if by doing so more words would appear to explain what 'she' could have been thinking to keep this away from him, or that words would seem to say how deeply pained the man on the other side of this letter was. The letter had so many words with double meanings in it, words like fear and sadness, but no explanation of what he feared or what made him sad. Was he sad about what he read in my letter written years ago? Did he own his part in setting up a situation where my only recourse was to write a letter on paper to someone who gave me life and was, at least by traditional standards, supposed to be there to nurture and steer that life to a safe place, and yet was a total stranger to me.

Blain could feel some anger welling up in him as he read the letter for the tenth time in the past week. He was angry at so many things. Angry at his mother, whom he knew would only back her decision to keep his father's response to his letter from him for so long, and this by saying it was for his protection, that she was only seeking to provide him with some of the safety that his father was supposed to supply. Blain knew that the truth was somewhere in the middle, that it was probably more of his mother's anger at his father that kept her from giving him the letter, and not wanting to admit to herself that his father was a good man that cared about his son. And that she chose to leave, not him. Blain knew he could not be hateful towards her, because after all, wasn't she only doing what hurt people do? He remembered a saying he once heard, "Hurting people are only human and lonely, hurting people are dangerously human. They do things that cause and deflect pain in that humanity." For this reason, he could not hate her.

It was for the same reason that he first wrote his father some seven years ago seeking to forgive him in homage to this mantra. Blain gave it to the family counselor who promised to have it forwarded to him. It was when he did not receive a response that he began to lose faith in his father and the seemingly wise mantra. Blain waited days at first, thinking that the mail was always like a watched pot. And then after a week and then a month went by, he began to feel the heaviness in his chest every time he saw something on TV or heard something on the radio about families. His thoughts were always the same, "Why not me? Why not my life? How can I have some of that happiness?" And his answers always hit him like bricks, "He doesn't want you. He can't want you. He isn't your hero."

Knowing now that his father had responded did not change everything that he or any person would have become after that kind of experience. All the pain and emotion that goes into molding who you are, because you lived through it, but it did give him freedom. Freedom to talk to his father. Freedom to reach out across time and distance to take a chance at healing old bitter wounds that, if left unattended, can fester and become cancers in a person's life.

Blain had known friends and acquaintances who never took the time or chance to root out some of their pain. He had watched it become cancerous and eventually devour them and everything light and desirable about them, leaving them broken, bitter, empty people that you almost pitied, if not for the understanding that it was their own choice never to challenge the pain or the circumstances that led to it. He was not them. He had challenged and questioned those circumstances, his own pain, and the challenges led him to the place he was now: standing here with a letter in his hand that had been delivered seven years ago but never received.

Blaine thought about his own letter and what he said, the questions he tried to ask in an artful manner as not to scare his father away. He remembered how challenging that endeavor was as a burgeoning young man in the midst of his teenage years needing a father around to help understand the physical and emotional changes that occur during that time of life, a father to be a guide during the first major transition in life.

Blain had resorted to various older male friends as surrogate fathers, even his grandfather, but somehow that did not seem the same as having his own father. It seemed like providence at this point in his life that he found this letter his father had written while looking for his baby stuff in the attic to use for his own baby. A time when he again needed a father, to discover he might actually have a father who might be willing to come back into his life.

If his father did decide to come back into his life, that would mean some explanation of how and why would have to be had with his mother, and that meant confrontation as well. They say the way life ebbs and flows are predicated on what causes the tides, or what pulls and pushes on life, such as the storms at sea that cause tides, where the storm itself is a confrontation between forces of nature.

In finding this letter from which Blain would write and send what must be a long awaited and nearly past hope reply, he knew that the forces of nature in his sea were about to create a confrontation which meant a storm, but a storm that Blain believed he could weather, and would gain from. With that thought, Blain looked at the letter one last time, put it back into his pocket, and went back up into the attic for the third time that week to continue the search for things of his life past that he might use now and for his future life.

CHAPTER FORTY-SEVEN
Gert Goes to Get Him

With the radio on, Gertrude Graves began her journey. She had a smile on her face and in her heart. Gert was feeling hopeful about the idea of a change in the dynamic of her relationship, and yet she had not thoroughly thought about what that change would look like or how it would play itself out. The truth was she hadn't actually examined her place in the relationship for some time. True, she had taken a look at herself and had even taken a look at J.H. himself, but to take a hard look at the real state of her marriage had been too overwhelming of thought for her to take on.

It could have been the prospect that any change in how she and J.H. talked to each other than through Bear would have seemed out of place if any of them attempted to do anything different, and who wanted to rock the proverbial boat for what would have appeared as out of the blue. How she and J.H. communicated worked; it was not ideal. It could be perhaps better, but it worked. If nothing changed their entire life, their life would still be okay as it always had been so far. True, there was no growth in their relationship, or really in their personal lives.

They had both been living in a routine, which was fine, but a routine nonetheless. And in such a routine, their life was an even-level plateau. They had the comfort of knowing that each of them was not alone. They had each other, even if their having each other had become a shell of a routine of living. It was comfortable. In reality, it was a comfortable loneliness, for even though they were together, they were living their lives only in the physical proximity of each other.

Long ago they had stopped really being with each other, talking to each other directly, living a life of routine individually with each other. With Bear looking like he had not much more life to live, and now J.H. having a heart attack which would require him to not work for a while, this was an opportunity for change. This opportunity also meant possibility, and it was both the opportunity and possibility that was the source of Gert's small light of hope she felt within that lightened the clump she felt.

They say an awakening is like an epiphany, a sudden realization of something previously unknown or at least unacknowledged. Gert was about to have an awakening, an awakening of her place in the relationship and of her own desires of her life. And then there was an acknowledgment of that this really was not working for her, this comfortable loneliness was not how she wanted to live the rest of her life. This awakening would crystallize into a desire, and this desire would manifest into a need, a need for more. More of what she was not sure; she did not know. All she knew was that she wanted more.

It seems that awakenings are like this for many. Once the desire for more is there, the more is not defined. In fact, it rarely is determined at the onset, but it is there. This beginning of the desire for more in our lives is itself an opportunity to create possibilities as we ponder and choose what that more is. What began on Gert's trip as the starting point or fresh start in creating the possibilities would not only change the now and the time that J.H. was out of work but also would be the catalyst for a change that would affect the rest of her life. Gert found herself incredibly pensive, so much so that she nearly missed the exit that was not marked with a place, but only a direction. That direction was east, east of here, east of where she was, east of anywhere.

The glimmer of hope, though a lightener of the clump she felt, also brought with it its own heaviness, the heaviness of self-examination, of responsibility, which often includes taking ownership for what we allow in our lives. For Gert, this burden of self-examination included the self-loathing, an acknowledgment that at any moment of her life in the past she could have challenged her own life, her fear, even cowardice, in approaching her life in full honesty of where it was at, and how it really did not work for her. It was not what she wanted. What Gertrude was lacking was not a better relationship. What she was lacking was courage.

Courage is defined as doing what we know is right for ourselves even though it is going to hurt. Courage is at any point being able to look at oneself honestly and authentically at any and all times regardless of how much it might hurt. Courage is acting on this honest and authentic way of being. It does not have any sincerity in it, for often sincerity consists of mere words without action, which is not courage at all.

As Gert was driving along the freeway, she began to notice the people in the other cars she passed, and that passed her. Are any of them living their life with courage? Or do they all just drive along with no real thought to their lives, real in that the thought is followed by action with intent? She passed one woman that seemed to be singing at the top of her lungs, a heavy-set man driving a silver Mercedes which appeared to be engaged in a conversation on the phone while shaving, and even texting on the phone at the same time. Then there was a large nondescript SUV with three children in the back that seemed to be drawing the driver's attention from the road. And then there was Gertrude, herself, driving on the freeway on her journey east of loathing, east of cowardice, east of less, east to more.

CHAPTER FORTY-EIGHT
Ordin – Pictures from the Past

Reaching to open the glove box of his car, Ordin was retrieving stamps to place on the letter before he entered the post office. A picture slid out just as he opened the glove box. The picture immediately sent chills inside Ordin's heart. The picture was taken by the bystander photographer, Laurence Lemn. It caught Ordin and his long-time friend, Peter Draingold, in what was intended to be friendly banter over who was going to have the last shot to break the wagered tie of who bagged the most fowl that day, but ended up being a true nightmare of the death of a friend. Heavy beads of sweat broke out on Ordin's brow, and once again it took over. It was the constant barrage of daymares that had come to haunt his waking life, just as much as they had his sleep, leaving him exhausted and spent.

He dropped the gun, then picked it up as if picking it up again would somehow silence the boom that came from its end, then dropped it again. The grunting and gurgling that came from Peter, who was nearly five feet away and squirming, was deafening to Ordin's ears. He walked in what seemed like slow motion over to the body, now ceasing to move at all. Ordin looked down and what his eyes first caught caused him to retch immediately. Peter was gray and still, his chest bore a gaping wound like some kind of deer or bear that these woods had come to know as the spirits of lost nature. There were bits of lung that were exposed to the smell of gunpowder, blood, and bile wafting thick and heavy in Ordin's nose. He knelt next to him and in an anguished rage shouted, "Damn fool! Damn fool, look what you have done!" He nearly pounded on the corpse before he caught himself and began to weep. He could hear a voice in the background shouting, "My god, my god!"

Ordin was in shock. In a moment he had gone from the would-be winner of a friendly wager to a would-be murderer. Nothing could have prepared him for this. Nothing can ever prepare one for a moment that changes everything you know and would know beyond that. He shook Peter's corpse, which was already starting to cool. It seemed much faster than Ordin thought it would be. "Is this how fragile life is, is this how quickly it leaves us?" Tears were now streaming down his face; his own shirt was covered in blood. He did not realize that he had been holding Peter's corpse tightly to his body and rocking rigorously, until someone tapped him on his shoulder and said, "Please let go. You have to let him go, he may be dead."

That someone turned out to be Laurence Lemn, who not only witnessed the shooting but also had the misfortune to be snapping pictures at the exact time that the gun went off. This would be the tie that bound Ordin to Laurence for life thereafter. It was these pictures that would be the key piece of evidence in both the prosecution's and the defense's case. And it was these pictures that would color the scope of both men's experience for the month during the trial and the years afterward.

For Laurence, it meant interrogation rooms and countless hours on the phone politely taking the calls from everyone involved in the trial from detectives to expert witnesses. It meant initially being on the various news stations (either by name or videotaped), and later requests for talk shows, as first the story of the day, then week, then month. He became a pawn for the N.R.A.'s stance that guns are harmless recreation tools that every citizen had the god given legal right to bear and that guns don't kill people, people kill people. He was also the new poster boy of the N.A.O.G.V.V.'s view that if there were no guns, there would be no death related to guns, and that guns don't' kill people, people with guns kill people.

The involvement the shooting brought Laurence pushed him down and wore him out. He began drinking and smoking. His partner, Albert, started to say he was not the same man he had fallen in love with, and that he had become a nervous shell of himself. His nights were filled with violent nightmares and constant tossing and turning. He became suspicious of everyone's motives. He even blamed Albert of being on the payroll of both the N.R.A. and the N.A.O.G.V.V., which was the breaking point for Albert, who left him to his misery. In the end and after the trial was over, and the news story had become back page fodder, he was still broken. He had not imagined that taking pictures of beautiful birds could turn out to be the event that changed the course of his life. At one point, some sleazy publishing agent talked him into writing his story and publishing it under the name, "What Fell from the Sky." It sold a whopping forty copies and was quickly shelved.

Laurence now lived in a small town with a new lover who took care of the bills and left him to his stamp collecting, which had become his new pastime. He did not imagine that he would ever hear from Ordin outside of the court, thinking that Ordin saw him as the man who destroyed his life, but his phone was about to ring, as a man miles away would attempt to release this ghost and do the same for Laurence.

Ordin looked carefully at the picture and turned it over to see the name of the photographer and the photographer's phone number. Here was a possible way to talk to the man who inadvertently had been a pawn in changing Ordin's life forever. Yet had he really? For even if Laurence had not taken the photo, Ordin would have still had to deal with the accidental death of his friend, Peter. The photo was only used as the primary evidence.

Would the phone number still reach Laurence after all these years? Likely not, but not trying to call it to even give it a chance was the same as doing nothing, and doing nothing was not relieving Ordin of the pain.

As he had put forth action towards his son, it was a good momentum to continue with others. Ordin picked up the phone and dialed the number on the back of the photo, almost like the action of an automaton, yet this action even with its appearance of being emotionless held with it the combination of fear and hope. Fear that he may not reach Laurence; fear of not knowing exactly what he was going to say, how, or even entirely the why. Fear that even if he reached Laurence, he might not even want to talk to him. Fear that this may all be in vain, that Laurence would not forgive and be willing to let the past go.

For Ordin, the hopes that he could actually reach Laurence, that there could be a chance for understanding and forgiveness for both of them, that there was a chance to let the past go, a chance to have a future empty of the problems of the past thus room for a future of possibilities was the reason why he found his fingers dialing the number and his voice whispering, "God, please let him answer."

It is strange how often circumstance dictates the situation. The circumstance of two friends engaged in a common pastime of wagering over bagged fowl combined with the event of an accidental discharge of a rifle, coupled with the circumstance of a hobbyist photographer being there at that exact moment taking photos of birds who just happened to catch the accident on film. All this created the situation of the lives of these two men being unintentionally entangled and thus resulting in an unforeseen and undesired change of course in life for both. Now was a chance, now was the place, and now was the time to begin to actively

113

create intention and life instead of being a victim of circumstance and situation.

CHAPTER FORTY-NINE
Circumstance

The mistaken notion that the circumstances of the past control the circumstances of the present, which thusly dictate the possibilities and circumstances of the future are not inherently true. Circumstance is often a result of a person's choices.

Even when circumstances are the results of others' choices or of things beyond anyone's control, the ultimate result of any circumstance is based on choice. The common thread, and thus the real truth, is choice. And with choice, a choice of the past may create the present circumstance; however, it does not dictate a choice of the present any more than the chooser allows.

The present choice is separate and distinct from the choices of the past or future or other choices. Regardless of how the past choices influenced the present circumstance, the present choice is controlled only in the now. The past is something you cannot change. The future you have no immediate control of or absolute promise. Only the now is under your control. Thus the only control is the choice of now. Inherent in choice is the full responsibility of that choice, and in that the responsibility of the choices made for any circumstance.

A person who grew up on a farm (that is where his/her parents decided to root the family), does not have to remain a farmer. At any point, the person can change their life's vocation if the reason is they no longer desire to be a farmer, never desired to be a farmer, disavowed a familial obligation to the family's vocation, or just wanted to branch out in their experience of life. Or for any reason they choose.

A person's future without a change in choice will be the result of present options. This is true, but the caveat here is without change in choice. If one decides to push self on a skateboard down a hill and does nothing else afterward, he or she will continue to roll until hitting something, changing course, or running out of momentum to move forward, thus coming to a complete and utter halt. Remember, it took courage and a sense of adventure to get on the skateboard in the first place, and even more so to push oneself down a hill on the skateboard. But if one chooses after that to just do nothing, he or she chooses to let go of their own power. At any point during the journey down the hill on the skateboard, one can choose to interact in a way to change the possible outcomes, even if that choice is to merely stop, change direction, attempt tricks, or whatever one can fathom to choose. Each possibility is directly related to one's choice.

In every choice there are three aspects: what you know, what you know you do not know, and even what you do not know that you do not know. The young farmer knows he knows how to milk a cow, which is a direct correlation to his learned experiences, which is what the past is. He knows he does not know how to swing a baseball bat professionally, but he can apply his learned disciplines of swinging an ax to receiving the education in swinging a baseball bat proficiently, which is what the present is, thus using our learned disciplines to something we do not know but wish to know. He can also step into the unknown with a single choice by being open to things he does not know that he does not know. This is the phenomenon of creating possibilities that were not there previously, or not known before by any one choice, also known as the unknown future.

116

Any future that is lived in the known is a future lived in past and the circumstances of his immediate present. This is living a life of limited choice and possibility, which many people mistake for the future. Since choice is always existent, it is inherent that future is never determined by the past or present any more than we choose it to be. At any given moment a choice can alter the future and even the moments in the future are possibilities of choice. Future exists as a possibility. Possibility and determinism do not co-exist at any given moment.

The choice is always yours, the individual. In everything there is choice. The free-will to choose a thought, response, and action are the truly empowering aspects of being human, of living as sentient beings.

CHAPTER FIFTY
Laurence Lemn

After Albert had left him, Laurence was left with only himself. Laurence was not comfortable with this as he had always had someone around, someone to care for him, to rely on, and to be loved by. "Why did Albert have to leave me now, of all times, now when I am going through one of my hardest times of my life? Seeing someone murdered before my eyes, being tied up into the legal and court process and all the public media, and now, Albert makes this time truly the darkest hour of my life by leaving me in my time of greatest need! How could he?!"

This was Laurence's lament for quite some time. He was unable to maintain a steady job. His condo that he purchased from the inheritance left by his parents who had passed away just three years prior looked as though it was besieged by a pack of animals wanton for only food and sleep. The floor that could not be distinguished from empty alcohol bottles and cans as well as a smell that readily told any guest they had stepped into an ashtray.

It was true that Laurence really never was by himself before. Laurence had met Albert while he was in college and still living with his parents. He was with Albert when his parents passed away in an automobile accident. Although the loss of his parents was an emotional hardship, Laurence felt bolstered by the love he shared with Albert. He was not alone, and that made it easier. Witnessing the moment of death, especially such a violent moment, is considerably different than seeing someone who has already died. Then the addition of all the press, the questioning, being dragged through the courts, the whole publicity of it all, was like a knife wound where the knife was still there and being jostled about, making the wound always fresh and never fully healing.

Shortly after Ordin's case was dissolved for insufficient evidence of mal-intent, and after Ordin had lost his wife and child to divorce, Laurence became a hermit, rarely coming out of the cave his condo had become. For Laurence, the whole ordeal was now even worse. For now, he felt partly responsible for what destroyed a loving family. His photo, name, and his story of what he experienced had become the focal drama that created a rift in his own life and in the life of Ordin. At times Laurence would shout out angrily, "Why could you not just let your friend have the gun, Ordin?! Why did you have to be such a typical man who had to win? Why did you bring this into my and your own life?!"

Laurence had shut himself away from the world and life, focusing on all the ways he was a victim, never forgiving himself nor any person or organization, or even society, who had all become part of the ordeal. When he received a letter from a publisher asking him to write his story, Laurence thought, "Finally, I can tell the world in my own way and in my own words about what happened in my life since. I can share it with them without anyone being able to change my words, and with them written down, I can share it as I want to share it not being a pawn to the prosecution or defense or the NRA or the N.A.O.G.V.V.!" It took Laurence only three months to write his book. Even though the book only sold 40 copies, the act of writing seemed to free up the angst within him, and it also opened up space for other thoughts, for moving on with his life.

Upon the completion of the book, Laurence cleaned up the condo, then sold it to his sister, Anabelle. The condo was no longer home to him. He needed to start fresh again with his life, leaving the past in the past. The condo held too much of the energies of the past Laurence needed to leave behind. It also seemed appropriate for the condo to develop new energy, energy of new life and a new family. His sister was newly expecting her first child with her new husband of only six months. Ana was the energy of new life the condo needed. For Laurence, his new life was a blank slate. He did not know where it would go to next. All he knew was it would not begin until he was out of the condo. This was a little frightening, but it even more exhilarating was the feeling of openness, of no longer being caved in, of a slate empty and full of possibilities.

By the time he became an uncle with the birth of his nephew, James, Laurence had met another wonderful guy who became his new love. After just a short five months of dating, Laurence moved in with Garreth. Still not finding a niche in the job market, Laurence spent his time collecting stamps, hosting parties, and volunteering with the local AIDS foundation of the small town they lived in. This is what Ana related to Ordin, once she figured out who Ordin was, "Laurence will be glad to hear from you," she said as she gave him the new phone number Laurence could be reached at, as it turned out that Ana kept Laurence's old phone number for the condo. Ordin wrote the new number down below the old number on the back of the photo, then decided to wait to call Laurence's new number later when he reached home.

CHAPTER FIFTY-ONE
Karen - Look at me Now

When Karen's bag of pork rinds was finished, she headed for the kitchen to fetch another. "Why not," she thought I'll be a celebrity and have a personal trainer to get me in shape for my appearances, so why not indulge in a little more?" While Karen was reaching up into the cabinet, she had a flash of a memory cross her mind. Karen had been in this same spot reaching into the cabinet for a can of Progresso's tomato bisque soup which was to be the appetizer for a meal of meat loaf al-a-carte. A side of toasted bread spread with butter and garlic salt would be the finishing touch to a meal she had planned for Sam Waterford before she was to ask him if they were ready to take their fledgling relationship to the next level and become exclusive. Karen was naturally already exclusive, but in her mind, men needed a little prodding to get to that stage. And, she had always heard that the way to a man's heart was through his stomach. While Karen was not a whiz in the kitchen, she had her druthers that a woman should be able to at least cook one home meal, even if it was not gourmet.

This memory gave Karen a pinch of sadness as she recalled its outcome. Sam's reaction was both comical and tragic at the same time. First, Karen had to convince Sam that this dinner was one that was needed at the table rather than sitting down in front of the TV as they usually did. Sam seemed suspicious of this but gave in when Karen refused to bring the food to him on the couch.

"Sam, how long has it been since we began seeing each other?" Of course, she knew the answer but felt this was a good way to break into the topic of conversation she desired.

"Hmm... I'm not quite sure. It has been a little while now, maybe a couple weeks."

"Yes, it has been, 17 days to be exact, which is a good amount of time to really get a feel for someone."

"Yeah, it can be a good amount of time for a beginning," Sam replied a little cautiously.

"Exactly, a beginning. I feel we have had a great beginning and that it is time to move onward."

"Onward? Yes, you mean to continue as we have been right?"

"Well, yes... and no... continue yes, but now that we have had our beginning, I think we are ready to be exclusive to each other. I know I want you in my life and only you. I do not want anyone else, and I think we are already exclusive to each other. I just want it to be a formal agreement."

With this, Sam nearly choked on the soup he was sipping through the large tablespoon Karen had supplied as a soup spoon, his eyes wide and now starting to water from the choking, which Karen, of course, mistook as a sign of great emotion of happiness from Sam. "Uh... uh... listen, Karen, I appreciate the thought, but right now..."

"Right now? Is something wrong with now?" Karen asked in alarm.

"Uh... yeah... it's... it's my cousin, you see. He is very ill in the hospital and needs a kidney, and well... I am the only donor match.... And well, I do not feel right to be making promises of a serious relationship when I have to go through this operation that I may not even come back from.... I might not make it back, you know, having my kidney taken out. Deaths happen on the hospital surgery table all the time. My chances are about... you know... 20-60-20... so, I would really like to ... like... you know... give you what you want... but it would not be fair to you, Karen. You deserve so much more. I mean, you are so, so... yeah.. and you are so sweet to try hard too... Maybe if I come back from the surgery, and both me and my cousin fully recuperate, then we can look at this again. But I will write... and thanks for the dinner and... uh... everything...."

Sam said this as he hit his knee on the underside of the table and practically dragged the table cloth with him as he scurried up and away from the table toward the door. As Sam opened the front door, he looked back at Karen and said, "You know, Karen meatloaf is supposed to have fresh onions and garlic, and it is not meant to be dry as... a real loaf of bread."

Karen looked sad and flustered. "But... but... you didn't even get to have any of my meatloaf tonight..., as she sniffled. Karen stared at the door that Sam had just left through, sitting motionless at the table. Her gaze spoke volumes of the feeling of longing and the wish for a someone who would just stay.

Karen decided not to pick up the bag of snacks. "Pork rinds are for fat people, and Karen Miller is not fat. She's beautiful, and it's about time the world knew it." With that, Karen marched right for the living room and picked up the telephone. With a steely look in her eyes, she dialed Sam's number and held her breath while it rang. When Sam picked up after several rings, Karen was so flustered and indignant that she simply blurted out in a loud and somewhat cracked voice,

"Ha! and double ha to you, Sam Waterford. I'm going to be a star, and you will never get any of this. Oh, and by the way, I give killer head and make a great meatloaf. Maybe some people like their loaf to actually be a 'loaf'."

Karen quickly and ferociously hung up the phone. She raised her arms in a "V" for victory, then ran her hands down the length of her hips and legs and did her best impersonation of Gloria Gainer's "I will survive," singing at the top of her lungs and waving her hands like Diana Ross from her Supremes days. Then

Karen laughed until tears flew from her eyes and snot jutted from her nose as she snorted, as she is prone to do when she laughed in joy. Karen let out a long sigh, flopped on the couch, kicked up her legs and grabbed a tissue, saying to herself, "Karen, old girl, things are going our way."

CHAPTER FIFTY-TWO
Paul's Conversation with Willow

Checking the rearview mirror, Paul snapped to attention and immediately noticed that his hands were gripped white-knuckled around the steering wheel of the car. How long had he been driving in this sub-conscious state he did not know. It seemed to him that this trip was spent more in daydreams than in the conscious awareness of where he was going and for what purpose.

In truth, Paul did not really want to tackle that question, so he needed some sort of distraction from it, and he needed something to keep him more alert while driving. Paul no longer had Detective Graves to bounce off of. What Paul needed was a conversation with someone. Paul instinctively picked up the phone to dial, then thought... "Who will I call?" He then decided in the same brief moment to call his daughter, Willow. She would hopefully be available to answer the phone. Willow always had a way of helping Paul forget his stress by bringing a smile to his face as well as having such a fresh child-like perspective on the world around her.

Willow picked up the phone on the fourth ring, answering cheerfully, "Johnson's residence." The sound of her voice sounded like the happy bluebirds singing in the early morning outside of the bedroom window.

"Hello Willow, this is Daddy."

"Hi, Daddy! When are you coming home?"

Paul thought to himself, when am I coming home? What a sweet and yet complicated question. No matter how many times Willow asked me this he felt a yearning to be already home embracing her and never wanting to leave her, and yet this was not the reality of life. "Willow I will likely not be able to get home today as I had to drive out of town... out of state. I will need to stay overnight before heading back tomorrow."

"So what time tomorrow will you be home, Daddy?"

"Uh... honey... it would not be until. ..."

"Can we go ride horses tomorrow then, Daddy?"

"I wish we could, but I will not be home until very late tomorrow when it will be dark already."

"Daddy, what's a lemming? Mom always says that the reason you are not home is because you are a lemming."

"Uh... a lemming is a video game character that works a lot to help the other lemmings get to their destination."

"So where do you help people get to, Daddy?"

"Different places, sometimes good places, at times bad places. Sometimes the people make the choice for themselves. Sometimes I have to make the decisions for them. As much as I do not like having to make the choice for them, it seems that I am stuck in the position where I have to make their choice for them because they choose not to choose or they make a choice that is not safe or good for others."

"I don't understand, Daddy."

"Willow, neither do I."

"Is it like the time I heard you talking to mom about the hom-ni-size?"

"Yeah, sorta like that, except that is more a place where Daddy really has no choice, and in fact, neither does the other people involved have a choice." You see, honey, there are good and bad people. I know I told you that good things happen to good people, but sometimes bad things happen to good people, and sometimes even good people do bad things. But bad people sometimes hurt others in a way where they cannot take it back, and that is one of those times when the hurt is permanent. It cannot be taken back, so the choice to hurt in this way makes it so others have no choice."

Inquisitively, as Willow is prone to be, a quality that Paul and Kristine really enjoyed about their seven going on fifteen-year-old daughter, she asked, "Daddy, have you ever did a hom-ni-size? Have you ever taken away someone's choice? Have you hurt someone in a way that could not be taken back?"

"Wow, Willow, that is complicated, and probably too much for you to hear right now. But to be honest, I have had to make choices for others that I did not always like. That is a part of what I am expected to do. It seems a part of what I am and who I have become. There is so much I wish I could tell you. You always lighten my heart when you listen to me, and you could probably teach most of us a thing or two about listening and understanding."

"Does Mom listen and understand Daddy?"

"I think mom listens and tries to understand, but our world has so much more attached to it than just listening and understanding. Your life is in a place where you still have time and magic to listen and understand. I enjoy that about you and only hope you do not become too rushed or pushed into our world, the adult world, sooner than your time. You know, Willow, I was thinking that the next time I come home that I just may stay awhile, a while longer. I know I am not home a lot honey, and we have missed a lot of time. I don't want to miss out of any more time with you than I absolutely have to. Maybe you can show me and teach me more of that magic. It seems I have forgotten what it is like and that can be your gift to me."

"I am only seven, Dad, how can I give you a gift? I have no money."

"Willow, the best gifts money cannot buy, and you have more of the best gifts than you know… more than you know.... I'll be home tomorrow, okay, honey? And I will call you again soon. Be good. Bye, Angel."

"Okay, Daddy, you be good."

With that, Paul hung up the phone with a smile and again noticed his hands on the steering wheel, but this time, they were not tense and white-knuckled. They were relaxed and merely resting, guiding him onward on his journey, and perhaps to absolution.

Paul wondered whether the man he was going to investigate and possibly apprehend had a daughter or a son, as well as whether his daughter or son would ever have to ask him the same question, that is, if he was ever coming home. Will Paul's choice cause hurt that cannot be taken back? Paul did not know the answer, but he knew he would have to make a choice, and very soon.

With this thought, he looked over at the empty seat and spied Detective Graves' hat still left on the seat, an old weathered fedora that somehow embodied Graves, where once it was sort of this token of strength and coolness and now just looked empty, sad, and alone.

CHAPTER FIFTY-THREE
Questions of God

Ordin took another look at the picture in his hand and placed it back in the glove compartment, exchanging it for the letter to Blain he had come to mail. He habitually closed his eyes and bowed his head and began as he always had. "Father God, I come to you in prayer, boldly approaching your throne of grace, asking for mercy and grace in my time of need. Father, I pray in the power of the Holy Spirit, according to your perfect will, and ask these petitions in the name of Jesus Christ, my high priest. Lord, I need,"

I need... Ordin found himself at a loss for words knew what he wanted to say and what his needs were, but there was a part that was missing: it was his heart. His heart was not in it. Ordin had felt this way several times in the past year when he went to pray. The truth was he had felt this way for the last several years. For Ordin, there were many reasons he felt this way: his loss of freedom, the questions of how God could allow the death of his best friend, the death of his family as he knew it, the death of his dignity, and the loss of his power as a man. These were all things that Ordin felt about his walk with God. But what it all added up to was a loss of faith, a loss of faith in God, a loss of faith in humanity, and ultimately a loss of faith in himself and his ability to even hear God.

Ordin remembered that as a child, then as a kid and young man, whenever he had reached out to God he heard back from him in some way, be it tangible or just metaphorically. However, Ordin could not recall having had a conversation with God, from whence he felt or heard an answer since he moved from being a young man to an adult. This troubled him, for it seemed that when Ordin needed God the most, God was not there. For Ordin, it was not clear as to the reasons why this communication had ceased. Was it because he had lost or given up his ability to hear Him? Was it that God had decided to give up on Ordin, or to just allow him to walk alone? Though it was not clear to him at this time, this was the root of Ordin's loss of faith.

...What the hell am I doing? This is a waste of time, right? You're not going to say anything, are you? Heck, I don't even know if you're up there anymore, if you just don't like me, or if you ever did. I mean, to take Sonya and Blain away was cruel. I know I wasn't a great man in my marriage and that I did things to hurt her and to hurt the marriage, but I did love her. You know that.

And Blain, what did he do to deserve not having a father? Or does a person have to deserve the bad things that happen in their life, huh? Are they all just tests of faith that are designed to build character? That's the way you work these days, isn't it? You don't speak in a booming voice or provide a cloud by day to shade the sun and a pillar of fire by night to warm the bones. You use people and their frailties to illustrate our need for you, our need to reach up and out of our own strengths and to rely on your strength. I know these things. I just don't entirely agree.

I mean, isn't that how the human growth pattern works? We live with and through our parents until we can provide for ourselves, and not just sustenance, but in all things that make us adults in this human sense. So why wouldn't that be true in our spiritual lives? If we see ourselves in the analogy of all things being possible then what controls the possibilities? If you are the archer and the universe is the bow, I am the arrow, and the target becomes the realm of all possibilities. Or is the universe the bow, with me as the archer and the arrow being a possibility and wherever aimed being the realm of possibility that I choose?

This is what I have asked myself and you for as long as I can remember. But you won't answer anymore. If I answer, then am I taking away your divine guidance, and if I leave it up to you to answer, am I then negating my free will? All I want is to hear from you again, or do I really want to hear from you? What does it mean to me if I do hear from you and what does it mean if I don't ever hear from you again?

Is it wrong to ask why? Lord, I feel so out of control and human, and all of this is tearing at me. These damn daymares won't go away, and now this urge to go back and heal the wounds that were inflicted, to release Sonya and Blain from their torture, that seems to be at my hands but won't subside either. I want to release this man that has changed his life with a camera and a moment. I want to live again outside of the shell of the ghost that I am. How do I do these things without you and your guidance?"

Ordin went silent and waited. He closed his eyes and pressed his head against the dashboard, and still, nothing came. Ordin opened his eyes and stepped out of his car. His hands were shaking, and his brow was furrowed and moist. The people around him looked with a mix of alarm and concern as if he were some walking ailment. Ordin noticed this, but gave no further thought to them, as he could only focus right now on all the energy it was taking him to simply walk in and slip the now stamped envelope letter in the outgoing domestic mail slot.

With the letter sliding into the slot, out of his hand, out of his control, Ordin felt light-headed and yet alert to a seemingly light and cooling breeze that seemed to chill his beads of sweat. Somehow, Ordin felt lighter, as if an unseen weight was lifted off his shoulders. As he walked back to the car, his heart felt like a confusing mix of lightness and heaviness. He had now sent his first communication to his son in several years. This felt good, and yet what would be the result? Would the fruit of this letter bring him joy or add to the despair he had felt all this time?

He instinctively knew it would bring joy, but the work he had to do had just begun with the letter. The letter was only a beginning step, an important and necessary step, but still just beginning, rather than an end. What the end was, or the possibilities of the result of the letter, Ordin could not know; he had to just trust. Was this trust an action of faith?

As he placed his foot back into his car and began to sit down, Ordin felt more than heard the world slip from his mouth, "Okay, Lord, I'm listening. I did what you said. I trust you." Ordin knew he would receive no response, and still, the lightness in his heart filled in the void, for now.

CHAPTER FIFTY-FOUR
Gert's Call to Winslow

Sometimes it seems as if the phone itself knows what you're waiting for, or who you want to pick up for. The tone of the ringer may sound sad, excited, anxious, or even apprehensive. For Gertrude Graves, the tone of the ring sounded unsure, unsure whether it wanted to be answered, unsure of what it would do once picked up, unsure if it was even right to be ringing.

Gert had a quality that some mistook for resilience, but what it was a glossing over of the facts. The facts were that her adopted son Winslow hadn't phoned home in almost seven years now, nor had he written or even returned a letter. She saw this as a young man undertaking his journey into self-reliance and his rite-of-passage. This was how Gert filtered most things that she could not control. She would ignore the facts and then place warm feelings and cliché sayings in their place. This time, however, there was a strange feeling in the pit of her gut as the phone rang that would not allow her to ignore the truth of the moment, that she was about to talk to the son she took on to soothe the longings she had for motherhood and womanhood twenty-four long years ago. It had been an experiment in love and companionship that turned into a struggle for independence and identity.

Winslow's perspective grew out of the awareness of his being less the fulfillment of a lonely, loving woman's longings, and more of being the sounding board between two people who were simply and sadly out of touch with each other. Winslow never questioned Gert's love for him or the desire she had to create a place of peace and happiness for him. But the fact that she was woefully unable to create peace for herself went a long way to set the tone for how their relationship would play out. Winslow knew by the age of twelve that he would not end up calling this small besieged woman "mom" as much as she would always be just "Gert." In so many ways, she was the personification of her name. It probably did not help at all that J.H. Graves never referred to Gert as mom in relation to him.

However, these things were not the determining factor as to why Winslow hadn't called since he left for college seven years ago. For Winslow, the rift was his inability to talk to either J.H. or Gert about his life. As much as he wanted to share what his life was like, what he was excited about, who his friends were, and even who his love interest was, neither J.H. nor Gert seemed capable or willing to hear the truth about his life. When something fundamental to one's life cannot be discussed, it makes any and all conversation nothing but an empty shell and thus meaningless to have. For Gert and J.H., Winslow being gay was a truth that was a scary and unknown territory that they felt was better ignored than dealt with.

This was clearly evident to Winslow when he wanted to ask a guy out to the senior prom as his date, the date that never happened. When they asked him who he was going to ask out for senior prom, Winslow chose to tell them he was going to ask Alan, a guy Gert and J.H. saw as Winslow's best friend. They were shocked, alarmed, and adamant that they would not be known as the parents of a gay son. How could a respected detective on the police force and his wife be known in the community as the parents of a gay son? No, they would not have it. Yes, living in the San Francisco Bay Area, the idea that homosexuals existed was not new. But to have one in their own home, to be associated with them, was something neither could or wanted to fathom. They were respected in their community and among their friends. How could they still be respected if this was known?

Gert had tried to mollify the situation by suggesting that for the prom, which was a traditional formal dance, Winslow should take Andrea instead. Taking her would not have to mean anything other than that they were acquainted. And Andrea was a lovely girl, and prom really is for young guys and girls. Besides, Andrea was the daughter of J.H.'s boss, the chief of police, whose mother happened to be the principal at Winslow's school. This was the proper and expected thing to do. The Graves wanted a dutiful son who honored them. Not going to the prom with Andrea because Winslow wanted to go with Alan was neither respectful nor honoring. They would not have it. If Winslow would not go with Andrea or some other nice girl they approved of, he would not go to the prom at all.

For Winslow, this was his dream of his high school prom turned nightmare. Prom was to be a dance of celebration, of young love and hope for the future beyond high school. Without Alan, senior prom would not mean any of those things, so it was just as well if he could not take Alan to not go to the prom at all. This seemed to be the only thing Gert, J.H., and Winslow agreed on at this point: Winslow would not be going to his senior prom.

From this point on, even with Winslow in the house during his last two months of high school, Winslow was no longer available to be the sounding board for Gert, and J.H. Conversation between them was brought down to the absolute minimum required to co-habit the house. It is no longer felt like home to Winslow. In truth, it did not have the same feeling of home as it had before for Gert or J.H., but they chose to ignore this reality. It seemed they were at an impasse, where they could not talk about anything without thinking about and thus focusing the conversation on the unpleasant truth that Winslow was a homosexual. So life would go on, they fell into their routines, and barely acknowledged each other.

A week after this pivotal argument, J.H. brought home "Bear," a sturdy brown and white British bulldog, which remarkably resembled J.H. and was probably the reason why Bear got his respite from the kennels with an otherwise sure death sentence. Bear was fetched from a dog rescue adoption that was held as a community public relations event at the force. Gert and J.H. now had something new to focus on, something new to talk to and use as a sounding board. A semblance of normalcy had been brought back into their household, for they now could communicate to each other through Bear, replacing their need to communicate through Winslow. For Winslow, normalcy would never be a feeling associated with this household again.

Gert heard the final beep of the messaging service of Winslow's phone indicating the time allotment for her message was over. How long it had been beeping at her, she did not know. Did she say anything into the phone as a message for Winslow? No, she likely did not; she was not sure what she wanted to say. She almost forgot why she even called. Certainly Gert was not surprised Winslow did not pick up the phone.

"If you are not satisfied with your message and want to re-record, press three to delete and re-record," Gert heard again. She pressed three and," then spoke, "Hi, Winslow, it's Gert. I know this is an unexpected call, but I thought you should know J.H. is in a hospital. He has suffered a heart attack, and I am on my way to get him." Gert did not know what else to say. After some short duration of silence, she heard, "If you are satisfied with your message, please press pound or just hang up." Gert pressed the pound key and then hung up her phone.

What or even if something would come of it, Gert did not know. The call itself felt like an autonomous action out of what she felt was the duty and the normal or right thing to do. And yet much to her surprise and for the second time today, Gert could not help but feel a glimmer of hope. Perhaps this could be the seed of change in her relationship with her son Winslow as well.

CHAPTER FIFTY-FIVE
Conner James of Cold Case Killers

"Brent, get me my coffee, then make sure the Henderson file gets on my desk by two tomorrow, or it's your ass! Just kidding, but I really need that file." Conner James was the senior producer of "Cold Case Killers," For Conner, this was his third attempt at a show and his cou't te grait. His first two TV shows he produced had flopped, not because they were bad ideas he liked to say, but rather because they were ahead of their time.

The first show, "Derrick O'Malley," was a drama about a surgeon who had moved from rural Ireland to practice veterinary husbandry in the big city. The other, "Space Cadets," was a quirky game show where pre-teen contestants competed in physical and intellectual challenges to determine who would win the right to enter NASA's junior space cadet program. Conner had almost lost the credentials as a credible producer of the two failed shows, but Cold Case Killers was his saving grace.

Conner was in a conversation with a buddy over dinner when the topic came up about all the old case files that get placed in the basement of the police departments that were just collecting dust, most of them never coming to a full resolution. Conner felt that there needed to be something done, for it was not right to have all the hard work of the police department just become forgotten in some old basement because they could never be solved. The best attention anything could get was through the media, and particularly his field, television. Was there not now even a whole station offered through cable or satellite services that focused on this and similar dilemmas? It had changed names a couple of times. Currently, the station was called "Investigation Discovery." This station aired shows indigenous to it and some that began on regular network TV such as CSI. With such a following already, it was a proven topic to work with TV viewers.

All Conner had to do was to bring in some slightly different angle that would differentiate Cold Case Killers from other similar productions. For Conner, this unique angle was combining two already existing angles in one, the angle used in "America's Most Wanted" combined with the angle used in CSI. It would undoubtedly be a winning combination. Plus, the show would present the "Cold Case Tipster" with a cash award and a cameo appearance on the show. This bonus angle was the anchoring third screw that made the show hold.

It was not until after the third episode that Conner was confronted with the reality of the consequences of bringing up old cold case files. Where Conner had felt he would be giving the nation and the nation's police force final justice on all of these forgotten and buried investigations, he did not take into account the disruption of the lives of people that ended up being good people caught up in unfortunate circumstances. Conner wasn't aware there would be a price to be paid. And so what if the price resulted in him profiting. He finally had a winning idea that the networks and TV viewers loved. In his mind, if these people were originally investigated, surely they must have been guilty, at least enough to warrant being investigated in the first place. Therefore, they were not innocent and deserved to reap the full consequences and not allowed to live life "getting away with murder," which happened to be the tagline of the show: 'No one gets away with Murder."

The day to the running of the show gave Conner such a charge you would have thought he was the dictator of a small country. He would bark out orders, slam doors, yell profanities, and this was all before seven a.m. when most had not even arrived at work. Today's tirade centered on getting the updates for the next week's shows. Conner liked to keep a tight window between when a case was re-opened and when it could be aired on the show. Several legal considerations had to be taken into account, and there was constantly something coming up that needed to be filed last minute, so Conner prided himself on running a tight ship with lots of forethought.

When Brent came back into the room, Conner launched himself at him, poking his index finger in the young assistant's chest. It was not the first time this had happened, and Brent had the bruises to prove it. Not that he ever would. Everybody knew that in this town complaining about harsh treatment from a successful producer was tantamount to writing oneself right out of a future and career in the 'business' as it was referred to.

"Brent, damn it! What is going on with the Aire case? Is he behind bars yet crying for his mommy? And what about that cow that called about him? Is she primed and prepped yet? I want the answer today! And find out what's up with that name, Ordin Aire. I swear I couldn't write it better if I tried. The guy's name is literally ordinary, like every man. Boy, I tell ya, this show never ceases to amaze me. And find out what kind of man he is...or was. I want the background. Any wife and kid in the loop? I want drama and heart strings here, and get me the skinny on the guy he off'd, whether he had a family."

What Conner could not know was that the very question he'd just asked about Ordin was swirling around in Ordin's head and heart, "What kind of man am I?" There was no clear answer to this question. In fact, this had been the crux of Ordin's struggles for the last twenty odd years, and no fledgling producer's assistant was going to answer it in one day no matter how many fingers poked his chest or how high his ambitions rose.

"Brent. Brent, are you listening to me? Damn, boy, do you think I got this far on my good looks and charm alone? No, it was by listening and taking directions. Place a call to the S.F.P.D. and ask for Smith. Find out what's going on with this case, as it's to be our central piece for next week's hundredth episode special." Brent Simmons dropped his pen, dashed down the hall to his cubicle, and began to dial the phone in the hope of getting answers to the questions.

Brent Simmons was not the only one who would be disappointed by the lack of answers. Somewhere driving a car was another soul who was searching for the same answers and asking the same questions, and who would soon have to make some tough choices.

CHAPTER FIFTY-SIX
Ordin - The Separation

Ordin inserted his car key into the ignition switch. Suddenly, he was sitting in his old car, ready to drive away to a new identity, a new life away from the hectic mess his life here had become, but also away from his wife Sonya and his son Blain. How did he get here? His life had seemed like such a torrential blur ever since the death of his friend Peter.

The only semblance of peace Ordin had found since that incident was when he was locked up in a jail cell during that thirty-day period. Between the time of harassment from the other prisoners and the guards, Ordin had time to himself. Yet these times were not peaceful, as Ordin would consistently fall into his daymares of reliving the horror of Peter's death.

Outside of the jail cell, out in the real world, Ordin not only still had the daymares, but he also had the direct barrage of reporters and neighbors who proved to not be concerned about Ordin's wellbeing rather their own perceived safety of having a "murderer" among them, strangers who would stop, stare, whisper, look alarmed, and who kept their distance. A phone that would not stop ringing when plugged in. Multitudes of post and non-post mail that came to their mailbox and doorstep, that Sonya referred to as "nasty grams". And seeing the effect of the extra stress on his wife and son all became part of the nightmare Ordin's life had become. He could not find peace.

His wife had been battling with the reporters, neighbors, family, friends, and total strangers whenever she went out in public. And the nasty grams during the whole time Ordin was locked up behind bars. For Sonya, there was no more energy left, no more patience, no more personal strength to support her through the turmoil her life had become, for something she had absolutely nothing to do with, only for the mere fact that she was married to the man. A man that she had already stopped being entirely honest with, a man to whom their relationship had become more smoke and mirrors than a real feeling of relatedness. About the only thing that they really shared a mutual interest in anymore was their son who was now only three years old. And how could she continually subject herself and Blain at such a young and impressionable age to such an unmanageable hell their life had become? Sonya believed and perceived the only real way out of this was to separate herself entirely from her husband. And not only for a brief time, for she knew this accidental shooting seen by too many as murder would never be forgotten, but entirely in space and any association with the man and his name.

It was not a question of who would take custody of Blain. She would be of course, for to allow her only son to live life under the shadow his father's life had become was unthinkable. Sonya sought to be given a separate identity and life from her husband by taking full custody of Blain in her divorce. She would take her maiden name again as would her son. The judge did grant Gordon, who was to change his name to Ordin, to have the right to contact his son, but not for another 10 years, at which time, Ordin and Sonya would be apprised of each other's address location by the court at that point. Even this was too soon for Sonya but was mandated by the judge. Blain would be told that his father left and that they did not know where he was until and if it was ever felt he could or should know the full truth.

Ordin begged Sonya to stay with him, to not take his son away from him. Yes, their marriage was not ideal. They had come to a point where their communication was less and less complete honesty and openness. All that could change. A simple relocation could be a totally fresh start for the whole family. Blain could have a mother and father as well as a happy home to grow up with, and maybe even another sibling. They would go to marriage counseling, have a new name, a new home, a new location, and even new jobs. They could survive anything together. Did not the marriage vows include "in sickness and in health," and was not this time in their life like a sickness that they should stick together through to enjoy the times of health that would surely come? They did get married out of love. The love still was there, just not the communication. Instead of running away from it all, stay together, work it through, and grow together stronger than before. This is what marriage is supposed to be about. Life is hard. You never know what it will throw at you, but as long as you have someone there to share it with, anything is possible.

Sonya would not listen. She did not want to start fresh again with Ordin. Sonya wanted a total fresh start. When asked if she still loved him, Sonya had no response. She felt like a victim, a victim at the hands of Ordin. It did not matter that it was an accident. It did not matter that Ordin had lost his best friend. It did not matter that neither of them asked for all the turmoil created by the press, the political groups, the neighbors, or any of it. Sonya could not, in truth would not separate the true reality from her perceived reality. Her personal friends and her family were all behind her with regard to leaving Ordin. They did not want to lose her to him, nor did they want any association with the man who they believed did not accidentally kill his best friend. It was in their best interest for Sonya to leave Ordin. If they had the choice, they would never have Blain know his father.

Ordin had said his last goodbyes to his son Blain, crying and promising to be there for him as soon as he could, saying that 10 years really would not be that long. He tried to say goodbye to Sonya, but she would not look him in the eyes and did not respond vocally to him at all. After only one minute of Ordin giving Blain a hug and kiss, Sonya reached in to pull Blain away, and then took him immediately inside the house closing the front door behind her. Defeated and heart-torn, Ordin was led by Agent Tim away and inside the car, where the agent then closed the door for him.

"Sonya, please! Don't take him away! Don't leave me!" Ordin was back at the post office sitting in his car. He noticed that a few of the townsfolk had stopped and were staring at him, whispering their concern and wondering if he was okay. Ordin had left the car door open, had been sweating, and had started yelling. Ordin stated almost inaudibly that he was sorry, wiped the sweat from the brow of his face, closed the door, turned the key, and then drove back towards home.

CHAPTER FIFTY-SEVEN
Detective Graves – The "A" in Life

Detective Graves' eyes were heavy and would not remain open as he slid back into sleep moments after he turned over on his side. J.H. was excited about his school paper. Ms. Miller, his 7th grade English teacher, told the class to write a full research essay on their dream job. She encouraged them to dream big, to reach for the seemingly impossible, to not let fears or others' opinions deter them. The essay would require research of what it takes to actually do the job. Research could include not only books and periodicals but also interviewing people, preferably someone in the career field or someone who would have clear knowledge about their chosen career. "Get creative, be thorough, and make me live your dream with you in your research essay," intoned Ms. Miller. The class had four weeks to turn it in.

For J.H., this dream job that seemed impossible was to be a U.S. Congressman. He wanted to be where the laws were made. He wanted to represent his community in Washington D.C. No one in his family has ever done this before, and he would be the first. "I can hear it now... 'and the floor will now recognize Congressman Graves.' Being the first meant J.H. had no one in his family that really knew anything about being a congressman. At first, J.H. thought it would be just placing himself in situations where he would give impromptu speeches to the community to get himself heard, known, liked, and voted in. However, he began to learn as he browsed and read parts of books, periodicals, and reports of the U.S. Congress, elections, and campaigns, that in today's world it takes a considerable amount of time, who you know, and money to run a campaign with no guarantee of results. How would he do this?

J.H.'s mother offered up the idea that he could go the route of becoming the Chief of Police in law enforcement, and then get well known that way and backed by other politicians. J.H.'s own father, Harold James, was also a police officer who had become Chief of Police by J.H.'s senior year of High School.

"James Harold, let me tell you, son, this is the life a man should lead: a strong provider and a role model to his wife and family. For many generations now, our family has had a history of having at least one male, typically the oldest, take on the mantle and tradition of being in law enforcement. Now, don't get me wrong, you may choose whatever you want to do, but consider the honor it is to be in law enforcement and to carry on our family heritage. It is the laws of the land that bring cohesion in our society. Imagine what our world would be like without laws and without those whose sole duty it is to ensure those laws are enforced? It would be life with reckless abandon. It would be chaos, and it would be a society and a world where no one was either safe or free. In truth, laws that seem to confine actually bring freedom and fruits for one's efforts. For example, if there was not a law against theft, how safe would it be to even try to pursue owning things that may get stolen? And why would you even bother with working towards owning something that someone could just take from you without earning it? Would you ever drive a car or even care to walk across the street if there were no laws and those to enforce them regarding speed and when to stop and when to go? It is one of the highest ways to serve the society we live in, to be a part of enforcing laws that protect us. Now you can go on to making laws, but son, let me tell you, it is enough of a task enforcing the laws we already have. That is where the real heart and meat is."

To this, Lillian had replied, "Now, now Harold, enforcing laws is vital and necessary, but do not discourage young J.H. here, as people's needs and circumstances change, so must laws at times. I think it is a grand goal in life for J.H. to have. To think our very first congressman in the family, and J.H. could get there first by helping to enforce the laws, then onto making the laws."

Encouraged, J.H. then thought and said aloud to his parents, "Is there not a movie somewhere about some Chief of Police winning the hearts of his community to go on and represent them in Congress, or maybe that was part of the comic story of Batman or some other superhero? Shoot, Dad, you're already Chief of Police. Why don't you go for being a congressman?"

"For me son, enforcing the laws is the real task. Besides, why would I want to get involved with all those politics?"

"Because it is a step higher, dad. Isn't it better to be in on the making of the laws that you enforce?"

"J.H., you may find out, as I have, that going higher is not always worth it, that staying where you already are is surer footed and is well enough in life without the disappointment of trying for more only to not get it."

Ms. Miller really liked J.H.'s idea and felt his enthusiasm, and had the essay been graded on this alone, he would have received an "A." Except there were too many grammatical mistakes, misspellings, and missing information as to how he would become the Chief of Police, and who he would have to befriend politically, as well as what issues he would present as his platform. For these errors, J.H. received a B-." J.H. was very disappointed. He strove for the "A" and did not get it, even though he had an "A" idea. He saw this not as an experience to learn from and strive to do better next time, but rather saw this as proof of his father's warning of disappointment.

J.H. woke from the dream with wet eyes. "No! NO!" he thought I could not have been crying in my sleep. It must be something in the hospital air, maybe some dust got in my eyes or something. Still, J.H. could not shake the feeling of disappointment he had as a child. He was close to retirement age now and still he had not made Chief of Police. His father had made this much seem so easy, and yet J.H. had failed to even accomplish that. His father had been right all these years. J.H. learned to accept where he was at in his station of life. He was a good police officer and a good detective, and that was good enough. To try for more would be a sure effort in only feeling disappointed, and that was definitely not acceptable to Detective Graves.

J.H. reached for the glass of water sitting on the standing tray next to his bed and drank it down to soothe his parched throat. With all the effort it took him to drink the glass of water, J.H. again felt fatigued, turned over on his other side (the pillow was wet on the side he had been sleeping), and quickly slid back into a sound sleep.

CHAPTER FIFTY-EIGHT
Blain Writes the Letter

Seven days earlier Blain at his desk in his bedroom...

What does one call a man who fathered your birth, but you have not known all your life? What was this man? Was he just a provider of half of the chromosomes to create a life, to create a life that would result in me? Was he a father? He has not been there for me all of my life, so he is not really my dad. But then again, reading his letters that I found hidden away in the attic expressed, along with regret and pain, true love. Isn't a Dad someone who not only brings you in the world but loves you as a son? Does loving you as a son have to mean that he has to be there to raise you regardless of circumstance?

The first letter I found was from seven years ago. This seems to be the last, but it was not the first letter written, that was when I was 12 years old. My mother kept his letters from me, so my mom, in essence, kept my father from me. Does this make him any less my dad? I know I want to call him Dad, will he want that as well? I feel he will, though I cannot know, but I feel he will. More than that I feel, I want to, and I have learned I should trust my heart and be true to it. Okay... here it goes.

"Dad, how are you? It has been some time, hasn't it?" Ah, I like the way that sounds, the way it feels, as if we were old buds and not total strangers. The truth of the reality is that we are strangers; still, I feel a closeness to him from reading the few letters he did write. I know this feeling may be just a yearning, but I will take that yearning and trust in putting down what I feel in my heart and not my fears or logic of reason. Yes, many times logic and reason are appropriate, and it may be wise to allow logic to temper emotions, but never to trump emotions that are genuine and good.

"Dad, I need to talk to you, and if not in person, then this will have to do."

I do want to meet him in person. I want to get to know him, and I want to have a chance to have him in my life and in the life of my child. But I do not know what took him away, if he can come into my life in person or not, or if he is willing and ready for that. So I will give him the chance to at least communicate with me through letters, to pick up what was once started but ended before it really began many years ago.

"Dad, so many things have happened in my life over these past twenty years. Things were really tough, and there were times when I thought I wouldn't make it and times when I didn't want to make it. There were times when mom's anger with you seemed to control our lives. I grew up believing that you wanted to break our family, to break me. I didn't know what I had done, but now I think that it wasn't me you were running from, that maybe it was you running from yourself."

Wow, I hope this does not scare him, the up-front honesty and all, but I do not want to be anything but totally honest and open with him. All of my life much has been held back in communication about and with my father due in part by mom. If there is a chance for our relationship to grow, it cannot be without honesty, openness, and forgiveness. This is an opportunity to let the past be the past, but not avoiding it as well.

"There were bright spots too, like graduating college early and winning sports awards."

I cannot let him think that all my life was bad.

"I have had good things, too, and many things to be grateful for, but it seems like just when I get it all together, something comes in to steal away my joy, like now. I have this girlfriend, and that's part of the problem. You see, dad, my girlfriend is pregnant, and we just found out that we are having a son."

I sure hope he understands that I need him in my life and in my son's life. That I want him in our lives, even if he cannot do anything but be here, that is enough.

"Dad, I don't know what to do. We were only going out for five months before she got pregnant. And I don't know how to tell mom, or if I even should. Oh, by the way, mom is fine, dad. I don't know what to do. I do know that I need you and your advice. I mean, I can barely remember you, but I know you're my dad, and I need my dad. I want my son to know his grandfather. I don't think I could forgive myself if I took that away from him because of what was done to me. Dad, would you write back or think about coming to see me? Father, there has been an emptiness lately. I can't explain it. I can only feel it."

Wow, this is true. I have not really thought about it, but sitting down and writing to him somehow makes it clear to me that I have been feeling an emptiness, and that I have not felt whole and complete.

"I know a few things, though: I know that love fills the emptiness. I know that love creates hope and that if anything can; love can heal even the old pains. I have found out in my twenty-two years that some men can move mountains, and some can move and control the sky itself, but some men, that is, the men who have love, can move the world. No, the whole universe, and space, and even time. They can make it stand still, and then it wouldn't matter how long they have been gone, they could still be the root and the bringer of love, just like God. Dad, they can bring love, just like God. I am smart enough, and I have learned enough to know that. Dad, it has been too long, and I need "your" love. I need you to bring your love, and I know it is overdue."

This is really what I am asking for. I have not felt loved by my father all these years, and now after coming across the letters, I have a hope of that love, of feeling it, expressing it, and experiencing that love, and a chance for a family that is whole and complete. I do not expect my mother or my father to get back together again. And I am too old for that to matter anymore. I do want my child, the grandchild of my mother and father, to feel and experience the love and strength of family, even from a broken state, that regardless of circumstances, they are loved and supported by all in the family. And I want to experience the strength and support of that love as well.

"Thank you. Your son, Blain."

Sitting there with the pen held tightly in his hand and the tip of the pen still held at a point on the paper, Blain caught a fleeting glimpse of what his new family could look like, what it could feel like. To be his father's son, and to be the father of his son, to share that circular bond of love was what had been missing in his life, and this letter was Blain's reaching out to create that possibility, knowing full well that possibility held no certainties or guarantees, only hope. Writing this letter was an action to create possibility and that action came from faith and hope in the possibility.

It seems strange that this logic, this reality, this gem of truth was indeed circular. Faith is not had without actions and actions are performed with faith. They both co-exist simultaneously and feed off each other. Yet this caveat of truth lies within faith and possibility, and any created possibility is not based on real faith or hope if it seeks to control another's choice, if it aims to take away in whole or part the free will of another. My hope with my father is that he will want the same as I do and that he will act upon that desire accordingly. I know he may not want it. I know he may want it but choose to live his life in fear, as I believe he has been doing. And if for these or any other reasons he chooses to not write back to me or to be involved in my life and the life of his grandchild now, I cannot hold him wrong nor can I love him any less. I cannot judge this for him or on him. I can only express my hopes and desires to him, being true to myself, and to him, to create the space for him to choose to be a part of my life, to be my dad, and for me to be his son.

Reading over what he had just written before placing it in the addressed and stamped envelope and into the mailbox, Blain felt a new strength. He felt emboldened in his action and with the hope for the desired fruits or results, even if nothing came of it. Blain was true to himself, and this is where one's inner strength comes from.

CHAPTER FIFTY-NINE
The Attending Physician

"How young are you, Mr. Wright?" Alan Wright had finished undergraduate school in only three years and his master's program in two years and was currently in his second year of the doctorate program for general medicine. The bulk of his doctorate program was to work directly with doctors in a hospital. This was Alan Wright's classroom three days of the five days a week. "I am 25 going on 26, Dr. Thomas."

"Well, you must be a quick study then."

"I tend to be very focused on what I want, sir."

"You do not have to call me sir, but I do appreciate the respect. Just call me Dr. Thomas."

"Yes, sir... err... I mean, yes, Dr. Thomas."

Dr. Thomas smirked. "Alright then, it looks like the first case I need you to look at is an out-of-state police officer who was just brought in a couple of hours ago. He has been stabilized and appears to have suffered a heart attack. I am sure you already know that the protocol is to keep heart attack victims under our direct supervision for a minimum of twelve hours. His wife is on her way from San Francisco as we speak. I want you to look at his x-rays and charts then come to me with your prognosis. After that, I need you to research for any prior medical records you can find for him."

"Yes, Dr. Thomas. May I have the patient's name?"

"His name is James Harold Graves. He's from the San Francisco police department."

The name James Harold Graves hit Alan Wright like a ton of bricks. How many James Harold Graves of the San Francisco police could there be? It had to be the same J.H. that he knew from his childhood as the father of his best friend and later his lover. It had been a good seven years since he had seen Mr. Graves, and that last time was not a desirable memory. "Mr. Wright? Are you okay? You look like you recognize the name. Do you know Mr. Graves?"

"Uhm… I am fine. The name is familiar, but what are the chances it is the same person I know?"

"Well, check on the patient first then to see if you know him. And if it will be a problem for you, I can assign you to another patient."

"No, no. I mean, I will check on Mr. Graves, of course, but it will not matter if I recognize him or not, as I will not have a problem."

"Okay, good. Carry on then."

CHAPTER SIXTY
Sonya Discovers the Opened Letters

Sonya arrived home in the middle of the day from a much needed week-long vacation. Waiting to wash her clothes was not an option because Sonya left all of her work outfits unlaundered before she left on her vacation. White blouse, black pants, and black shoes was the dress code for the upscale restaurant she now managed. "Well, since I am washing a load of whites, I might as well check Blain's room to see if he has any whites I can throw in as well," Sonya thought as she climbed the stairs.

This was not particularly unusual for Sonya to do; however, whenever possible, she just asked Blain to bring down any whites he had. This time, Blain was not home. He had been not home a lot as of late. In fact, in the past couple weeks, Sonya had not even seen Jessica, Blain's girlfriend. The two were going out and hanging out elsewhere it seemed. "Could they have broken up? No, if they had, I am sure I would have heard about it. Oh well, I will just have to check his room myself for any whites he may have." Little did Sonya know that this simple act was going to bring with it an unwelcome surprise while at the same time an open door to what was previously shut.

When she opened Blain's bedroom door, she saw laying on the bed a handful of letters but paid little attention to them since she was there to look for whites. "Lord, that boy, when will he ever learn to use the hamper and not the floor for his dirty clothes?!" As she bent down to pick up a pair of dirty white socks, Sonya accidentally bumped the bed, and one of the letters fell off. When she picked up the letter to put it back, a name stuck out at her as if it were lit in orange neon lights: Ordin. "This can't be!" Sonya exclaimed within her mind as her heart raced with fear. But there it was. In fact, there they all were, all the letters on Blain's bed were from Ordin. All of the letters she had kept hidden away, meaning to throw them away, but for some unexplainable reason could not and instead settled for hiding them where no one ever goes: the attic.

Sonya stared blankly at the pile of letters. I knew that someday Blain would have to know the truth about his father, but I was hoping, all the same, he would not. Now what will I do? What is Blain's reaction? Will he just leave it at that? I suspect he will not. He will likely want to seek his father out. Is there anything I can do or say now that will keep Blain from doing so? Or is it too late already? If Ordin becomes a part of Blain's life, that means I will have to deal with him, too. How can I? How can I face the man I left over twenty years ago? Our relationship then is but a faint shadow of the past, but a shadow that is coming back to haunt me now. Why would God do this to me now?! I do not want this. I cannot handle this. Why did I not have the strength of will to destroy those letters? Why did God keep me from doing it?"

Life for Sonya was about to change, a change she did not want, a change she did not know the outcome of, did not have any answer for and a change she feared. Sonya did not want to take any responsibility for her choices in the past for leaving Ordin, of telling Blain a lie regarding his father, of keeping Ordin's letters from Blain. For all of these options made her appear bad, perhaps even evil.

Would Blain understand and forgive? Would Ordin? Would God? Could she forgive herself? Sonya felt a pit in her stomach that was growing and painful, like hunger and pain that would not be satisfied by eating, resting, or any manner of medication. Sonya did not know the answer to these questions. Little was she aware that this was indeed an opportunity for a change that was needed to move forward in growth and in life, with self, family, and God.

That this was itself a challenge intended to increase who a person is, though painful and hard to endure, it could be the doorway to more peace and harmony. A real peace and harmony that cannot be felt with the past still being kept alive in the present and future that could only be experienced by taking responsibility and letting go, not pushed away and not dealt with like sweeping dirt under a carpet.

CHAPTER SIXTY-ONE
Jessica Riley – Mother to Be

"Okay, now, mothers, breathe real deep, followed by three quick, powerful breaths. Breath deep again... and Push!" On and on the interesting personality the Lamaze instructor encouraged.

"Wow, I cannot believe this is me here on the floor, that it is me who is being called a mother. I do not feel ready for this. It has only been five months. Oh, how I wish I had not forgotten to pick up the pill. I thought for sure Blain would have brought a condom, but he seemed to have accidentally left it behind. But my God, how much pain and pleasure it was to have him inside of me, how natural it felt to go from making out, and in the moment of the heat of passion, throwing caution to the wind and allowing my guy to become one with me physically. I guess I had hoped that we would somehow escape the natural and logical consequence; that somehow we could manage to have sex and not get pregnant. Look at me now!"

"Now husbands, keep support of your wife. Hold her hand, and if needed, help her lean up. Keep telling her how much you love her."

"Blain is not even my husband. We have not really discussed whether or not we will get married. This is all too soon, but then we both agreed that abortion was not the answer that we wanted. Was this the right decision?"

"Jessica, I love you, and I am here for you and our baby."

"I know, honey."

"Breathe, Breathe. I wonder if he truly loves me, or is he now just following the rest of the group in following the Lamaze teacher's instructions? I do know that he is here for our baby and for me. I do know that there is a reason why I have been dating

Blain for a year now. Maybe he really does love me. Maybe I actually love him too."

"Now just remember fathers, that no matter what your wife screams at you when delivering the baby, she really does love you and the baby. So hold onto her hand no matter how tightly she squeezes, or how greatly she protests, or no matter how loud she screams."

Hmm. Blain a father. I never met Blain's own father, and Blain does not remember his own father either. I wonder what type of father Blain will be? How does him not growing up with a father affect him and his ability to be a father? Will he end up abandoning his child and me like his own father did?"

"Jessica, honey, I will never let go of your hand."

Ah... there he goes again, Blain and his beautiful smile and eyes. It is hard to imagine that as sweet as he has been to me that he would be any different with our child. Well, whatever this adventure in life leads us, it's sure an interesting one what with all of its uncertainties and unknowns along with all of its possibilities. I don't know if either of us are ready to be parents, but here we are, and somehow I get the feeling things will be alright."

CHAPTER SIXTY-TWO
Physician Alan Wright Checks on Mr. Graves

Alan first took a look at the x-rays and the initial physician report. The patient definitely had all the symptoms of a heart attack. Blood work had been drawn and was being processed in the lab. It was time to submit a request across the medical information network from the hospitals in San Francisco. If this was indeed the same J.H. Alan knew that had he lived in the San Francisco Bay area for more than 20 years, having moved there shortly before adopting Winslow, so any records would have to be there. The requests could take a couple hours or up to a full day to come in so nothing more could be done in this regard for now.

The steps to the patient's room seemed more slow and deliberate than usual. "Is it really J.H.? What if it is? But then again, it might not be, but how could it not be? "Alan felt a great trepidation and yet among that feeling was also a sense of relief. If this was J.H., then maybe finally there could be a break in the wall from communication that had been built seven years ago.

But what if it was the same J.H., literally the same, meaning the J.H. who would not be accepting, who did not want to listen, and who created the wall, to begin with? What if J.H. still did not want to take down the wall and try to rebuild his relationship with his son, who was also Alan's partner?" Winslow had long stopped talking about J.H. and Gert, the parents who raised him, but Alan occasionally caught forlorn looks when Winslow would zone out into the world of his own thoughts. Alan could tell that Winslow deep down really wanted to have a relationship with his parents again, that as much as Winslow loved him, Winslow still needed the love of his parents, the love of J.H. and Gert.

"Alright." Standing at the door, Alan took one last deep breath and a sigh of reserve then turned the handle to open the patient's room door. Lying on his side facing the door fast asleep was indeed J.H.

Suddenly, Alan was back seven years ago. He had come to the Graves' home to pick up Winslow for their movie date, which was announced as just the boys going out to a movie. Something was different this time, though when Alan rang the doorbell. He could not tell what exactly, but something felt strained and stressed.

Mr. Graves answered the door but instead of a friendly hello and a heartfelt slap across the back shoulder, Mr. Graves stated, with a concerted effort to maintain volume and dignity, "Alan, I would appreciate it if you do not come to my house ever again. I know about you and Winslow, and I do not approve. And I do not want that in my house or on my property." Mr. Graves then succinctly shut the door without further discussion.

Baffled and shaken, Alan had walked back to his car. Winslow had caught up to him and got in the car, horrified about how his dad had talked to Alan. He had cried into Alan's shoulders. Things were never the same afterward. All Alan knew was that he truly loved Winslow and could not nor would he ever imagine life without him.

Just then the nurse came up to check on Physician Alan Wright. "Is there anything I can do for you, sir?" Taken out of the flashback and feeling a little bit disoriented, Alan Wright answered, "Yes, nurse, will you let me know when patient Graves is awake? With the IV in him, there is no need to wake him early."

"Will do doctor."

Regardless of how this might come across, or how it might be received, Alan knew he had to call Winslow to let him know that J.H., that is, his dad, was in his hospital. Gert had obviously already been contacted since she was on her way. This could be one interesting and long-needed family reunion, and yet it could be another dramatic disaster in familial relationships, or nothing could happen at all.

The possibilities would be up to the collective choices of each person, but it had to begin with Winslow making the choice to come see J.H. and Gert. Right now it was Alan's decision to open the door to these possibilities by calling Winslow. Winslow would likely be home now on a break between college classes and the internship, probably feeding their cat that hadn't been fed that morning. Alan dialed to get an outside line then proceeded to dial the house.

CHAPTER SIXTY-THREE
Ordin - "Today"

Ordin arrived home, still feeling a little shaken by the daymare episodes at the post office, decided to take the photograph inside his house to make the call. He had enough stressful experiences in his car today. The old chair Ordin sat in had permanent worn indentations and some holes in the fabric but was still just as comfortable if not more so to Ordin as it had been for the past twenty years. He had already made the call once, so it should not be that hard to make it again. And yet here Ordin was, pausing with the phone in his hand ready to have a number dialed, but seemingly unable to move his fingers to do so. "Maybe I need to go to the kitchen and get myself a snack, something to settle my nerves a bit."

When Ordin opened the refrigerator, he discovered that the only food in it consisted of a few condiments, milk, bread, butter, limes, and the fish he had caught that morning at the lake. "Well, it's a bit early to eat the fish, since I was saving it for dinner, but I don't want to go back out to get more food right now." As Ordin was finishing cleaning of the fish, he remembered how peaceful it was on his lake, and how much he was grateful for it.

The lake and his conversations with God there was the only real respite Ordin had all these years. "Thank you, Lord, for providing me such a place of peace to go to out in nature where I feel closest to you and to life. Without it, I think I would have gone insane many years ago," Ordin stated aloud as he sliced the butter into the hot pan readying it to fry the fish. Ordin placed the fish cut into halves into the pan, then grabbed the garlic powder, pepper, and salt to season it with. Ideally, he should have some type of vegetable to go with this, but that would have to wait for dinner.

As the fish was frying, Ordin thought about his day. It began like any other day; and yet, somehow this day had turned out completely different. Somehow that day doors were opening that were shut with no sign of ever being open. Today, Ordin had the chance to create a relationship with his son. Today, Ordin had an opportunity to let go of the past with Laurence, the photographer. Today, Ordin had a chance to create a future of possibilities he had long given up any hope of hoping for.

Instead of filling the day with mundane tasks, Ordin felt fresh, new energy in the changes from today and the possibilities those changes may have for him in the future. Even if nothing else came of today other than what it had been so far, today, the load on Ordin's shoulders felt lighter and easier to bear. Today had been a day of actively choosing to create possibility, by following through on what was provided, a letter from his son, and finding the courage to call the number on the back of Laurence's photograph. Ordin turned off the stove, walked determinedly back to his chair, picked up the phone and dialed the new number. "Be with me, Lord, be with me," he sputtered breathlessly.

CHAPTER SIXTY-FOUR
Winslow Gets the Message

During a one-and-a-half-hour break between morning classes and the afternoon internship as a teacher's assistant at a local middle school, Winslow had run home to feed Sebastian, a black cat with white feet and a white spot on his belly and forehead. The house that he and Alan were buying was a mere two bedrooms, mid-western ranch style house on a half-acre of land in Washoe City, Nevada. It was a quiet town with its own lake and far enough away from Lake Tahoe to not be bothered much with tourists. As a mountain desert region, there was not much greenery; however, there were a few trees and shrubs that were mostly indigenous and a small greenhouse in which they grow vegetables and herbs. As Winslow opened the door, Sebastian gave him a disgruntled meow. "Yes Sebastian, I know you are hungry, I am sorry we forgot to feed you this morning, but you will have to wait just a minute longer. I have to go to the bathroom before I burst."

Alan had to work an early shift that morning, and Winslow also had early classes at the University of Nevada – Reno. Both he and Alan worked and were finishing their graduate studies in Reno, Nevada (a half-hour away). Neither minded the 30-minute drive each way, though, because the house was exactly what they wanted. Also, they were allowed to lease-to-own the house until they were both finished with their graduate studies. When the time came, he and Alan were already making plans of adding a study, creating an upstairs master bedroom, and creating a 'great room' giving an open flow and feeling between the kitchen, dining area, and living room with a combination of removing walls and expanding the room. And by the time Winslow was done with his graduate studies, he would be a full-time teacher and eligible for a

167

state-assisted housing program for an education faculty, which included lower interest rates, as well as deposit assistance up to half the cost of the house. They would use this created buffer between debt and value to pay for the expansion.

After going to the bathroom, Winslow grabbed a half-used can of Iams cat food from the refrigerator and mixed it with a half-cup of Iams dry cat food. As he was mixing them together, he looked up to see a picture above the telephone of him and Alan holding each other when he saw the message light blink. With one hand still stirring, Winslow reached with his other hand to press the play message button.

"Hi, Winslow, this is Gert. I know this is an unexpected call, but I thought you should know that J.H. is in a hospital in Nevada. He suffered a heart attack, and I am on my way to get him."

With the "Hi, Winslow" before he heard "This is Gert," Winslow knew immediately who it was. A voice from so long ago and yet, all the same, a voice so familiar, and a voice that brought with it rivers of emotion, mainly of sadness and regret. Winslow focused so much on this alone that he did not hear the rest of the message. In fact, Winslow had to re-play the message three times before he could really get all that was said. J.H. in the hospital... well, it could not be just any regular doctor visit, or Gert would never have bothered to call him. Oh, yeah... she said a heart attack, but she did not say which hospital. All the same, Winslow did not know if he really wanted to see J.H. or Gert again after all these years, and under these circumstances where it would seem nearly an induced excuse. What would he say?

Surprisingly, Winslow was now feeling concerned for J.H. and even for Gert. What she must be going through, and how severe was this heart attack? What would she do if J.H. did die? Who would she have? It would be awkward for her to come into his life after all these years of not talking. It would not feel real. What would I say to J.H.? He would likely not want me there. In fact, he would probably be angry enough to have another heart attack and maybe even die during it just for having me there. Still, in a situation like this, I should be there for them. They were there for me during my life raising me as their own son when I could have been stuck in the foster care system all my childhood life.

Winslow picked up the receiver as if the action itself was on automatic, but paused as his fingers reached the buttons to dial *69. "Am I ready for this now? Do I have much time to wait? I know I should call, but honestly what more can I say to her right now?" Winslow heard the annoying sound you get after holding the phone off the hook for too long. Just as he put the phone back on the receiver, it rang. It was Alan.

CHAPTER SIXTY-FIVE
Brent Simmons Call to the S.F.P.D.

"San Francisco Police Department, may I help you?"

"Yes, I am looking for Officer Smith. Is he available?"

"Who may I say is calling?"

"This is Brent Simmons calling on behalf of Conner James from the television production of Cold Case Killers."

"Hold on, I will ring his phone."

"Thank you."

Sarah was like any stereotypical police dispatcher. Her tone and the way she carried about the duties of her job to whoever was on the other side of the phone was to the point, dry with no hint of the possibility of humor, like one who carries on their work as an automaton devoid of human personality and emotion. This was deemed a necessary and desired work ethic with the idea being that unemotional in the line of police work was required to diffuse rather than exacerbate any situation. Since most people called the police department with some sort of drama or problem, the last thing needed was to add anything to it.

Officer Smith was stuck to his desk most of the time these days, more being the in-house go-to-guy for several of the detectives out in the field. Smith could be out there now in the role of a traffic cop; but after 10 years of that, he was ready for a change. He figured the best way now for him to become a detective was to work for them at the base, getting to know how they worked, and how the system worked including the in-house research and handling of calls when the detectives were otherwise not available. Officer Smith hoped this stint of being behind a desk would not last that long, but so far it had been a year. Just how much longer before he would be called into action in the field as a detective he did not know. He needed a detective to retire, quit, or at least be out of commission for a while to have his chance. And today, after Smith got the call from the field detective in training, Officer Johnson, informing the department that Detective Graves was in the hospital and that he would continue alone on the trek to investigate the Ordin Aire case for Cold Case Killers, Officer Smith felt a glimmer of hope that he just might have his chance sooner than he imagined.

"Officer Smith here. How may I help you, Mr. Simmons?"

"I'm calling to obtain a progress report on the Ordin Aire case."

"Mr. Simmons, one of the two detectives assigned had to retire early from the case. We currently have the other detective still en-route, though he is now delayed an hour and a half longer than originally anticipated. He should still arrive there by tomorrow morning. I will give you a call as soon as we learn more."

"Had to retire early? What can you tell me about that? And which detective is out of the investigation? Who is the one still on the case?"

"Normally that's not something we can share until we have more information on the situation. I'm working on bare bones, just like everyone else."

"Um... you don't seem to understand," Simmons scoffed, "I have a nationally syndicated program that must air in five days' time. There are no bare bones on the information and don't tell me you all really talk like that. Just give me the information so I can do my job."

"Mr. Simmons, right? I don't really care about your program, and I really, really don't care for your tone of voice. But if you must know, and you didn't hear this from me, Detective Graves has suffered a minor heart attack and is currently under a doctor's supervision in a hospital in Reno, Nevada, which is where we got the latest progress report and call from. Junior Detective Johnson is the one who is still on the case and is expected to call in within four hours from the last time he called. But we do not expect anything noteworthy to report to you until later tomorrow morning after Detective Johnson has had a chance to investigate the Aire case. Now if it were me, and I depended on this case to be solved, I would push for the captain to get someone else out there right away that could help close this thing out. You know, you might want to request someone that had some knowledge about both the case and cold case killers. I'm familiar with the case and your show. I'll leave that up to you. Good day, Mr. Simmons, and good luck."

"Thank you, Officer Smith."

"You're welcome. I know the network must be anxious, and I wish I had more to report to you, but the location of the suspect, unfortunately, takes a day's drive to get any information or results. If you want information quicker, you may have to fly someone out there. You are lucky that these two detectives said yes to working on days they were to have off since no one else was available for this last minute request."

"Yes, we do appreciate the effort and willingness of S.F.P.D. in working with us here at the network and the Cold Case Killers show, for which we will definitely give credit to the department. Please call me as soon as you hear from Detective Johnson."

"Of course, Mr. Simmons."

Brent Simmons feared it would be too early to have any results. However, he felt that the heart attack of one of the detectives, requiring the other of two to drive on alone added great drama. It already had some dramatic flair because the two detectives were driving to a location three states away to investigate the possible perpetrator of this cold case, the Aire case for Cold Case Killers 100th episode. After working so long with Conner James, Brent knew the producer of Cold Case Killers would feel the same way. He also knew he had to start throwing his weight around. After all, Cold Case Killers had given the S.F.P.D thousands of dollars in kickbacks as donations for their speedy processing of investigations often leading to indictments. Some might have said that that kind of interactive relationship between the police and a syndicate was unethical and even illegal, but Brent knew that for Conner James it was just good proactive journalism.

CHAPTER SIXTY-SIX
Your Father is in My Hospital

"Hello, Alan. You have great timing. I just got home. How is work today?"

"Well, that's part of the reason why I called, honey, other than to tell you that I love you. Something a little different happened today at work that I feel might be of interest to you."

"Ah.... You know I love you, too. I have some news as well that might interest you. So something different, eh... like a different type of accident or injury?"

"No, more of who came in and is under my care."

"Not my boss or one of my teachers, I hope."

Alan had to chuckle at this because he knew that, unlike many people, Winslow actually really did enjoy his classes and his work. And he surely wouldn't want anything to happen to his boss or teachers. Speaking softly, Alan answered, "No, Winslow, it is J.H., your father." Alan spoke again after a long and thick silence from Winslow. "Honey..."

"Yeah, I know why he's there. And please do not call me honey. You know I do not like it when you call me honey in public, and I do not want it to become a habit by saying it even in private."

"I know. I forgot in my effort to make this as easy for you as I can."

"I appreciate your desire to help, Alan, but some things you just cannot make easier, especially by calling me honey. Anyhow, that was my news. Gert called and left me a message telling me that J.H. had a heart attack and was in a hospital, but she did not say which one. I guess I know which one now. How sadistically ironic it happens to be here."

"Do you think either of them knows that is where I work?" asked Alan.

"No. no, they wouldn't. We haven't spoken in seven years. They only have our phone number in case of an emergency. Besides, Gert probably just found out you, and I are still together from answering the message on our voicemail if she paid any attention to it that is." The truth was, Gert did not even hear the message of the voicemail. She only heard the prompting to leave a message.

"I know it's been a very long time, and I wouldn't even think to place any guilt on you if you did not want to see your parents even now; but here is an opportunity literally placed in your lap."

"Guilt? Guilt for what, Alan?! I was not the one who threw me out as soon as I graduated from high school when they would have thrown me out much earlier if they did not fear more the reactions of others! I was not the one who did not allow me to go to our senior prom with you. And I was surely not the one who after all this time never apologized for how you were treated after it was revealed that we were romantically involved. It is they that should feel guilty, Alan, not me!"

Alan at this point did not know if he really should bring up Winslow's reactionary response to his parents' unwillingness and arguably their inability at that time to accept their relationship. Although Winslow certainly acted within his rights, the intent in writing the expose for the school's newspaper announcing his relationship publically to all, while denouncing his parent's refusal to allow him to go to his senior prom with Alan, was maybe not altogether benign. Winslow felt he needed some way to vent, and he certainly could not talk about it any further with his parents. The fact that the school's principle was the wife of his father's boss, and would certainly read the school's paper, did not escape Winslow's attention either. It had seemed like the perfect way to passively get back at his parents while venting his feelings openly. Winslow did not want to keep himself any longer in the box created to satisfy societal expectations. Writing about it had been the best way he could think of to express himself openly with less of a chance of having his words misconstrued.

"I know all of that's true, Winslow, and regardless of who did what to whom, the lack of communication in any relationship is not just one-sided. But I'm not trying to pick a fight here. I just know that here is an opportunity to perhaps change the present and future relationship with your parents. J.H. will at some point recognize me, and there is bound to be some words that will hopefully be more of a discussion rather than another tongue lashing. This is really in your court of what to do. It's your decision. Your father has been here nearly four of the twelve hours required to keep him here, so you have some time to think about it. I have seen and felt your sadness many times. I also believe you miss having them in your life and wish it was possible otherwise. Maybe after all this time and under these circumstances, we both have a chance to start to build a bridge rather than enforce the wall that exists now."

"It was they that built the wall, Alan."

"I know. And sometimes we have to be bigger than others to bring out the good."

"You don't need to tell me how to be bigger than others, Alan. I could sit here and do nothing and still be bigger than my dad has been for the past seven years of my life."

"Either way, Winslow, I love you, and I will always love you and be by your side."

"Thank you, Alan. I'm sorry I have been lashing out at you. I know you love me and that you are on my side. I love you and will always be on your side, too. I have to think this over. I have some time as you said. I'll go on with my day and call you either way before you leave the hospital to let you know."

"Okay. my love, I will talk to you soon."

Winslow placed the now well-mixed cat food down on the floor for Sebastian. Wow, this was a lot to take in. What had started like any other day had suddenly become a day that Winslow both feared and hoped for.

Winslow did not want a confrontation with either Gert or J.H., but then again, Alan was right. Winslow did miss having his parents in his life. He loved them, too, and appreciated all that they had done for him. Winslow could not understand how they seemingly so easily stopped caring. But then again, J.H. was always about himself, even with his wife. She fulfilled a role, what was expected in this society, and from J.H.'s family, married to a woman and father to a child, being the man of his household.

There seemed to be little to no room for J.H. to accept anything different, to acknowledge that people are all individuals who are not meant to just be cogs in a wheel or part of a puzzle. Each individual was their own puzzle, not to be contrived to fit a particular shape, size, belief, or set of roles, no matter how a family, society, or religion would try to dictate otherwise. Each person was a free agent unto themselves. Free will was truly the only real law governing man provided by the universe or God and was the greatest gift and truth.

How could a man that Winslow was raised by and respected in his youth not know this? But again, Winslow had to admit, it was J.H.'s own free will and right to believe and act as he chooses. Winslow just wished that J.H. and Gert could accept and respect his free will as well while not creating a vast chasm of disconnection between him and them.

"I do want to see them, and they are literally in my own backyard, although unknowingly, they are here." Winslow knew that he would go see them, but he was uncertain about how it would go down. What would their reaction be? Would they respond or just react? If they just reacted, there would be little that could be accomplished. If they would respond, there would then be space for creating the possibility of communication.

"Well, cannot control their choices, but I can control my own." Winslow felt comforted in that he would do what he felt he should do to create the possibility he desired. He would go see them, and he would talk lovingly with them, be happy to see them, glad that circumstance has provided an opportunity. Winslow did not know whether the circumstance was just that or if God or some higher energy put it all together to give them all a chance to rebuild their relationship, to forgive each other, and themselves so that they could all move on and perhaps even move forward.

CHAPTER SIXTY-SEVEN
After Lamaze

"Okay, parents that is it for today. Remember to practice breathing with each other daily. Have your go-bag ready so you just have to grab it and go when the time comes for your child, the beautiful new life to come out into the world from the mother's womb. I will see you again next week on Wednesday evening and then again Saturday morning. Have a blessed week."

That was the end of today's class. With that, Blain got up and helped Jessica up, as did all the fathers in the room with each of the respective mothers. It had been an incredibly emotional few days, and Blain was feeling a little uncertain about his state of mind. Jessica thanked him with her customary kiss, except this time she was a few inches further away than last month. Her belly was more swollen with the new life inside of it. Blain felt the roundness of her belly with his hand and drew back from the kiss. He looked long and lovingly at Jessica, took a deliberate breath, and let flow some silent tears.

"Blain, what's wrong? What has happened?"

"Jess, I am just so full right now. My head, my heart, I can feel the baby's life in you, and I wonder if I have what it takes. It's no secret that my father was not there for me for a long time, but I found letters from him that I never knew he wrote. Even though I don't know him, or anything about his life yet, I feel I know him through his letters. I feel him and can feel why he left. I mean, I don't have the facts, but I don't need the facts. I have the feelings, and they tell me that a man's journey is fraught with pitfalls and missteps that are part of imperfections that exist naturally as well as those that are created. I wanted a perfect story as to why he left. I wanted a perfect reason why I would not be like him and yet I'm scared to death that I will be, for better or worse. Jess, you are all the pureness I have in my life, and I am afraid of tainting that pureness with the imperfections I inherited from him. And yet I know I can run away in my own way and style if I let my head lead me to the place where the fear lives. I guess what I'm saying is I never wanted to be a father because I never want to be my father. I never wanted there to be a little version of me with a heart and head mired in thoughts of insecurity and uncertainty about his role in my absence. I felt that doubt for most of my life and now I stand on the verge of being that same man. I just want to get it right, but how do you get it right? Are there any real answers?"

Jessica touched Blain's lips with her fingers and then held his hand and guided it to first her heart and then her belly. And with a knowing smile that contained the wisdom of a life-weary sage, she closed her eyes and held his hand tighter and more forcefully against her belly. Blain did not move his hand, and his heart beat faster as he felt the pressure Jessica was applying. Blain was not sure what she was doing or why, but he felt her flinch and instinctively tried to draw his hand back, but Jessica would not let him and pressed all the more. Blain was confused, and just as he was about to withdraw his hand from her belly, she opened her eyes sharply and gave a short gasp and let her mouth go to a natural position.

"Blain, just as I do. You have the power of life-or-death over this little one that grows inside me. Not just his physical life, but also the life or death of his dreams, his emotions, his challenges. Blain, honey, this child is a part of you and of me, but does not come from or for us, but through us for God's purpose. Painful to you and I or not, we are only the bow and he is the arrow. And we only aim and shoot and where he flies and lands is God's grace. So, yes, my husband to be, you should be affected and afraid, but not fearful. You love me, and you love the life inside of me, so run if you must, but like your father, return, return to me, to your child, to your life, but return when you are ready. His life, my life, will be here. No matter where we run and no matter what we do, you hold on to me, and I'll hold on to you. Regardless of where we land, you hold on to me, and I'll hold on to you, and the two will make a strong cord for the third to climb."

Where these words came from Jessica did not know. But its effect on Blain was palpable, and Blain stood back as if he had been hit with a blow by a heavyweight boxer. His eyes welled up with tears, and he knew he could never leave this woman and child. No matter how hard it would be, no matter what a reconnection with his own father would bring him, in that moment, with his hand pressed against Jessica's swollen belly teaming with the life they were ushering into the world, Blain crossed the threshold from boy to man, from single male to father. He would never go back and would never run. Never.

CHAPTER SIXTY-EIGHT
Reaction and Response

If you were to look up the definition for the words reaction and response, you would find them almost identical. If they are defined the same, why then do we have two terms for the same meaning? What is the differentiation in the use between them?

The term reaction is used to infer that the action a person takes is on the level of an automated action having no real thought or consciousness behind it. On the physical level, an example would be when a doctor tests your knee for reflex. The doctor hits the knee with a small, rubber-covered hammer just above the knee to compel it to jerk in reflex, in a direct reaction to the stimulus. If you accidentally slam your fingers in a door, your first reaction is to yell and perhaps curse. A reaction generally is the very first action taken without pausing to think about it. Many reactions are based upon fears. Fear is on the same level as the flight or fight survival mentality and instincts, which of themselves are reactions. Whenever someone fears something real or imagined, substantial or insubstantial, they are more likely to act out on that fear.

At a clothing optional beach, there was a friend who chose to be without clothes who saw someone they thought they knew. As this friend was coming up to the other person who chose to wear clothes, the other person immediately yelled at the guy, calling him a faggot and cursing. The clothed guy acted without thinking through his action, assumed my friend approaching had another intent other than to say hello, and thus acted without checking the reality of that assumption. The clothed guy reacted.

A response differs in that it is not automatic. There does exist a pause wherein a person thinks and chooses their action or non-action. With a response, a person gives more thought to the effect or possible results of what they say or do in conjunction to what they really want, what is needed, or what has more potential to provide them with more desirable results. Typically, a response is more conscientious, whereas a reaction has no inherent conscientious thought behind it. A response usually has the appearance and effect of being softer, more thoughtful, more caring, more open and honest than a reaction. In simpler understanding, a response is more human (more sentient), and a reaction is more animalistic (more pure instinct without thought). Of course, humans have the ability to operate on both levels of interaction with their world.

CHAPTER SIXTY-NINE
Blain and Sonya Talk

Blain came home from dinner with Jessica to shower and get changed for his graveyard security shift when he spied his white clothes clean and folded at the end of his bed. "Oh, my God! Mom is back, and I forgot to put the letters away. Mom! Mom, where are you?" Sonya heard Blain yell down the stairs and knew immediately why he was calling for her. The pits in her stomach instantly grew larger and at the same time made her stomach feel more empty and uneasy. True, she could have left the clothes downstairs on the couch or placed them on the floor at Blain's bedroom door, but instead, she felt it best to deal with the unpleasantness now rather than having it fester inside. And the easiest way to bring it up was to make it readily apparent that she had seen the letters.

"I'm down here in the kitchen, Blain."

"Will you come upstairs for a minute?" With that, Blain heard his mom's slow but deliberate footsteps on the stairs. What would he say to her? He did not know, but now the present moment was as good of time as any to talk about the letters.

Blain's door was ajar as Sonya reached his bedroom. It was about all she could do to keep her hand from shaking as she reached to push the door further open when she stepped inside. Blain was standing near the corner of the bed. He had given thought to put the clean clothes away but felt awkward in not having them still there in their place as a conversation bridge.

"Thanks for washing my whites, mom. I really appreciate it."

"You're welcome, son. It wasn't much more effort to add them to my own whites."

"I assume when you came in to retrieve my clothes you saw the letters laying on my bed."

Here it is, Sonya thought. "I did."

Blain remained quiet, leaving the space of no words to create an opening for further thoughts to be expressed from his mother without the constraints of any words he could add at this point.

"You see, Blain, I didn't know when to bring up the topic of your father to you. I wasn't sure that having his influence in your life when you were already going through so much would have been a wise extra complication."

Blain still kept his silence, giving his mother a look that spoke, "Go ahead, keep on talking."

"Well, the truth of the matter is, I also did not want to have to have your father in my life again as well. If he were in yours, he would have to in some form be in mine as well, and I was not ready for that."

"What really went on between you and my father, mom? Did he really just leave? From his letters, he does not sound like the type of person who would just leave by his own choice. I want the truth, mother. I have already sent him a letter, and I expect to hear back from him sooner or later."

Sonya had been deliberating possible scenarios of this conversation the entire day ever since she saw the letters, and even more so when she made the decision to leave the clothes folded on Blain's bed. And as much as she wanted to be able to gloss over the truth, she knew she could not. If she did gloss over the truth again and even now, Blain would eventually learn the truth, and anything she would have said contrary to the truth would only create a greater chasm in her relationship with her son. So as much as the truth would cause her pain now, further avoidance of it would only create greater pain and perhaps even irreparable damage. Sonya truly loved Blain, and the very thought of any

185

possibility of not having him in her life and she in his was much more of a nightmare to fathom than being forthright now with the truth and ghosts of her past relationship with Gordon, now known as Ordin.

"Your father had a shooting accident in which his best friend was killed when you were only two. This put our lives in a whirlwind of nightmares between the courts, publicity, various organizations, neighbors, and people from all over that we never knew. They suddenly became entangled in our lives and would not leave us alone. It became unbearable. Your father and I had already started to have problems in our relationship before this happened, and the whole situation was not only something that broke us individually but also the last few strands that held us together. At one point things got violent. Both your father and I knew that we could not continue this way. We either had to move and try to recreate life somewhere no one knew us together or create new lives separately. Instead of staying with your father and going on what seemed like the run from everything that we knew as a life, I chose a divorce at that time, and I held onto your custody so that you would not have to deal with any aftermath of the whole situation."

"You say my father had a shooting accident. It was an accident, right?"

"Yes, Blain, it was an accident. Your father loved his friend very much and would have never intentionally harmed him." Just speaking those words brought about a tinge of guilt in Sonya as she now recognized that she had treated Gordon as if he had purposely shot and killed his friend. How horrible she had been to him. She now recalled her sharp words said to Gordon, "I cannot have my son grow up with a father who killed his best friend."

"It would seem, mother, that I still had to deal with the aftermath of what I am sure was a nightmare of an experience for both of you, for I have had to live without a father."

This was true, and something Sonya had thought of before, but for Sonya, the aftermath of staying with Gordon or having him in her life still outweighed then what she felt the consequences would have been to not have him in Blain's life. But now she was not so sure.

"I know, son, and I am truly sorry for that. I just did what I felt was best at the time."

"Why then did you keep these letters from me the whole time, mother? Are there any more letters he wrote that are not here? Any letters to me or cards since I was twelve?"

"I was afraid, son. I didn't want to have to see your father again, nor did I want any of the past to hang over you through your impressionable teenage years. I mean, I wasn't even sure if I could see him if that would endanger our lives, his life, or what was going to happen. No, there are no other letters. The courts kept him from writing to you before your twelfth birthday. It was not until then that either of us knew where the other was or that your father had changed his name to help him live a separate life from the incident. We were forbidden to even attempt to seek each other out before then."

"So, you have known how to get in contact with him since I was twelve?! That was thirteen years ago, mom! How could you continue to keep this from me for so long? Did you not think that during my teenage years was when I needed a father the most?"

"I was afraid, son. That really is all there is to it. I was afraid."

"So your fear cost me the possibility of knowing my father for the past thirteen years. Your fears undoubtedly were what directed you to run away from my father twenty-three years ago, and thus is the cause of me not knowing my father my entire life! How selfish you have been, mother, putting your fears above me, above another."

With this, Sonya began to cry uncontrollably. All this time she had been living her life through her fears. She had tried to run away from them, ignore them, live as if they did not exist, and yet the undeniable truth was they did exist. Every act of feigning otherwise had only increased the stronghold her fears had on her and her life.

Sonya's tears softened Blain's heart. Even though he was still angry, he could not bear to see her cry. "Mother, you cannot have been living life all that happily with the weight, strength, and control you have given your fears."

"You're right, son; you are right," Sonya acknowledged between sniffles. "Though I have been happy, Blain, you have given me reasons to experience happiness and joy. I want you to know that."

"I know, mom, and I love you, too. I want you to truly be happy. The type of inner happiness and joy that needs no other to experience it, but is only further enhanced by others. I don't believe you have had the experience of this true inner happiness that sits with you when you are alone in your thoughts about you and your life with no dependency on another. And what about God? What about his love? Isn't that what you taught me, that God's love is happiness and that through any kind of pain if we only have faith, faith in him, faith in ourselves, faith in love, that all wounds will heal? Isn't that what you taught me, mother? Where did that go? Where was that when the fear came?"

"I think I remember feeling that way once for a time in my childhood, and even for a time when I met your father, but I have forgotten it. Have you experienced this for yourself, Blain?"

"I think I have in brief moments, but I have felt incomplete for the longest time. I think I have felt incomplete because I felt incomplete about my relationship or lack thereof with my father, of not really knowing who he was."

"I am sorry about this Blain. I am sorry for my part in it." Sonya broke down and cried.

Blain wanted to just stand there coldly watching the tears run down his mother's face; yet he could not. All the anger he felt melted with every tear. "Thank you, mom. I know you are sorry. I'm glad that we now have this out in the open and hope that we can continue to be more honest with each other in our communication."

"I would like that. Well, I guess if you wrote him, I would have to see him at one point sooner than later. I am not sure what I will have to say to him. I don't know if he would even talk to me if he would ever forgive me."

"I have hope he will, too. Somehow, I feel he will mom. I also have a hope that he will write back to me soon and that he will want to be a part of my life and the life of my child."

"Your child?" Sonya whispered in surprise.

"Yeah, mom. As part of the new leaf of having a more open and honest communication between us, Jessica is pregnant with my child. I wrote my father asking for him to be a part of my life and the life of my son. I do not want my son to grow up without a father nor without knowing my father."

"Oh, Blain, I'm so happy for you! You are going to be a father! Knowing you, and as is evident from how grown up you are in our conversation today, I know you are going to be a great father. I don't know where you learned it from, but I am very grateful to God that you are who you are despite my own faults as a person and a mother."

"Mother, you have always shown me, love. And it's your love and the love of God that I have learned and experienced that has taught me what I know and am today."

"Thank you, son," Sonya smiled warmly. Both Blain and Sonya felt lighter and more fulfilled at this moment than they had for some time.

"Blain, you must not wait for a letter from your father. You should call him."

"You have his phone number, mom?"

"I do, part of the information shared from the court upon your 12th birthday, was not only the current name and address but also each other's phone number. So unless he has changed it over this past year's update, I have it. And since your father does not know that I kept his letters from you, he may think that calling you is not welcome. He likely also wants to avoid talking directly with me much as I have been wanting to avoid talking with him. I will get it for you now before you leave for work."

Beaming now with a new possibility that just opened of not having to wait for a return letter, Blain's mind was racing with what he would say. If he could get a hold of his father, what would the conversation be like? Again, Blain did not know the outcome, but he had a hope that was bolstered now as a result of the conversation he just had with his mother. "Thanks, mom. That would mean the world to me."

CHAPTER SEVENTY
Detective Graves – Awake

Detective Graves woke when the nurse was taking his blood pressure reading. "How long have I been sleeping?"

"I really don't know that Mr. Graves," the nurse replied. "I just got on shift an hour ago, and as far as i am aware you have been asleep the whole time I have been here."

Detective Graves studied the nurse for a moment. A young male about the age of 27, with dirty blonde hair and hazel green eyes standing about 5'10" tall with a slim frame of about 150 pounds, a fair complexion and hands that he noticed were soft when the nurse lifted his arm to get the pressure cuff off. "Do you know what time my partner left? Um, what's your name, kid?"

"I don't know what time your partner left. I can check the guest logbook for you. My name is Jason."

"Well, that doesn't really matter right now, Jason. But maybe you can tell me how long I've been admitted into this hospital and when I can be released."

"Mr. Graves, you have been checked in now for four hours, and you can be released after 12 hours of observation, that is, pending no further problems are experienced. Also, you have to have someone to take you home, as well as have a discharge physical examination by your doctor. Is your partner going to be taking you home?"

"No, my partner has gone on to complete the investigation. Unfortunately, Gert, my wife, is on her way to pick me up."

"Oh, my apologies. I thought when you said your partner, you meant your live-in partner, you know, as in domestic partner," Jason said embarrassed. "I'm guessing now that you are either a law enforcement officer or a detective."

"Do I look gay? How can you insult me so?"

"No, Mr. Graves, you do not particularly look gay; however, in my experience, there is no one particular look or type that is gay, and I saw on your chart that you are from San Francisco. I meant no insult, as I personally do not see being gay or even straight as an insult, just a preference. I am glad that you have someone in your life who loves you enough to come and pick you up from the hospital this far from your home."

"Yeah, well I would prefer her not to come here. I would actually prefer to leave on my own and leave her doting out of this."

"I think you are fortunate all the same. I wish I had someone in my life who cared enough to dote over me."

"Humph," Graves brooded while Jason finished his medical notations before leaving the room. Just why is everyone telling me I should be glad that Gert dotes over me? Graves thought. I am my own man, like my father, who doesn't need doting, who only needs to be the man of his own household, to bring home the money and provide for my wife and … child. J.H.'s face became disturbed as he thought about his son. "I have not heard from my son for seven years, he thought. He's a grown man by now, and no longer should have need of me to provide for him. But still… is there not more to provide to one's son, one's family, besides a roof over their heads and food on the table?

J.H.'s father, Harold James, always provided a solid example of being a man who took care of himself, his household, and others. Harold James judged things as black and white as the colors of a police car.

"James Harold, let me tell you, son, this is the life a man should lead: a strong provider and a role model to his wife and family." J.H. looked up to his father and felt his father's pride and love whenever he did things like him. A man should never cry; a man is the provider; a man is the strong arm of the law of his household just like being a police officer is being the strong arm of the law in its enforcement of the laws of the land. For the successful execution of these duties, a man should expect to have a dutiful wife and children, a home in order, a place to kick off the shoes and uniform at the end of the day, to have a warm meal prepared, and to have the household chores taken care of by his wife and children, not to mention a son to carry on the traditions of the family name and of being a man. It wasn't even a question for J.H. that he would also follow in his father's footsteps by becoming a police officer to be an enforcer of the laws.

It was J.H.'s hope and expectation that his own son, though adopted, would also carry on the family heritage, be an example of manhood, and take on the mantle of being in law enforcement. So it was with utter disappointment and a great feeling of failing to be the father his father was when J.H. learned that Winslow was gay. How could anyone gay ever be in law enforcement, where all men are men - the stereotypical alpha-male type of man? And just how did J.H. fail to raise a son to be a man, not a wussy gay boy?

CHAPTER SEVENTY-ONE
Paul - Pit Stop in Carlin, Nevada

'Carlin next exit' the sign read. It was perfect timing for the fuel gauge indicated low fuel, and it was about time for Paul to check back into home base. Conveniently, a Pilot Travel Center was located just off the exit. As Paul stood up and paused from sitting in the car, he could feel all his leg and back muscles slowly release their tension. Just why exactly did the department send us out on this long drive? I know they could have just as well sent the case file over to the police department local to the suspect. But Paul knew that it was for the network that produced Cold Case Killers that the S.F.P.D. wanted a more direct interaction with the case and that Detective Graves's ego was somewhere in the mix. Exactly where he did not know, but he was sure that if there was a way to snag any glory out of this situation that Graves would be on the hunt.

There were bigger payoffs for being directly involved rather than handling it over to another police department. For Paul, it meant one step closer to being a full detective, one step closer to his next advancement. And for that, Paul tried to convince himself, it was worth having to disappoint his little girl one more time. He could make it up to her later. Being a full detective was a spot Paul knew many would love to have. If he said no, there would have easily been one to step up and take it from him.

"You know, Willow, I was thinking that the next time I come home, that I just may stay awhile, a while longer. I know I am not home a lot, honey, and we have missed a lot of time together. I do not want to miss out on any more time with you than I absolutely have to...."

These words he spoke to his daughter, Willow earlier that morning came unbidden while Paul stood staring blankly out at the horizon. Paul had to wonder, "So what if someone else had stood in?" He was obviously having doubts about even staying in the police force. He really did feel like he had not been spending enough time with his daughter and Paul really was no longer happy on the force as it no longer felt like home nor like the space he wanted to be in, that is, in the service of others.

There had to be some other option he could choose. Just what, Paul did not readily know, and this may have been part of the reason he had stuck it out for so long. But waiting longer was only creating a greater gulf between him and Willow as well as between him and his wife Kristine, not to mention the person he was and the person he wanted to be.

"Just a little more time in and my time will be my own," he mused. When I'm a full detective, I can make my own schedule and then I can spend more time at home." How many other detectives had had that thought there was no way of knowing, but Paul felt that a change was coming. He really believed in his words and that to him was what separated him from the self-serving detectives that polluted the force. But what he felt and what the reality of the force was were two very different things.

The pump stopped automatically indicating the car's tank was full. Paul put the spout back into the pump's slot and stepped into his vehicle. "Well, I know I must at least fulfill this assignment, and then I can decide. There is no reason to seemingly irrationally choose to leave the force in the middle of an investigation." Paul picked up his cell phone and dialed home base. Sarah answered the phone in her usual manner.

"Hello, Sarah, this is Officer Johnson calling in to report I have made it to Carlin, Nevada. The next time I call will be when I have reached Salt Lake City."

"Oh, hello Paul. Smith wants to speak with you, he was waiting for your check-in call. Cold Case Killers called for an update not long ago."

"Okay, thanks, Sarah, I'll hold."

"Hello, Johnson! Well, I guess Sarah already mentioned to you that Cold Case Killers called for an update not more than thirty minutes ago."

"Yeah, Smith, is there anything, in particular, you need to tell me? There's nothing more to report on my end other than that I am on schedule."

"Well, nothing really. I just thought you might be interested in hearing that they are giving thought to fly me out there to join you to aid in the investigation now that you are alone on the case, just in case the suspect gets hostile."

"Really, Smith? Was this their own idea or what?"

"Well, I may have mentioned it to them that it might be a good idea and ensure their cold case highlight for their 100th episode goes down without a hitch."

"Well, if they decide that they need that, though it would be just as well to have me team up with a local police officer, one that might know the suspect more personally and thus increase chances of minimal hostility, so be it."

Smith did not want to admit it, but Johnson actually had a valid point, though he would not say so because he still wanted to be out on the case to get his shot at becoming a detective. "Well, yeah, it is in the network's hands as to how they want this handled," Smith replied.

"Thanks, Smith, for the update. Make sure the network knows of my suggestion as well so that they can make a more informed decision."

"Okay, Johnson, I will."

"I best get going. I still need to use the restroom and get a refresh on my coffee before hitting the road again."

"Alright, Johnson, I will keep you informed when you call in from Salt Lake City."

After going to the restroom and getting a refill of coffee in his thermos mug, Paul headed to the car and thought to himself, "See, you were right. There's always someone ready to jump in to take your place like Smith."

Well, he had not planned on using the local police force to aid him in investigating the suspect, but now that he said it, he was more or less obliged to do so. In all actuality, Paul did not believe he was going to need the backup. If he had to have backuup, he preferred a local officer who would allow him to call the shots rather than Smith who would be so gung-ho on getting the promotion that he would jump to arresting the suspect without any real proof other than the say so of Cold Case Killers. With this thought in mind, Paul drove back to Highway 80 and towards his next destination: Salt Lake City, 250 miles away.

CHAPTER SEVENTY-TWO
Smith Updates Brent Simmons

"Hello? This is Officer Smith of the San Francisco Police Department calling for Brent Simmons as he requested."

"Officer Smith, this is Simmons." Brent was awaiting this phone call and recognized the number he had stored in his quick dial at once. He thus took the call personally before forwarding it onto his assistant.

"I am calling to report that Jr. Detective Johnson has called in to report and that he is on schedule."

"Thank you, Officer Smith. Is there anything else to report?"

"Well, actually there is something to report in regards to our previous conversation about the detective being on his own. Johnson has suggested that he team up with an officer from the suspect's local police department with the idea that they may already be somewhat acquainted with the perp, being such a small town and all. Of course, I feel that they would not be familiar with Cold Case Killers and how you like things handled, so it may still be a better choice to fly someone out there from the San Francisco Police Department who could fly to Salt Lake City and meet Johnson there. Someone familiar with both Cold Case Killers and the case, someone like... I don't know... myself?"

"Thank you, Officer Smith. I'll keep both ideas under consideration as I bring them up to Connor James." Brent was not dumb to the push in which Smith was attempting to get himself more involved, and although Smith points were good, he felt an angle of getting the point of view from someone else who might know the suspect other than the neighbor who called in the suspect was likely the better option. That someone would be on the local police force combining their efforts and knowledge with that of the S.F.P.D. where the case originated and would bring about much more network and audience appeal.

Another great idea, Brent, he thought to himself. This 100th episode will be the one that really puts me over, then it's "1,000 ways to murder someone" produced by Brent Simons, airing Tuesdays at 8 p.m. The sound of it was like music to the ears of Brent, and all he had to do was finish this episode, put it at the top of his resume, and head out to the other networks with his masterpiece. Brent thought about telling Connor the truth about the idea, then thought again. It was kind of my idea anyway, and I need some credit as an independent producer with that asshole Connor anyway. No more talking down to me. No more taking his shit.

As Brent discussed the Aire case handling options with Connor, he could hear it in Connor's voice; he just did not respect him, even after Brent told Connor his great idea of having a local come out. He half wanted the episode to fail so he could ruin Connor, but Brent knew that would mean he could not use a nationally televised show as the crème de la crème of his resume. He reluctantly sucked it up and affirmatively nodded as Connor agreed to have the S.F.P.D. contact the local police department to see whether they could have an officer join up with Detective Johnson on the investigation when he arrived Sunday morning. As long as they could, this would be the option they would choose, holding the flying out of another office to meet Johnson in Salt Lake City as the last option.

Brent immediately called back the S.F.P.D. Sarah again answered in her usual manner. "This is Mr. Simmons from Cold Case Killers calling again for Officer Smith."

"Smith here."

"Officer Smith, this is Brent Simmons again. I have discussed it over with Connor James, and we are both in agreement that we will have you contact the local police department to see whether they can get a local officer to join Detective Johnson on the case. Assuming they can, this is the route we want to proceed with. If they cannot, we will hold the option of flying you out to join Detective Johnson."

"Of course, Mr. Simmons," Smith, responded somewhat let down and yet slightly hopeful. What he felt, however, was another in the long litany of him shooting himself in the foot, a litany that included him getting himself passed up for promotion after promotion, all the while trying to seem coy about tooting his own horn and meaning to railroad everyone in his way. This just appears to be the way his life went. Under his breath he muttered, Oh, well, easy come easy go. Such is the life of a damned fool." With, that Smith hung up the phone, walked into the cafeteria and ordered his regular lunch, except this time he thought, "I'll also have some salt to go with that foot." A small township just might be too busy to help out on a last minute notice, and if this was the case, he just might have his chance!

CHAPTER SEVENTY-THREE
Dr. Thomas and Attending Physician Wright Discuss Patient J.H. Graves

After Jason, the attending nurse, left J.H. Graves' room, he went up to the nurse's station to place a call to Physician Alan Wright. "Hello, Dr. Wright? This is Jason at the nurse's station. You asked me to let you know when patient Graves awoke. He woke up about 10 minutes ago while I was doing my rounds."

"Thank you, Jason. How are his vitals?"

"They're all within normal range, Dr. Wright."

"Good to hear. Dr. Thomas and I will be visiting the patient shortly."

"I will let him know."

"Thank you, Jason."

With this, the call ended. It was time to speak with Dr. Thomas again. As Alan walked to Dr. Thomas' office, he began to wonder whether J.H. Graves would recognize him, and if he did, how he would choose to respond or react. There was really nothing that Alan could do right now or would do any differently.

Sure, he would inform Dr. Thomas that he did indeed know the patient, and to be completely fair and honest, Alan would provide him with a brief history as to how he knew the patient. And yes, Alan could at that time opt to have the patient taken from his care. If Dr. Thomas insisted on this, Alan would obey; however, Alan felt it would create a better chance of building a bridge for Winslow and his father if he remained on as J.H.'s attending physician. It was Alan's hope that J.H. would not recognize him. In this manner. He could just do his job professionally, thus postponing the reunion until Gert and Winslow would arrive. This would also give J.H. a chance to recognize Alan as just Dr. Wright, a professional. On the other hand, if J.H. did recognize him, Alan really had no idea of what he would do or say. Alan's plan was to just keep it professional and non-personal as possible for now.

Wright knocked on Dr. Thomas' door "It's Physician Wright. Patient J.H. Graves is now awake and ready to be visited."

"Yes, Wright, come on in."

As Alan peered through the open door, Dr. Thomas' stared at him askance. "I have submitted a medical history check in San Francisco. As it turns out, I do have personal knowledge of the patient from my childhood, as he is the father of my childhood's best friend whom I have not seen in seven years. From what I know of patient Graves, he has lived in the San Francisco Bay area for over 20 years, so all of his medical records should be there and available."

"Do you know anything yourself of his medical history?"

"I know that he has always been healthy overall, though he has gained some weight since last I saw him. I know his own father worked for the police department as well and died relatively early into his retirement years. I believe it was from heart complications, but I am not entirely sure of that."

"And will there be any problem with keeping Graves on as your patient?"

"I do not have any problem with that myself, sir. I'm not sure how Graves will respond if he recognizes me, as the last conversation we had seven years ago was not so pleasant. I would appreciate the chance to stay on as his attending physician as I still know the patient's son very well, who I have contacted so that they might have a reunion of sorts."

Looking intently into Wright's eyes, Dr. Thomas saw how much this meant to him. "Okay, Wright, I will keep him on your schedule. Despite this, I feel it best that I accompany you in case the patient responds in a way that threatens his current health."

"Understood, sir. I mean, Dr. Thomas (Alan said with an embarrassed giggle), and thank you. I expected nothing less than your support and caution. Thank you."

CHAPTER SEVENTY-FOUR
Dr. Thomas and Attending Physician Visit J.H. Graves

Graves turned on the TV mounted on the opposing wall with the remote in hand and had come across an airing of COPS he had seen before, but felt he could never tire of watching the show. And it certainly had to be better than the so called victims on such shows as "Monty." Graves really enjoyed the fact that most of the action was caught live on tape. Indeed, these cases and situations were exactly why being in law enforcement was so necessary as a service for the public good. He felt proud to be a detective since it was his duty to investigate crime scenes and possible suspects. The heart monitor registered annoyingly to Graves as a result of his excitement as he watched a police officer chase down an escaping suspect.

Dr. Thomas and Physician Wright knocked politely on the door as they entered the room. "Hello, Mr. Graves. May we come in?" Hearing the escalated rate of beeping from the heart monitor, and noticing the chase scene on the TV, before Graves could reply Dr. Thomas reached for the remote and turned off the TV.

"Sorry to disturb your show there, but seeing as how it gets your heart all excited it might be best not to watch it for the time while you are here under observation. I'm Doctor Thomas, and this is your attending physician, Wright, who will be working directly with you during your stay here. I will let Wright take over now."

"Hello, Mr. Graves. I am sure you are already aware that you were brought here after suffering from a moderate heart attack. You were stabilized as soon as you got here and have been under mild sedatives to help you sleep and to recover. Now that you are awake, we will take you to cardiac catheterization laboratory to directly evaluate the status of you heart, arteries, and the amount of heart damage. Your nurse, Jason, who I believe you have met already, will take you there in about 15 minutes. In the meantime, I need to ask you some questions that we were unable to obtain earlier from your law enforcement partner who brought you in."

"Sure, whatever I can do to be of help, especially if it will get me out of here sooner. I was in the middle of a case you know."

Graves did not like being in the hospital for even one minute, especially when he was not here under official capacity, but rather as a patient himself. Having the occasional need to be in hospitals to help investigate suspects and victims, Graves knew well that complete cooperation with the doctors would have more a chance of shortening the stay.

"I believe your partner mentioned that as the reason you were so far away from your home jurisdiction. We have submitted a medical history search on your behalf, which was originally signed for by your partner. We will need now your authorization to continue to do so since you are now in capacity. In the meantime, we need to know if you have had any prior complications with your heart and if so what, when, and to what extent."

"No, this is my first time."

"To your knowledge, has anyone in your family history ever had any heart complications?"

"My father did. He died nine years ago from sudden heart failure shortly after his retirement."

"Did he show or have any symptoms, such as mild heart attacks or similar ones to what you just experienced before this?"

"Not to my knowledge. But then again, he would be the type to never tell me if he had. The only reason I knew of the last one was because my mother had passed away the year before from cancer, and as the only next of kin, the hospital had to call me."

"Do you know of anyone else in your family having any history of heart complications, like your grandfather?"

"You know, it's possible, but the men in my family never talked about their health other than to say they were just as fit as ever. We have all been men of the law and could never be seen as anything but our best."

"Okay, that is enough for now. Later the nurse will bring you the full review of medical questionnaire to fill out to the best of your knowledge along with the medical records search waiver. Do you have any questions for me?"

Already knowing the answer, Graves thought he should ask it anyways, just to be certain there was no way of being let out early. "Yeah, how much longer will I need to stay here before I am released?" Wow, the need to be released almost felt as if he was in prison.

"You have been here a little over four hours so far. Assuming we can obtain a confirmatory cardiology tests and of your heart and surrounding circulatory system that may be needed, and assuming you maintain stability, we will be able to release you to your wife in a little under eight more hours. Protocol dictates that we are required to keep you under observation for a minimum of twelve hours. Any more questions, Mr. Graves?"

"No, but I guess I will need to find something to watch that does not get my heart monitor all excited."

Both Doctor Thomas and Physician Wright chuckled at this. "Yes, it will help the hospital records to report stability," Doctor Thomas replied.

As the two left the room, J.H. thought to himself that Wright looked familiar. But to his disappointment, he could not recollect if he had actually met Wright before or if he just had a familiar looking face that reminded him of someone else he had met. Who knew? In his line of work, he saw a lot of faces. Considering where Wright worked and lived so far from San Francisco, J.H. conceded that it was unlikely he had met Wright before now.

CHAPTER SEVENTY-FIVE
Forgiveness

What is forgiveness? Is it peace in the center of the soul? Is it the realization of faith? Or is it a lightness of heart that comes when you release the pain of the past or the guilt of the moment?

People have tried for eons to define forgiveness. Famous authors such as Yates, Hemmingway and Poe had attempted to describe it through their literary works. Fine artists have used endless forms of expression to interpret and recreate on canvases and in mediums of all kinds. Musicians have written some of the world's more profound, beautiful, and recognizable songs about it. Religions of the world have gone through many changes regarding forgiveness throughout centuries with what some would still say to this day is their attempt at trying to own, corrupt and sell it. Forgiveness has gone through as many transformations as the sins that inspire its need.

Forgiveness is an amalgam of feelings, ideas, emotions, and action. For example, to the Christian, forgiveness is strongly tied to the notion that in the spiritual sense only God on high can grant it while on the earthly plain, the act of forgiveness is a commandment to be obeyed. Merely obeying does not take into account that we humans in all our frailty must still find a way to reach into our psyche and understand, process, and then make peace with the wrong and the person that perpetrated our perceived wrong before we can even begin to attempt to embrace the idea that we would hold no harm over our perpetrator.

In many forms of Buddhism and Hinduism, there seems to be no exact equivalent concept. The closest views these two faiths have in the concept of forgiveness concerns the death of the old self, which paves the way for the birth of a new self. The philosophy here is that on the idea of progression, there can be no real progression while holding onto the old self. Therefore, the adherents of these faiths seek to continually let go, or lay to death the parts of the old self which hold them back from progression, and in that act create a new self.

In essence, the fruit or results of most religious views regarding forgiveness create a new self for the person or for another by letting go of the things that are undesirable from the past. In true forgiveness, the past is the past and is laid to rest so it no longer occupies the present. Only in this sense may a person begin anew with a clean slate.

This clean slate is also replete in other non-religious and non-faith schools of thought/philosophy. An example is Erhard, who presents the idea that what keeps a person from living a life full of possibility, with each moment being a clean slate, is that they actually do not live in the present. Instead, they are actually living in the past by clinging onto things of the past that they are unable to change and filing it as part of their present; or by living in the present as if it was the future which has not yet come and thus they have no control over. To truly live in the present, to truly live a life full of possibility, is to have the present clear of all past and all future to truly be a clean slate. If a person holds onto any part of their past, (in the religious context by not forgiving, or in Buddhism by not letting the old self die), they do not have a clean slate to live in the present. Without living a life full of possibility, their own personal growth, as well as those around them who are influenced by them, is greatly inhibited.

Another notion is that the energy it takes to hold harm against someone is akin to using one's hands to grasp the hurt in the past. By using a hand to grasp the past, a person is taking away his/her ability to grasp anything else. Furthermore, the realization that one's future is writhed with possibilities, so many in fact that to truly take advantage of all the possibilities, one must use both hands and all of their strength to grab onto them. Thus to use one hand and half of one's power to grasp the past is to render oneself incapable to fully grasp the present and the possible future. Therefore, to hold the past is to constrain the possibilities and potency of one's present and future.

Whichever philosophy resonates most, you must take it as your own. Your experiences in life may drive which you might choose, or you may connect with you a combination of these philosophies. You may start out with one philosophy resonating, and as you advance through life and more experiences, another may resonate more. Each person creates their own concept of forgiveness, but in any and all kinds of philosophy you will find that the narrative thread that binds them all to a greater notion and purpose is that they all have at their root, humanity and the need for it. The word humanity has always had the implication of gentleness and frailty, which in the grand analysis we as "humans" are. Consequently, forgiveness is human. You are human!

CHAPTER SEVENTY-SIX
Laurence Lemn Receives Forgiveness

Laurence found the final Jenny stamp of the 1918 three-stamp set. He already had the non-inverted red and blue 24¢ stamp, the green 16¢, and now a collector with the orange 3¢ Jenny stamp was willing to give it up in exchange for the BATUM GEORGIA 1 BLOC MNH CAR / MASERATI. Laurence had no real interest in cars, but he definitely wanted to complete his Jenny collection. And it so happened that Laurence had previously that year come across this stamp from the country of Georgia of the Maserati. At the time he acquired the BATUM GEORGIA, he thought to himself, that although he did not care about cars, having a stamp from the small and relatively unknown country of Georgia had to be worth something. In this case, 1.5€ or ~$3. His dream was to someday be able to just see in person (he could not fathom himself being willing or able to pay over $800,000 to own) the inverted Jenny 24¢. Laurence was in the middle of writing the email to the holder of the 3¢ Jenny stamp when the phone rang.

He did not recognize the number and wondered who with an out-of-state phone number would be calling him. Perhaps it was for his partner, Gareth. It was more likely to be a telemarketer because anyone who really wanted to get in touch with Gareth during the day would call him on his cell phone. Normally Laurence would just let the call go to voicemail to screen out calls from unknown phone numbers; however, this time, he found himself picking up the phone right after the third ring and just before the fourth ring (where it would have gone to voicemail). "Hello?" There was silence on the other end. "Hello? May I help you?" Still silence. And yet there was a faint hesitant, audible sigh on the other end. "Look, if you are not going to talk, then I will have to hang up," Laurence warned.

With the determination that Ordin had dialed Laurence's phone number, he was amazed that as soon as he heard his voice, he froze, seemingly unable to speak. Yet he had to speak now, for surely the next time Laurence would not answer a call from a phone number the caller was nothing but silent the time before. Now was Ordin's chance.

"Uh, hello? Mr. Lemn?"

"Yes, may I ask who this is?"

"This is Ordin, but you knew me as Gordon." With that both were silent.

Laurence had long given up on the idea that the man who now called himself Ordin would ever call, or rather that is what he had told himself. In truth, he had asked his sister to keep his old phone number so that if "Ordin" ever did call, he could find him, and now he had. Laurence was nevertheless not prepared for this, and yet he had wanted, perhaps even needed it, even though the exact purpose and result could not be known. "Hello, Ordin. How have you been?"

"I've been fine. Well, I've been, just been. The days and years seem to go on by with indifference to each other. How have you been?"

"I've been fine as well, and I know what you mean by the passing of time."

"I understand from your sister who gave me your new phone number that you have a new love in your life since the last time we saw... talked."

"Yes, he is a good man and has been a stronghold for me."

"I am glad you have someone in your life."

"What about you? Do you still have someone in your life? I know the damage it did to my life back then."

"No, I've just been keeping to myself."

"I am sorry to hear that, but I understand."

"Yeah…well today has been an exciting day for me, a day in which I have found new courage and energy. And as part of this new courage and energy I need to tell you that I hold no blame towards you for any part, you serendipitously had in my life. I never really did. All this time I blamed my friend, my God, and society overall, but mainly I blamed myself and would not forgive myself."

Ordin sighed audibly and said in a cracked voice, "me too, but I'm free now of that as well."

Laurence did not respond but continued to speak. "The only thing I hated about you was not about you, but rather it was about how the picture; engrained so fully the horror of the moment that would not let me forget even if I could block out my own mental picture of the moment."

Ordin replied assuringly, "In a way, your photograph was necessary, as it became the specter of responsibility. Without it, I may have well fallen into the trap of denial. Even with it, I have still tried to run away from it, to not accept, to hide myself from society, family, friends, and even myself. I know that my choices in the moments before the accident could have created a different outcome; nevertheless, I cannot change those choices nor can I change the outcome. For all my life and all, I hold dear I wish I could."

Ordin paused, then continued. "I feel that my best friend who died, as a result of the choices he and I made in the preceding moments, would not want me to hold myself in the mental, emotional, and spiritual prison that I have lived in for the past twenty years. I died in many ways that day with him. He loved life and would want me to continue to live in the love of life.

"We all died a little that day, I understand." Laurence's words were a strange mix of, bravery and retreat to Ordin. Ordin could feel the words beginning to become thicker in the back of his throat, but he spoke on.

"No one knows when our time on this earth will end, which makes living in the moment, living and loving with the time given us all the more precious and valuable. I have squandered the past twenty years of my life and do not want to waste any more time. I am glad you have found the love and support you have with your partner in your life. I hope that if there is any part of your life that you had put on hold in any relation to the experience of when our life paths crossed, that you will accept my forgiveness, be able to forgive yourself, and move on to live life more fully. I am truly sorry for not having done this earlier, for not helping release any undue guilt and responsibility that was not yours to shoulder. I hope that you will forgive me for having wronged you in not expressing my release of responsibility upon you much earlier."

"I forgive you Laurence said, I forgive you in so many ways; with my heart, with my mind, with my life, I forgive you, and I forgive that moment and God, who saw our moment before time began and chose to let it stand."

Tears had welled up for both Ordin and Laurence as Ordin spoke expressing for the first time aloud the forgiveness of himself as he asked for forgiveness of the guilt laid upon Laurence. For Laurence, these were the words he had wanted and needed to hear.

He had thought he had moved on and stopped putting his life on hold years ago when he wrote the book "The Broken Forever" and moved out of his condo. In some ways he had. But when Ordin expressed genuine sorrow for any effect the unreleased guilt may have had with regard to Laurence not living life more fully, Laurence realized his inability to find a niche in life was the signpost that he had not been living life more fully. That he had still kept with him the guilt, that he had been still living in the past and was thus not able to have a clear slate in which to live in the present, which is living life more fully.

Both men were silent. It seemed to be a good few minutes of silence, but in reality, it was not much more than 30 seconds. Even though no words were spoken, the silence spoke volumes as sniffles and sighs of acceptance and release were felt and heard.

"Thank you." Laurence softly and warmly spoke in breaking the silence. In those two simple words, Ordin felt and knew Laurence had just truly forgiven him.

"Thank you," Ordin intoned. With that, the two mutually disconnected the call.

Laurence went on to finish the email. Ordin went back to the stove and turned it back on to finish cooking the lake trout he had caught earlier that morning. Somehow, though, they both felt lighter, more aware of the moment, more alive. At that very moment, both Ordin and Laurence looked back at the phone and motioned to pick it up, as if there was more to say, but then and in sync, both men turned away. Enough had been said, enough had been felt. The release was a gift that both men had given to each other this day; release of guilt, the release of stagnation, the release of fear, release of the blame. No longer would the media, our culture, our society and even our God bare the weight of two men's lives and the intersection in which they met.

CHAPTER SEVENTY-SEVEN
Gert Arrives

Gert reached the hospital and parked the car. She paused there with her hand on the keys ready to take them out and in that pause fell deep into her thoughts as sort of a daydream.

The drive seemed to pass as both an eternity and a mere moment. Indeed, even our time on earth is a mere moment in the realm of time in the existence of the universe. But while we are here, our life has the experience of being both an eternity and a brief moment. Each minute, each breath, can be either ignored or blurred into each successive minute, and breath or each may be experienced as a moment, a singularly recognized experience.

The drive felt like three recognizable moments: the beginning of the drive, the call to Winslow, and the rest of the drive. "Where did all that time go? How did I spend it?" Gert seemed unable to recall, yet here she was parked in the parking lot of the hospital hours away from home.

It struck Gert how her life since Winslow leave the house seven years ago, had become one big blurred moment of the repetitive motion of a scheduled week happening again and again with no real differentiation. And even when Winslow did live with them, it was now apparent to Gert that she had relied solely on Winslow to provide her distinguishable moments in her life. When did she lose her own distinction of self? Gert could not remember. As she felt a cool tear run down the cheek of her face, Gert realized how sad she really was.

Gert became aware that she had fallen into an introspective daydream for a few minutes and now realized she had chosen the moment of introspection and respite to gather up the courage to get out of the car and walk into the emergency room of the hospital.

As Gert walked through the Emergency Room doors, the distinct smell of sanitization mixed with medicine, blood, and all the odors coming from the various people in the waiting room and the nurses and doctors wafted strongly in her nose causing her stomach to grow more uneasy. Gert had not been in an emergency room since Winslow had broken his arm skateboarding when he was ten years old. A faint smile cracked her lips at that memory momentarily breaking the numbed emotions of the moment.

"May I help you, ma'am?"

"Yes, I am Ms. Graves. My husband, Detective J.H. Graves was brought in here several hours ago for a heart attack."

Gert had to pause and swallow the reality of what she had just said. Her husband had a stroke. She thought she had already dealt with that fact during her drive, and yet when she had to actually say it in a hospital, the fact became more real.

"Oh, yes, Ms. Graves. I will have the attending physician be with you in a few minutes. While you are waiting, will you please fill out these papers for us?"

"Yes, of course."

While Gert was seated filling out the papers, her thoughts went back to the last time she was doing this for Winslow. Even though the broken arm was not a life-or-death matter, it certainly did create some anxiety for Gert. She felt, seemingly all at once, the mixed emotions tied with the varying thoughts of 'I knew Winslow would break something from riding that skateboard', 'boys will be boys', 'should I keep him from riding the skateboard ever again', 'what if something worse had happened like he lost control and could not stop before a car hit him', 'what if instead of his arm he broke his neck, 'he could have been paralyzed or even dead!' Gert advised herself, "You cannot be watching your son every minute of his life. You'll have to let him live and make mistakes on his own. You will need to trust that when the time comes, he will remember and listen to everything you have told him to keep himself safe, even if he breaks an arm or a leg at times in the process."

When Gert had gone to Winslow's bedside with his arm being prepared in a temporary cast while the more permanent cast mold was being set and readied, all she could say was, "I love you, son." This was one of the moments where Gert honestly felt like Winslow's mother and not just a surrogate parent / legal guardian. Even though she would not wish for any harm to come to him ever, when harm did come, it created an environment in which Gert could easily recognize her love of Winslow as a son. This was a good singular moment of her life.

Gert completed all of the initial paperwork given to her by the receptionist when she heard her name called from a young man in doctor's garb standing near her. "Ms. Graves? I am physician Wright, your husband's attending physician." Gert stood up and instinctively handed the clipboard with the completed paperwork to him, and then as she looked into his eyes, a glint of recognition hit her. "Alan?"

CHAPTER SEVENTY-EIGHT
Ordin Receives a Phone Call

Ordin had just finished washing lunch dishes when the phone rang. The phone sat conveniently near his comfortable chair. Thus Ordin sat down as he picked up the receiver. "Hello, this is Ordin." Silence met him on the other end. Usually, Ordin would hang up the phone if he had no response or greetings from a caller. However, since he had been silent for a moment on the call he previously made before lunch, he felt obligated to be more patient himself. Maybe this was Laurence calling him back, Ordin thought to himself. "Laurence?"

On the other end of the phone sat a young man who was making a call to someone he had never spoken to before or at least spoken to at an age of remembrance. For if, he had talked to him before he would have been between two and three years old. And for the most people, the majority if not all memories before four years of age and for many even six years of age become part of a memory void where no real recollection is retained unless the event was particularly emotionally dramatic.

For Blain, all he could remember was that his dad had left one day never to return, seemingly disappearing not only from his life but also from life itself. To the mind of a young child in their third year of life, the recollection of his father seemed more like a phantom of a dream where its reality was only made certain by the conversations with others which held very little information. When Blain picked up the phone to call his father, he had a slew of questions to barrage him with. However, as soon as Blain heard his father's voice, all of that vanished so swiftly he could not muster much to catch any of them before it was too late and he was held speechless.

"Uh, no. This is not Laurence."

Ordin waited for more of a response before he replied. "So am I the person you wanted to call?"

"Yyesss... I am just not sure what to say. I wrote you a letter. I'm not sure if you received it yet, if you read it, or... This is Blain."

With that, it was Ordin's turn to be speechless. He had written Blain a letter in response, only hoping to receive another letter in return and perhaps start communication with his son through letters for a time before actually talking with him in person. Yet on the same day he received Blain's letter and had written and mailed a reply back to him, now remarkably he was talking to his son on the phone. Well, so far not really talking, yet more talking than he had the courage to hope for after all these 20 some years. Ordin's first thought was God was working, if not speaking, then working all the same.

"Blain? I just got your letter this morning, and I have already written and mailed you a letter in return. I had long ago given up hope of ever hearing your voice again until this morning, and definitely did not think I would hear your voice today." The thickness of the moment was almost palpable for both men for the joy they were feeling.

"Dad, I hope I can call you that. We have much to catch up on. I know some of the past from talking with Mom not long before me calling you. I got your number from her. I do not care about the past. I care about creating a future with you as a part of my life and the life of my child as part of my family. I want to see you in person. I want to get to know you. I want you to get to know me. I hope you want these things too, but if you do not, I understand." In his rambling, emotional dumping, Blain realized he had not even given his father a chance to respond. He was as overwhelmed as he had ever been with anything.

"Oh, Blain, my son. I so much do want these things. I had given up all hope until I got your letter today. Your letter gave me hope. It gave me courage. It has filled my day with a new strength that is only realized with a new hope. Thank you."

With this, both men wept for what seemed like an eternity. In that moment all the angst through all the years built up over the lack of a relationship they had with each other was released. In that moment, a great relief was felt where literally it felt like every cell in their body was lighter, lifted, energized, and filled with hope and a new energy. In that moment, their souls were made stronger. In that moment they both felt a true happiness, an inner joy that cannot be borrowed, stolen, purchased, or bargained for. Indeed, this type of happiness came only when true forgiveness was given regardless of the grievousness or the pain experienced in the past, when the slate of possibility was clean from hanging onto the unhappiness and stress, and when the stories that both have been living their life through are released.

An instant exhaustion came over Ordin. So much release of emotional baggage in one day made it seem as if he had lived another lifetime in the last few hours. And yet here he was, realizing for the third time in one day an answered prayer, a chance for redemption. Ordin almost laughed to himself through his exhaustion thinking what would come next. Will Sonya call me and say I'm forgiven? Then his thoughts and attention returned to the son, his son he was now speaking to.

"Dad, how soon can you come to San Francisco?"

"How long do you want me there?"

"Dad, I have not had you my whole life. I do not want any more of my life without you in it. I want you to come here, possibly to stay."

"That may take a while to prepare to sell what I do not need, and pack up what I need and want. But I can leave there as soon as

Monday at first for a couple weeks, then come back and get the house here sold or leased out later."

"I would love that! I'm not sure if you can stay here with Mom and me, but maybe you can get a weekly rental for a couple of weeks while we figure it out otherwise."

"Of course. I would not assume nor would I be ready for staying over at your mom's."

"I am looking to move out on my own with my girlfriend soon anyways before she has our baby."

"Nice. So you are planning on marrying her?"

"I believe so, but we have not discussed that yet."

"That is an important discussion to have soon son, but also when you feel the time is right."

"You're right, dad. I'm excited and happier now than I could have imagined. Thank you."

"Thank you, son. I'm happier now than I would have ever thought possible when I woke up this morning."

"Same here, dad."

Both paused experiencing the silence of the moment. The silence was not the same silence felt at the beginning of the call, which had been filled with trepidation. This silence was full of the energies of hope and love. Each lost track of the time they held the phone open in the silence before disconnecting the call, and each could not tell who disconnected the call first, or if by chance they disconnected the call at the exact same time. Even after the call was disconnected, the silence was still experienced as each man sat down looking into a future with greater possibility. For Blain, the possibility of having a father in his life, and for Ordin, the possibility of being reunited with his son and being part of a family, his son's family.

CHAPTER SEVENTY-NINE
Karen Miller's Call to S.F.P.D.

Karen could not stop pacing back and forth. She tried watching her favorite show, and she tried wine. Nothing calmed her down or made her waiting any easier. She thought she should call someone, anyone. She thought she should call her mother again and really give her what for. Then she thought she should call one of her old boyfriends and tell them exactly what they would be missing, though Karen knew inside that none of them would care or would think that they would be missing out on that much regardless of how famous and rich she became.

She just wanted to know what was next and when that next would happen. She got it. She would call the S.F.P.D. and ask them how far away the camera crew was. They always seemed to know on Cold Case Killers exactly how far they were away from the perp. She would call them up and just say, "I'm Karen Miller, the Karen Miller, star of the next big episode of Cold Case Killers, and I want to know when the camera crew will be here so I can be ready."

To Karen, this made perfect sense. Never mind that the actual S.F.P.D. had little or nothing to do with where the camera crews were at any given time, or the fact that they probably had much more important things to do besides taking phone calls from impatient women regarding their moment in the sun. Karen picked up the phone and dialed the number she had had on the card by the phone for days. It had been given to her in case the perp found out that she had given their information to them and decided to run, threaten, or attempt to harm her.

The phone rang several times much to Karen's consternation. "Hurry up, you stupid phone. Why don't you just cooperate? It was if the phone itself along with most of the world were in on some cruel joke just to not give her what she wanted.

When the operator finally picked up, it was Sarah, answering in her pleasant, unattached, monotone voice she reserved for work. "Hello, S.F.P.D." Karen was immediately thrown. She couldn't figure out what all the letters she was saying spelled or meant. Karen thought she had dialed the wrong number. Sarah spoke again, "San Francisco Police Department," She enunciated slowly and a bit louder, realizing that some people would be calling in shock, panic or desperation and might not put the acronym together.

Karen's voice cracked then rang out, "Oh, God, it is you. I thought you would never find me." Confused, Sarah lightly smiled behind the phone and said, "Ma'am, can I help you? Are you alright?"

"I most certainly am not alright" Karen rushed the words. "I'm Karen Miller the star of Cold Case Killers, and I'm trying to get ready for the cameras. Do you know when they will be here? They are coming to catch my friend Ordy next door and put me on TV." Sarah only knew partially what the frazzled woman was talking about because of her conversations with Brent Simmons and Detective Johnson.

"Ma'am, I don't have that information, but let me get you over to Detective Johnson. He might be able to help you. Hold the line, please."

Before Karen could tell the woman on the phone who acted like she did not recognize how important she was to the show, she was listening to a version of the Police's "Roxanne," the 'muzak' version.

Detective Johnson picked up the phone and answered quickly, "Johnson," and then went silent. Again, Karen was thrown off and did not know how to react. She stammered and started to repeat her Karen Miller Cold Case speech when Detective Johnson stated matter of factly, "Hold the line," and went silent again.

Karen was completely at her wits end and was about to hang up when Detective Johnson came back on the line. "Is this Ms. Miller?" Karen answered "yes" right away, afraid to be put on hold again.

"Ms. Miller, I understand we have a situation here. Let me see if I have this right. You are going to be on this mess of a show that is screwing things up around here, and you want to know when our guys and the camera is going to be there so you can be all gussied up for it."

"Yes." Karen chirped.

"And you're starting to wonder whether it's going to happen at all, correct?"

"Yes," Karen said sheepishly.

"Okay, I can't help you. Call this guy. He's the associate or main producer or something, and he'll give you an answer."

Detective Johnson sputtered out the phone number and disconnected the call so fast that Karen had to rely on the one good thing about her mind. Karen had a near photographic short-term memory when it came to numbers. That was why she fancied herself a banker even though she only worked at a check cashing store for people who could not or did not have a bank account.

Karen hurried and wrote the number down to doubly ensure she would not forget it. She wasn't really aware she had a near photographic memory and had Karen been aware of it, she might have done better in school and actually had a career as a banker. Karen picked up the phone again and dialed the number. Hope was in her heart again; she was getting closer to her debut.

CHAPTER EIGHTY
Local Police Force to Join Efforts with S.F.P.D.'s Officer Johnson

"Another salt flat and I'll die," Paul thought to himself. He was about ten miles or so out of Salt Lake City. "Hey, the old Saltair." The Saltair was an old time hot spot from back when travelers would be welcomed to the Mormon refuge of Utah by the pleasant façade of the edifice. The East Indian architecture was stunning when new and was referred to as the "Coney Island of the West." Salt Lake City, Utah was one of America's biggest small towns with a homogenous population and a deeply entrenched version of family values. It felt as if one had just driven into a neighborhood in Anywhere, Indiana or Kansas, except most of the people here worshiped at the various tabernacles that are synonymous with the Mormon religion that dominated the region. Paul thought it looked like a good place to gamble if they even allowed that sort of thing here.

Like most people, Paul really didn't know much about Utah, Mormons or Tabernacles. He, like a lot of people, believed that the people were just short of Stepford wives and that all of the men had multiple marriages and families of fourteen or more kids. Most of this thinking could not be further from the truth, although that was the image that Utah had.

Paul had no sense of the culture he was stepping into on his way to complete his mission where he then would start anew in an attempt to keep some of the promises he had made to his own wife and kid. Paul's promises and responsibilities to work and family sometimes seemed as if there were twenty people all tugging on him at once, wanting his time, wanting him to make a decision about this or that.

The gas station Paul stopped at to grab a quick snack looked like it belonged back in the 1950's. He could have driven the five miles or so to the Palace for a snack, but Paul was the kind of guy who thought, "I'm not getting caught in some tourist trap and paying those prices." As he walked into the gas station, he looked around and saw that there was no snack counter or refrigerator with the requisite drinks that decorated most gas station mini marts. There was just a long counter and a woman on the other side of it that reminded him of his Aunt Clara from the state of Washington. He walked over and, while making idle conversation he searched for what could be had for a snack, then asked the cashier about the place down the road with the Taj Mahal dome.

The lady tittered and said in the creaky voice of a long time smoker, "That place is the Saltair. It's a great little stop we have here to get a bite or get your family ready for some down time before getting into town. Used to be quite the little spot a ways back. Now it's just a place for music venues and the occasional travelers that stop."

"Oh, thanks. It sure does look a bit out of place for this part of the country, huh?"

"Yep, we get that a lot. They say the builder went to India on a vacation and the place just got under his skin, in a good way, ya know. And he wanted to bring a piece of it back home, but who knows, I just think of it as a nice little stop." Paul was nodding in agreement when his phone rang, and he excused himself to take the call.

"Hello, is this Officer Johnson of the S.F.P.D?"

"Well, it's Detective Johnson, but never mind. It is me. How may I help you?"

"Excuse me, Detective Johnson, my name is Officer Liam, from the Inwood County State Police Department. Detective Johnson, I've been assigned to meet up with you on your way in town to wrap up some business with a resident of the city here. I just wanted to touch base with you on it and get your take on what's going on and what you want to happen when you get here."

"Uh, okay. I wasn't aware that it was certain that I would be paired up with anyone else. I already have a partner on this, you know. But hey, the S.F.P.D. always keeps me in the 'not know' I always say."

"Well, detective, I'm not here to ruffle any feathers. I figured the brass here knows about the T.V. angle to this whole thing and just wanted as little interaction with the locals as possible. You'll see what I mean when you get here. We have a nice little place out here, where not much more than a bar fight or yearly fair gets people stirred up. And at risk of sounding cliché, we don't want any big city media circus here disrupting things."

"I understand fully, and I plan on being in and out in less than a day. I just have to come in and check out the story of a woman there named Karen Miller that involves this gentleman, Ordin Aire. Reportedly, he may have been previously known as Gordon Spitz, a guy from an old cold case. This also might just the T.V. people's idea of a dramatic finish to their season ending episode."

"Ah, I see. Well, let me know when you get in town, and we can sit down and have a cup of coffee and talk about it."

"Great. I'll be sure and give you a call when I'm a few miles out. Oh, and do me a small favor, will you? Can you guys wait on talking to this Karen Miller and Ordin guy until I get there?"

"Well, we certainly should be able to avoid talking with Ordin, but this Karen Miller gal has called the local station a few times over the last month or so trying to get on some show. We just kinda dismissed her as a kook of some sort. Says the show said call your local police and steer clear of any vigilante action. She probably didn't read the caption that had the contact number on it, but hey, that's small town folks for you, right?" Paul smiled on his side of the phone and just agreed with a "Humph" and a nod. "Okay, then, we'll talk soon."

"Yeah. Thanks a lot, detective."

Paul disconnected the call and turned to head out the door. Quickly as to ensure Paul did not miss what she had to say, the lady behind the counter with the raspy voice that would have made her a great jazz singer back in the twenties during pre-war Germany, bellowed out, "Stop and see the Palace. It's worth your time!"

"Worth my time," Paul thought. Was any of this worth my time? I don't know anymore. I just want to get this thing over with and figure out what I'm really doing. I can't help but feel this small tug in my chest telling me that I don't really even belong here, or anywhere for that matter. Sarah and Willow probably miss me like crazy. Well, Willow at least. Detective Graves is probably passed out in his hospital bed after dragging me across the country for some wild goose glory chase three states away to fulfill his dream of being somebody. And here I do not know who I am anymore going solo into something I don't agree with and feel conflicted about. Do I serve my duty to the force, or do I serve my heart and do what I feel is the right thing and just turn around and tell them to send someone else? Well, old boy, this all started with ideals and a few college buddies, right? Might as well see it through. Besides, if I quit now, they would just send someone else, and this is mine to finish anyway.

Paul got into his car and headed down the road. When he reached the parking lot of the Saltair, he thought, "You know, I'm not really hungry anymore anyway, and I'm not paying tourist prices." He sped up a little and noticed the peak of the crown of the Palace dome. It had a small needle protruding from it. "Nice touch," he thought, "nice touch." Paul thought about turning around and driving away, but for the distance, it took him from the freeway to get to the palace over its dilapidated and seemingly unkempt parking lot as if this place had been deserted for years. If it had not been for the few cars that were there already, Paul would have thought it was closed for business. "Well, perhaps taking time out to walk around the Saltair is just what I need to walk out my weary and cramping legs before heading to a highway motel further down the road."

As soon as Paul stepped out of the car, he smelled a pungent scent that almost churned his stomach. With the smell, which Paul learned later talking with the tour guide came from all the lake brine shrimp, he wondered how they could get anyone to buy and eat any food while here. Historically, Saltair was the first and only amusement park area west of New York City's Coney Island. This had been back in 1893-1925 until the first fire. The Palace had more of a palace feel to it then and was built right up to and slightly into the Great Salt Lake. It was rebuilt from the fire; even though the lake's waters had begun to recede, and World War I broke out and other entertainment venues closer to the city of Salt Lake itself became more readily available. And then another great fire in 1931 put the Saltair Palace to full dormancy for about 40 years. It was again rebuilt but this time from the old remnants of plane hangars. The train that had taken passengers from the city to the Saltair had been decommissioned during the previous 40-year dormancy period. The Great Salt Lake flooded the Palace then receded further than it ever had before. Today it had seen some life again, but not as an amusement park venue, but rather as a band/music venue hotspot and it still maintained its historical value. At the end of the tour, Paul was guided to a small souvenir and snack shop. A kind, older gentleman, greeted him across the room from behind a counter.

"Welcome to the Palace, the gateway to Salt Lake City and the West. I hope you enjoyed your tour. Can I get you something?"

With the still-wafting smell of the brine shrimp in his nose, Paul ordered the shrimp and fry basket commenting to the gentleman to "hold the shrimp."

CHAPTER EIGHTY-ONE
Alan and Gert

Alan had wondered whether Ms. Graves would recognize him. He didn't want to come out and blurt out whom he was. He wanted to keep it professional, so he decided to not bring it up that they were already well acquainted, that is, unless Ms. Graves initiated it by recognizing him without any help from himself.

"Alan?"

Who knows why Gert did so readily recognize and know Alan immediately upon looking into his eyes? Maybe it was because she had just recollected in a form of a daydream her son when he was younger and the fact that most of Winslow's childhood and teenage days were spent locked in as bosom buddies with Alan. In fact, although she did not recall it in her flashback, Alan, always by Winslow's side, had been there with her. Maybe it was the alluded to the idea (some say myth, some say real) of feminine intuition and connectedness to their children. And as much time as Alan had spent with Winslow, Gert had often felt as if Alan was a surrogate son and part of the family. The why did not matter at all. What mattered was that before Alan could talk about the business at hand, he now had to deal with reconnection of his life with Gert on a personal level.

"Yes, it's me. How are you, Ms. Graves?"

"Oh, Alan, my it has been so long! Well, you already know why I am here, so obviously I cannot say things are great. But for myself, I am well enough. But how are you? Wow, you are a doctor now? How long have you been here? Strange how it is you who ended up being the one to take care of J.H. Does he know yet? Have you talked to or seen Winslow lately?"

With this last question among the rapidly fired barrage of questions, Gert became quiet and immediately her eyes welled up with tears. How she has missed Winslow! Her life has seemed so sad and with so little purpose since he left home never to return again, since he walked out of her life, since she and J.H. stopped accepting Winslow for who he was when he did not fit the "acceptable" mold they had created for him.

"I am well, thank you for asking. I am not quite a doctor yet, I am an intern, a doctor in training. I have been here at the hospital nearly two years now. Fate or universal prudence perhaps took care of making me J.H.'s physician. He has not recognized me yet, and I have not told him. As for Winslow, well, he and I are still together. We live together, and I just talked to him earlier before you arrived."

It had become a good practice for Alan to be able to listen to all questions asked of him by a patient's family, no matter how fast or how many, and to then answer each in return in the same order. This practice became increasingly challenging the more family members, in turn, asked him questions with no sufficient pause for a reply. This time, however, automated the practice in responding to Gert's questions, Alan could not escape as this was on a much more personal level which was evident in the tone and facial expressions that came unbidden.

Alan reached out and pulled Gert into him. She seemed stiff at first, but then relented and even gave a slight sigh. For Gert, the welcome feel of the human touch was long overdue. She had not held Winslow in years. She had not held her parents in an even longer time. She tried to make an inside joke about the fact that J.H was not very affectionate. She would say when pressed by the few friends she spoke to of such things that "J.H. was not the holding kind; men of his generation expressed their love by paying the bills and keeping the communists at bay." But deep down, Gert longed to be held, even a simple hug would suffice.

At this moment, Alan had done what physicians and doctors do, that is to quickly analyze the situation and make an attempt to make the patient whole. Whether he had done so for that purpose or not, Gert felt better. "I have missed you, in many ways," she said and kept on holding.

Now it was Alan's turn to gather from Gert what a hug could mean after years of absence as he thought of his own mother. They were by no means estranged, but she had always been the busy type and a career woman. Alan had not seen her in years, and when on occasion he had the opportunity to make the trek back home for a holiday or just for a vacation, she always seemed to be on her way out of town. Alan was sure that this was not to avoid his company. In fact, she often asked him to meet her in whatever city she was flying to. The outcome of the invitation was always the same: Alan would politely turn down the invite with a kind joke about frequent flyer miles, when all he ever really wanted, was his mother at home for him.

With Gert's hug, Alan remembered how he came to think of Gert as a second mother all those years ago. She had represented everything his mother was not in that way. Gert was a stay-at-home wife and mother. She was not flying off to receive a random award for "women in business" or whatever new category it was that month, and she always seems to have dinner ready. For Alan, the first few years of his life that he could really recall, he thought that dinner was just something that was served to you by the polite Hispanic man, or teenage actor in the building with the men who took your car as you drove up. The idea that mothers made dinner at home was as foreign a notion as walking on the moon. It was these things that Gert left imprinted on his brain and heart, thus when they disengaged from the long embrace, Alan's first words were, "Why did I have to stop seeing you?"

The question drew the breath from Gert. She could picture Winslow's face in Alan's and even her own as she would put that same question to her son himself. Why? The answer came swiftly and betrayed Gert's real feelings regarding the matter. "J.H. forbade it." No sooner had the words come out of her mouth did she recognize the enormity of the hurt and wrongness of the stance she acquiesced to. Now it was time to choose otherwise. In this moment of the freedom and empowerment, Gert felt, she openly plunged her arms around Alan again. "How are you and my son?"

Alan did not want to betray any information that Winslow had not given her, so he replied, "We don't have a dog yet." The comment was both sweet and pointed, for it said that all those years ago Winslow was aware and conscious of his parents treating each other as strangers. Gert smiled in a saddened but grateful acknowledgment and said, "Good, dear."

"So how is it that you're here in this town? I didn't really know where Winny had moved to. The only time we talked was when he changed his phone number. It doesn't matter really. It's just good to see you. It shouldn't have been this long. Now how is my husband?"

With that, the moment had passed, and it took with it all the skeletons and elephants that pranced around one's life when too much is left unsaid at the end in any kind of relationship. Alan began to fill Gert in, and while she was listening to him, she was thinking behind her eyes that Winny had found a good friend and good man. She missed her son more at that moment than ever before and could not wait to see him.

CHAPTER EIGHTY-TWO
Blain and Jessica Talk

The phone rang three times before Blain took the call. He usually didn't take calls while at work until his break. Blain had planned to call Jessica on his break to tell her about the news he'd received earlier regarding his father and a potential reunion, but there she was calling him. His first thought was that something must have happened to the baby. Why else would she call him at work and before his break?

They had been over that time and again when Blain first started working for the company. At first, she called because she was lonely at home and generally not used to going to bed alone. Then she began to call because she thought Blain was purposely trying to avoid her. There was even an episode where Jessica had gone through Blain's phone looking for the number to his mother to ask a few questions about her impending pregnancy. She had found the number of a woman she did not recognize. After a brief but passionate confrontation, it was discovered that Blain had spoken with an ex-girlfriend from high school that he and everyone else always assumed would marry and have kids one day and whom he periodically kept in touch with. He wanted to tell her that his current girlfriend was pregnant.

For Blain, it was a kind of clearing of the old energy there and a beginning of a new chapter that left behind his old life and the dreams that went with it. Jessica was apologetic, and they set rules for when she could call. Not only did it keep their heads clear, but also it ensured that Blain wouldn't get in trouble at his job, which he needed now more than ever.

"Hey, Jess. What's wrong, what's going on? Is it Kyle? Is everything okay?"

Yeah, everything is fine. I... I mean, no it's not. I mean the baby is fine, but I'm not completely."

"Are you sick? Should I come home?"

"No, no nothing like that. It's just that I...I have been thinking a lot, and I'm scared that things are getting out of control, and we haven't got a clue about what's next and how we are going to tackle this. And my friend Ann-Marie went to get an abortion today. She is married and Sean her husband didn't even know she was pregnant because she just couldn't do it. I mean, 65% of marriages end in divorce, and well..."

"Slow down, Jess. What's all this about? I mean, you're not making sense. You're just a bit scrambled there. Is it those prenatal drugs or a bit of the old Big Mac madness going on here?"

"Blain, I'm not joking here. I really want to talk."

"Well, okay, but can it wait until my break? Or if this is a long conversation we need to have, until I get home? You know how short my break is, and I need to eat. I love talking to you face to face, and you know I love the way your little bunny nose scrunches when you try to explain stuff."

"Blain! Quit it. I'm serious."

"Okay, go on then."

"Blain, I need to know... I need to know that... that you're not going to run away like your father did. There, I said it. I just feel a bit vulnerable here... I mean, I have this thing...Kyle or Cliff or whatever name we have decided on running around in me, screwing up everything and making me look like I ate half of the state in one sitting and it's all making me nervous. I mean, everything is changing, from my body to my mind, to my heart, everything. And I don't see you changing with me. I mean, landing that job as a guard is going to help, but really, babe, how much can we count on with you working a night shift as a security guard? I mean, you are so smart and talented, and I know you have dreams. What if you wake up one day and look around you and start to feel trapped, like I ruined that, by forgetting to take the pill that night and you decide that you need to try your dream life of being a documentarian and traveling the world telling stories that are about life and people. What if just being a father and a security guard is not enough? What if I'm not enough?"

"Wow, that was a lot. But okay, I'll bite for now. Jess, I love you and have since we first kissed. I mean your butt was a little small, but hey, looks like Kyle is helping with that… and there is no way that I would leave unless I were dragged away kicking and screaming.

"I must say that you don't know anything about my dad and his life I mean I don't, well, didn't know anything about him until today. I mean there was a whole life he tried to share with me, and my mother hid it away from me. Every letter and every thought, and I thought he didn't love me, didn't want me. I figured I wasn't enough, just like you think you may not be enough for me."

"Jess, what I found out today is that it's not about not being enough. Sometimes it's about it being too much. There was this whole situation with my mom and dad that was out of control, and he didn't just leave, he went, and there is a difference. I will never just leave. I may go, I may go to film here or there, but I will always come back."

"Jess, I don't have to give up my dreams to support us. In fact, I see Kyle as adding onto my dream, expanding it, by expanding me, making me focus that much more on getting started and working harder, so I can be with you and Kyle as much as possible. I don't know what the future holds, and I'm not in the best shape that I've ever been in, but I know where I'm going, and it's not where I've been. It's a new understanding for me. I mean, until today I was scared, too."

"The truth is that we have only known each other for a year. You are pregnant and for most of my life, I have been running from the ghost of my father. And then the prospect of being a father made me doubt that I could ever outrun that ghost. But now, Jess, now I know that that ghost was never even mine."

"My father, he didn't just leave, he went, and when you go you can always come home, and I feel like he is coming home. So I understand how you feel, Jess, but my answer... my new answer is I will always be there, and if I ever go, I'll always find my way home and Jess, you and Kyle are my home."

Jessica was trembling on the other side of the phone. She could barely keep the tears from free flowing. Her heart had challenged her today, and she had won. Jessica had looked at an uncertain man and an uncertain future in the face and had found a self-assured leader in her life. She had her fear relieved in one conversation, just then Kyle kicked harder than he had before as if he had been listening to the whole conversation and was letting his mother-to-be know that he too would never leave and that he too was home.

CHAPTER EIGHTY-THREE
Paul's Call Home from Salt Lake City

Paul flipped his cell phone open only to discover his phone battery was dead, which aggravated Paul. Stopping at a local pay phone, Paul dug through his pockets as if he intended to find change in them. Virtually no one used a phone booth anymore, so no one carried change anymore. Paul thought about why didn't this pay phone accept credit and debit cards. He searched his ashtray in the car, pulling the last remnants of change from it. Having found two dollars' worth, Paul dialed his home number and dropped the change in. The phone rang several times then hung up, dropping the change back into the cup at the bottom of the phone. Paul tried the call again and this time, the phone rang only three times before Kristine picked up.

"Hello?"

Paul had always loved the sound of Kristina's voice. It had a slight lilt to it bringing to Paul's mind the sounds of a summer day and a tone that sounded like a Brazilian Bossa Nova when she sang. "Hey, Babe, hi." In her greeting was a tenderness that still existed after all the years. Paul felt that how they always greeted each other helped maintain a sweetness between them as well as helped them to remain faithful to each other, not to mention, stay married when so many he had known ended up separated or divorced and hurt.

"How's your day, officer?" Kristina asked. "Is everything okay? I thought I wouldn't hear from you for another day or so."

Her instant compassion rang in Paul's head and heart. "Why can't things stay the same?" There was a slight shaking in his voice and because of her connection to her husband, she knew he had made some sort of decision.

What Paul's impending decision was, there was no way that Kristina could know. She knew Paul was upset that he could not spend the day with Willow, but she also knew that he had to go on his assignment. She also knew that for Paul, this was the culmination of years of questioning and frustration for him. Paul had begun questioning his time on the force early on but had stood his ground.

Paul had been there when a young promising African-American football player had been arrested for the attempted rape of a white female classmate. Paul had seen the way the young man looked at him when he was telling him that she was his girlfriend and that she was just scared because her father had seen a pair of her underwear that had blood stains on them. Paul had been there during the questioning of the girl. In fact, he had asked several questions and was quite clear that the girl had panicked when interrogated by her father regarding the relationship she had with the young man. She feared his reaction to her dating someone out of her race and particularly someone of African-American descent. She had told her father that she had attended a football game after party and that the boy had made sure he plied her with alcohol and had taken advantage of her.

Paul had been on the force for over six years at that point and had become somewhat adept at seeing the truth in the information that he was receiving, which was why he was sure he would make a good detective. It was clear that she was lying and was covering up that she had wanted and invited having sex with the young man, her boyfriend. Paul saw how his captain had hidden parts of the statement that the girl made as the truth became clearer to her father. Paul's heart now looked back and lamented that he didn't do more to stop the case in its tracks and blow the whistle. Here had been a white girl accusing a black boy of raping her, when it was very clear that she willingly and consciously had engaged in sex with him. In hiding the truth, the girl chose to ruin the boy's life, whom she in private had expressed caring deeply for, in favor of saving face with her father's racist viewpoint and perception of black people.

Paul had observed a 14-year-old girl who had looked eighteen take her AIDS test because she had spent the last three years on the streets as a prostitute. Paul had reached a point where he didn't see anything in the world of the force that wasn't broken or corrupted.

Paul had spoken to Kristina on several occasions, speaking of his increasing desire to leave the police force and head back to school. He had come to realize that his desire to change the world one person at a time as a police officer was instead more full of ruining the world one life at a time. There was nothing else for Paul to accomplish in his present position, so he was giving up. He was ready to walk away, and this was the conversation that he would speak to Kristina about. He planned to tell her that she was right about him not being able to separate his life as an officer of the law and his life as a father. It was true that the two had merged, and it had become Paul's worst nightmare. Everything he hated about the force was now everything that he hated about his life.

At its worst, Paul had caught himself yelling at Kristina and trying to break down her point of view in the arguments that they had, the same way he had learned to twist a suspect's words to fit the accusation, levied against him. The arguments which were now at least twice a week, where once they had been twice every few months. This was the call where he cut the cord, and it was all prompted by the man that he had driven all this way to apprehend. Paul could not do it. He could not go through with it no matter how much it would do for J.H.'s career or even his own. Paul simply was not willing to break a life to make a career.

Paul spoke in a soft halting manner "So. So, I've been thinking that when this is over, we, that is the three of us, you know, you, me and Willow, we could go away for a week. I have some vacation time saved up, and we can go someplace and be in nature, or on the beach, just be alone and away from judgment and blame and expectation. I have been in a strange place the last few weeks. And in the last couple days, knowing I was going on this assignment really put my head in a strange place. I mean, I've been considering this whole career and thinking that whatever experiment I seem to have been undertaking was a mistake. Kris, the things I've seen, baby, the things I've seen." Paul sounded as if he were weeping as he spoke.

"Baby, are you okay?"

Paul continued. He had to get what he had to say off his chest." I tried to keep my problems at work, you know, lock them in my locker and put them away with my holster and uniform. You told me and I didn't hear you, couldn't listen, wouldn't hear you. You said that I would bring them home; every sight, every action. You said it would infest my head and then it would infect my heart, and that if I didn't know when to walk away, that it would eventually infect my soul."

"Paul, baby..."

No, babe, let me finish. You said I would be trading in my family in an attempt to prove that one man can make a difference and that in the process I would lose the very family I sought to protect the most, to save the most. But Kris, this week, these last few days, have made me realize this: What good is a hero if he cannot save his own home?

"Paul...I..."

"I look at the most influential people on the planet, the ones that have done the most to change this world, and I couldn't help but ask myself what were their families like behind closed doors?

Did they sacrifice them on the altar of Civil Rights, or Human Rights, or whatever greater cause they served? I also felt disconnected from my faith. I mean, didn't all of those people do what they did in the name of the notion that their God would be favorable towards them if they did the right thing or something like that? I thought about whether God wanted us to sacrifice for him, or each other, or everyone. Would he have us miss the one thing he makes clear for us to revel in and enjoy, our families? I don't know Kris, I don't, I can't do it anymore."

"Paul, think about what you're saying." Kristina had an inkling of what was coming.

"So I think I'm walking away. I still have to face this man, Airie. I have to decide whether I'm going to do it, or if I just drive off. I'm waiting for a sign. I don't know if God speaks that way anymore. Does he still provide a pillar of clouds to cool us in from the daytime sun and a pillar of fire to heat our bodies in the cold of night? Does God speak to us from a bush, or on the road, with angels all around? I guess that I'm asking whether he speaks out loud anymore, or whether it's the still, quiet voice that we must strain to hear? I don't know. I know I'm talking gibberish, babe, thanks for listening. I guess I've been rattling away and haven't even asked you how you feel today."

Finally, Kris got a chance to get a word in and made sure it was sweet but nevertheless direct and to the point. "Paul, this call isn't about how I'm feeling. I'm your wife, and I love you and stand by you when you're right and clear. And I'll stand up to you when I think you're wrong and not seeing the way clearly. I heard every word you said, and I have a feeling to it all, but today is not the time to tell you my perspective, because the truth is, honey, even though I'm your partner forever, there are some things you have to, we all have to, do alone. Paul, this decision about what to do with this man and his life, is yours and yours alone. I have

244

never doubted that if given all the information that you would always make the choice that best represents who you are inside. All you need to hear and feel from me is that I see your warrior spirit inside. I see who you are in your mirror, and I am here."

Paul hung up the phone. He didn't even say goodbye. He wasn't angry, shocked, or distracted. Paul had merely heard what he had hoped to hear, what we all hope to hear. That despite our best efforts to watch the infection spread, to let it spread and watch it happen, that there is someone who sees us and knows we want better for ourselves and those around us, who believe in us.

Paul prayed silently, "Father, reveal yourself in this. Let me hear from you. I will listen." Paul closed the door of the sedan and put the seat back, powered on the radio, turned up the volume as the deejay announced that one of his favorites was about to play. It was Colin Hay's "Waiting for my Real Life to Begin." Paul could feel his soul sink in his chest as the title lyric was sung. He, like a lot of people, was waking up and waiting for their real lives to begin. Paul's real life would start in what was a moment, the point after a decision that could result in a confrontation that would change his life, his family's life, and the life of a man fishing on a lake; a man that perhaps was fishing with God.

CHAPTER EIGHTY-FOUR
Winslow Decides

A thousand points of light. A thousand points of light we were told would draw us to an awakening, an awakening from a darkness that we as a country and as people had been in for too long. The time had passed since that iconic statement was uttered by President Bush Senior in his inaugural speech: "I have spoken of a thousand points of light, of all the community organizations that are spread like stars throughout the nation, doing good. We will work hand in hand, encouraging, sometimes leading, sometimes being led, rewarding. We will work on this in the White House, in the Cabinet agencies. I will go to the people and the programs that are the brighter points of light, and I will ask every member of my government to become involved. The old ideas are new again because they are not old, they are timeless: duty, sacrifice, commitment, and patriotism that finds its expression in taking part and pitching in." We all pitched in and got nothing in return, nothing but more of the same.

Winslow sat in his car with his stereo blasting his favorite Tool song. There was something effervescent about the band Tool and its lead singer, Maynard. He seemed to sing with abandon for all the lies of this life, to Winslow, he sang from a place that shrugged off the lies, the purposeful miscommunications and just whaled his truth. That's what Winslow longed to do right now. He had decided to talk to Gert and J.H. and be loving about it.

All the same, he and the unfinished hurt within his heart wanted nothing more than to whale... 'You liar, you a wretched liar. I was your son. You picked me out, chose me, and yet you turned me away because I did not love as you did. I did not want what you wanted for me, to make your ideas of being a man and a father real for you. You promised me, love, you signed the contract, and you let that woman believe in you professing that my presence could fill a void she felt. Deep down you must have known it never could. At a moment when I needed your unwavering embrace of love when you found out I was gay, you drew back from me reacting as if I had the plague. It broke my heart and tore hers out. Now look at you lying here, your stone heart failing you, your dreams unrealized, your life wasted. When did you do your part? When did you pitch in to fulfill the thousand points of light that the man you called your personal hero called on you to be? When!?!"

Winslow did not realize, but was now yelling at the top of his voice, so loud that he was drowning out the shrieks of Maynard's lyrical reprise from the poignant Tool song, Eulogy.' "He had a lot to say, he had a lot of nothing to say, we'll miss him."

"How ironic." Winslow thought that if J.H. died here today in this way, he would miss him. He hated all that he had been and still Winslow felt he would miss him. Or would it be that he would miss the chance to tell him that he broke his heart and shredded his mother's life? Maybe when we miss someone, it's not what they were that we miss, but what we wanted them to be that we miss. Right now, Winslow wanted J.H. to be sorry, to be regretful for turning him away, for making him feel that he had torn the whole family, but it was clear that he might not get that. Yet he had to prepare to speak lovingly and respond rather than react. He would stand there above J.H. steeled up with Gert beside him and open his mouth speaking outward words of love and forgiveness, while quelling the rage in his heart that lie not yet subsided. That there was a hope, though with no history of proof, that J.H. or even Gert could say something genuine and loving to calm the storm raging in his heart.

Winslow had grown past the need to believe in God, at least the God of any religious viewpoint he had come across. The God that he was taught loves all his children the same regardless, yet in the same breath by those who follow this God and in the moment of final separation between him and J.H. (and by default Gert), condemningly preach hatred toward him and would consign him to an eternity in hell for how he was built and whom he chose to love. Winslow would not choose to calm his rage, to forgive, and let the past be the past because the God of his parents' religion nor any god of any religion commanded him to.

Even though Winslow felt a longing to please his self and his rage, he would choose to quell this longing for what he had learned about the universe at large. The lessons of how the energies of life and the universe flow. That letting go of the past, moving forward, and expressing love creates growth and happiness. Holding onto the past, holding onto hatred and grief, and merely moving on creates continued pain and unhappiness. Winslow knew in his heart that this was what the principle of forgiveness was supposed to be as taught by many religious sects. However, their practice of it, and their relinquishing responsibility to an unknown and unseen God seemed to him as a spit in the eye of an even greater truth of life that supersedes any religious belief, that all of mankind have free-will and with that free-will complete responsibility for all of their choices.

To say any one person was responsible for your choice would naturally seem incredulous, and the same to lay upon an unknown and unseen God any responsibility for your choices. It matters not if any one person or entity desired or willed a person to do something, with free-will each individual is the complete arbitrator and as such entirely responsible.

If someone told another person, they acted against another because it was that other person's will, that someone's act would still be wholly their responsibility. If in truth the other person indeed did not ask them to act against another, then they would have been using the other person's name in untruth, or using their name in vain. Regardless of whether one asked them to or not, their act remains their own responsibility entirely. If one had not, then that person would have added to the injury from the action against another the injury of further untruth, of using another's name in vain.

Winslow believed this was what truly was intended to be the meaning of the Christian Bible commandment: "Thou shalt not use the Lord thy God's name in vain," not the use of foul language or cursing as is the commonly held belief. And yet religions are found most heinously guilty of this proclaimed commandment the most... Winslow now became aware that he had become lost in his thoughts and felt he needed to move forward. It was time.

As he left the car and began to walk back towards the door leading to the hospital, Winslow realized that he had left the music on playing full blast. Maynard's melodic chant was now to "wash it all away, wash it down," and Winslow thought, "Yeah, wash it all away, all the pain, all the anger, and wash it all down, but don't swallow it, spit it out and be rid of it. Winslow knew that come what may, today he had to move forward. He had to let go of the ghosts of J.H.'s disapproval and of Gert's inconsolable empty loneliness that had consumed so much of his youth and pushed him to pity her more than love her. Winslow had to walk away from the shell of a broken family and into the rest of a full, whole life. "Wash it all away," Maynard called in his head as he entered the hospital, and today he would.

CHAPTER EIGHTY-FIVE
Surmising J.H.

Alan finished surmising J.H.'s condition. "J.H. is lucky that this heart attack, though serious with possible implications for the future, was mild enough to not have created any permanent damage. And as such, it can serve as a firm but kind warning that something has to change in J.H.'s life."

Gert, knowing how stubborn and set in his ways J.H. was, did not know if this brush with possible death would be what would influence J.H. to make any changes.

"But these things are best discussed with J.H. and you both together. Let's head to J.H.'s room now."

J.H. had turned on the TV again. The television served as a distraction from thinking about the heart attack he just had earlier in the morning. He knew very well that the doctor would request that he reduce stress in his life in both his eating habits and work. Each day for J.H. was a routine that he had long ago become content with. The routines of his life created a sense of continuity and predictability. In the line of duty as a police officer, routines and automated gestures are what kept one alive and sane. How could he change that? Why would he change that? "I wish the doctor would hurry up already and give me the spill, to get this over with," J.H. thought to himself. As if God had heard him and decided right then to answer the request directly, physician Wright and Gert walked in the room.

"Hello, Mr. Graves. We have a visitor here who I think you know." Alan greeted J.H. in a tone of levity in an attempt to lighten the likely somber mood to follow.

"Hello, J.H., it's good to see you..." Gert did not know how to finish the sentence. It was good to see J.H., but it was also stressful. She wanted to say, "It's good to see you are well," but then she did not really know if he was or not. Maybe she could say, "It's good to see you are up and awake.' But J.H. was lying in bed and could have been awake for some time. There were likely many other ways she could have finished the thought, but instead, she became lost in it and let it hang with a pause after you.

"Hello, Gert," J.H. replied apprehensively. J.H. would have liked to be able to answer lovingly as he knew he should; still, he could not escape the truth of his apprehension. Why did talking with Gert stress him out so much? He had been married to her for nearly 30 years. J.H. could not recall exactly how many years it had been, but it seemed like a lifetime. Gert would know, yet J.H. would not ask her for he did not want to hurt her feelings that he did not know.

"If you two want some time alone, I can come back later to go over the prognosis, treatment, and recommendations," Alan spoke to break the awkwardness.

"No. No, please stay and go over it now," J.H. and Gert spoke in unison. It was indeed a rare occurrence for them to do so. Each welcomed a stay of time until they had no choice but to talk to each other directly. It was going to be an unavoidable event, but for now, they could still avoid the discomforting realization of their lack of communication.

"Well, as you already know, Mr. Graves, you had a heart attack, meaning your heart stopped functioning normally. It's sort of like when a car's engine stalls, then sputters, then chugs along but on only two of the four cylinders, then on all four cylinders but not in its usual timing, then back to its normal timing. Forgive me if I assumed erroneously you know how a car's engine works."

Alan remembered fondly that when he and Winslow had gone for their driver's license when they were 16, J.H. had made sure they both had some understanding of how a car worked to not only know how to drive one but to know how a car works, and the dangers and responsibility of driving a car. J.H. had to be sure that the boys under his tutelage were the type of drivers on the road that would make him proud rather than an embarrassment.

"Oh, no, no. Of course, I know how a car engine works!" Mr. Graves smiled with pride.

"From a coronary angiography performed using cardiac catheterization the x-rays indicated minor blockage of your coronary arteries. From this we performed a Percutaneous Coronary Intervention, essentially placed an expansion tube that ballooned once we set it at the point of blockage. This is a minor surgical procedure that was easily performed during the non-invasive coronary catheterization; however if you do not change certain elements of your life, the next time you may not be so lucky. The next time your heart may stay only operating on only two of its four cylinders or worse, stall and not start back up."

J.H. smiled as he recalled how proud he was of his two boys when they passed their written and driving tests for their first license to drive. He, of course, had taught them all they knew. J.H. would not have them learn how to drive any other way. Even though Winslow's best friend from childhood was not his son, J.H. often considered Alan just as much his adopted son as Winslow was. They were always with each other. How he missed them. BUT... they both totally disappointed him, they turned a wonderful and natural brotherly love of close friendship into a sick and perverted sexual love! How could they? A tear formed in J.H.'s eye-catching him aware that he was not alone, and both Physician Wright and Gert had stopped talking and were gazing upon him in the moment of his zoning. Embarrassed, J.H. held back his tear, sat up and with a muffled grunt. "Humph... as you were saying."

Intent on not embarrassing Mr. Graves, physician Wright carried on while Gert took up a note of possible joy in seeing J.H.

express more emotion than he had in years while the 'why' she could only guess.

"Mr. Graves, though I cannot tell you to change your employment, you are advised to find ways to reduce the stressors associated with work. Do you have a non-rigorous exercise routine like taking walks, bicycling, swimming, or cardio machines at a gym like the elliptical? Have you or would you consider stretching exercises like that aided in yoga and pilates? These type of activities will build your heart, reduce your physical stress, and even reduce mental/emotional stress..."

Physician Wright trailed off in his speaking as he noticed that both Gert and J.H. were no longer listening to him and instead had begun to really look at each other. "Well, all of this is spelled out in these brochures I will leave you, and you can follow-up with your primary care physician back home within a week. I will leave you now to be on your own. I will be back later to check on you and see what we can do to get you released." With this, Physician Wright left the room.

CHAPTER EIGHTY-SIX
Gert and J.H.

J.H. drifted back to sleep. Gert stood by J.H.'s bed looking down at her husband likely for a good hour or so. She had earlier learned something about her feelings in the talk she had with what Gert now knew was Winslow's boyfriend and she accepted it and him. As she looked at J.H.'s pale face, she noticed that for the first time J.H. looked weak and worn. Gert had known him to be so strong and capable. She had always had a bit of fear of his temper, but illness makes things different. Gert thought that J.H. could do just about anything he wanted, and she knew one thing he never wanted was to be weak. Gert felt sorry for him. Even though J.H. was having some realization of his situation, she knew that when J.H. did fully realize his situation that he would be embarrassed, and his pride would not let him lay there and be the one who needed help. Gert also knew that somehow she would get the brunt of his stubbornness. Nevertheless, she leaned closer to him and placed a light kiss on his forehead.

J.H. began to stir. He opened his eyes slowly and blinked a few times as if he didn't recognize Gert. Gert was quick to let him know that everything was going to be okay and reassured him that this was just a routine thing that was going to be over within no time. She could sense J.H.'s angst as he looked around the room taking in his surroundings. They were strange to him from this perspective. Usually, he would be the one leaning over a hospital bed talking to a victim or a perpetrator, asking a few easy questions, and attempting to obtain some cursory information. But this time, it was he that lay there looking up, with eyes staring down at him. "Gggert h-how, what's going on?" It seemed both strange and yet natural that he should ask Gert this question, although he knew already that he was stuck in a hospital somewhere in Nevada due to what the doctors were telling him was a heart attack. Yet he still did not want to accept this and hoped in some vain hope that Gert would tell him of a different story, a different reality.

Gert answered him right away. She wanted to avoid J.H. having to experience any unnecessary anxiety. "Honey," (she had not called J.H. 'Honey' in years), you had a heart… a mild heart attack and everything is going to be okay."

"Woman, get me the doctor and let me get signed out of this place. I have a case going, and it's one I ain't letting no dang rookie finish in my stead."

"Now, J.H. you can't just get up and walk out. You have to get the doctor's release, which will not happen until you have been in observation for at least 12 hours. I don't think you'll be going anywhere for a little while, especially not to go gallivanting out and about playing cops and robbers."

The look on J.H.'s face was telling. He never thought that Gert really understood how important his job was, and he became particularly testy when she called it cops and robbers. He felt that she was somehow belittling his career. Gert could sense J.H. about to go into one of his tirades and let her have it.

It was at that moment that Gert decided that she would change the way things happened between them. There was something about how weak J.H. looked and the talk she had previously had with Alan that had empowered her to take command of a situation. Her voice came out of her in a way it never had before, with a type of confidence and sternness she had never used, "J.H., you just lay right there and keep quiet. I want to say something to you."

J.H. attempted to sit up and retort Gert's statement, but a twinge of pain and his weakness stopped him. He fell back down on his pillow and rolled his eyes, preparing himself for yet another diatribe about her wanting to get out and travel more and do things. Gert had no intention of bellyaching, as J.H. called it.

"Honey, we've known each other for so many years and have been through a lot. This is the first time in years that it's been just you and I, without Bear, or something to distract you, and I want you to talk to me. No, I want to talk to you. Things are about to change J.H. I feel like for the longest time that I've just existed for you in some sort of shell of life. Looking out at real lives, real relationships, and real love, wanting so badly to be there on that other side of the fence. I know you've felt it, too. I know who I am to you. And I want you to know that I don't like it. J.H. Graves, I'm your wife, your one, and only wife. We've been married for over thirty years, and with God's grace we'll be married for thirty more, but I won't live it the same way I've lived these last thirty, loving from the outside. I need and want loving. I have been waiting for you to simply touch me, not just physically, but to touch my heart, with a word, any kind word, to touch my mind with a conversation about something that matters to me. You have acted like you never needed me before. I've cooked, cleaned, kept house kept up and kept quiet. I can't anymore, J.H. I want us to wake up and look at each other and somehow remember who we were, how you loved me."

As she spoke, tears were welling up in her eyes. J.H. had never seen Gert with so much conviction in her face. He wanted to say something, but she hadn't displayed this much passion in years, and he was too weak to interrupt, so he sank further in his pillow. This time, he began to listen, to actually listen to her, and somehow this woman had changed. She was not the kind of woman to pour out her heart or speak with any real passion. She was the quiet, accepting, and dowdy type, or at least that was the way he had always seen and treated her. So when Gert stood

256

sternly in front of him, he saw her for the first time again and this time differently.

She said, "I'm your wife." Right now in this very moment, with his bones feeling his age and his heart beating a bit more than he remembered it, J.H. wanted, no, needed a wife, his wife, the wife of his youth, the wife that his father and mother gave their blessing to. The woman he once kissed on the eyes as she stood in front of him in a pink dress, standing on the porch of an Alabama house that was his grandmother's and her mother's before her.

They had been on their way to get a malt at the local diner during a visit to his grandmother. J.H. wanted to introduce the girl he intended to make his wife, and possibly bear his children. The children, unfortunately, would depend on if J.H. could find a doctor to tell him that the sports injury that he had hidden from Gertrude Prudence Aligns was just a fluke and that he wasn't broken and that he was a real man. He had kissed her on the eyes then pressed her head into his chest and promised in his heart that if nothing else in this world, that he would get this one thing right. His reflection of that day brought tears to his eyes.

They were so young then, he thought, and they had wanted so much. This was all before J.H. accepted the opportunity to join the San Francisco police force. The acceptance meant a move and a fresh start to make a life for himself away from the shadow of his father, a shadow that evidently the move, in reality, could not provide an escape from and that which J.H. carried with him in heart and mind.

Now here they were, the heart attack making him feel like an old man still hoping for one last hurrah, lying in a hospital bed in a town he did not know, and barely able to breathe. And looking down at him, there she was. How she even found him, he did not know, that she found him was what mattered.

257

J.H. made a decision. He decided that his last hurrah would start here and that it would not be chasing down a 20-year old case and an elbowing aside of some young, idealistic junior detective with his own emotional life in the balance. His last hurrah would be to learn to love his wife before it was too late: too late to kiss her, too late to still connect to that feeling he had on that day on his grandmother's porch so long ago.

J.H. looked up at her with his usually downward parted lips, began to rise, and his teeth began to show. He was smiling ear to ear, and his eyes were tearing. And in the distance, he heard the wind and on it was a still quiet voice sounding like his father that said, "You are my son and of this direction, I approve."

Gert was looking down at him and was still expounding on her position in his life. She noticed first that he was smiling, which she took to mean condescension, but there was something else: he was also crying. She began to speak slower than not at all as she looked at her husband and him at her. "J.H., what is wrong? Are you in pain?"

He answered, "Yes, I am in pain. There's this place in my chest that's been frozen towards you for too long, and it hurts now. Hey Gerty, remember that day on my grandma's porch just before we got married? It was the day we saw the lady with the three babies in one carriage on the way to get that malt."

"Yes," Gert replied, "it was the first time you kissed me on the eyes." They both paused, letting the moment linger, and with each passing moment it seemed as if years were taken out of both their lives. He had never seemed so young and handsome, and she was suppler than ever, and her cheeks were full and rosy.

"We danced that night on the porch when we got back, and you didn't know it, but your grandma was watching, and she saw me see her. She smiled at me, J.H... and beckoned me to stay quiet and I did. She watched the whole time we were out there, and she smiled every second. I think it must have been the last happy thing she was ever a part of. She passed not more than a month later. I remember how you wanted her to know you were happy and would be okay, but you never knew that she knew. She knew J.H."

"Oh, Gert, you never told me that. Thank you. Gert, I'm so very sorry, for everything that we've missed, all those years without dancing, all those years, and yet you're still here."

"I'll always be here, J.H. I made her a promise in that silent moment, a promise that I would plant my flag and say, 'Upon this hill, I will make my stand,' and I'm still standing here."

Gert reached down to hold him, and he did his best to reach up. In this way, they reconnected, erased years of hurt and neglect. They stripped away ridicule and disappointment and held onto the notion that love in any form was the highest form of healing. He was looking for her love language and she his, and they were both speaking loud and clear. They were going to leave this place different than when they came. They would leave a couple, and if things went right and Winslow showed up, then they would also leave a family. Life has a rhythm and flow, and the dams that people build with their broken heart and torn emotions can only hold back the water for so long. This is because life is designed to use emotions to urge us to overcome obstacles, teaching us lessons along the way, sometimes about others and sometimes about ourselves, but always teaching. They were now listening loud and clear.

As J.H. and Gert embraced, J.H. thought of his love for his wife, then of his son, his family. "Wait a moment. What was Alan's last name? Alan... Alan... Alan Wright!" A beam of recognition hit J.H.'s face. At that moment, Gert saw J.H.'s face change with a type of look that could only be accompanied by a sudden realization that is accompanied with relief, regret, and confusion. There was a knock on the door of J.H.'s private hospital room.

CHAPTER EIGHTY-SEVEN
Winslow Reunited

Winslow wanted to go upstairs, but he wanted to see Alan before he went. He wanted to ask Alan whether he had seen J H. He also wanted to know what J.H. looked like now. Winslow wanted to hear that he had a still gravelly voice that just made you feel judged and guilty all at the same time like the jury would not need to be declared 'out,' because, for J.H., the jury would never even have been in. He decided and moved on his decision automatically.

Winslow knew what J.H. had decided that he was a disappointment to him. People use the word disappointment to describe a person or situation that they believe does not live up to their expectations in order to describe a taste in their mouths left by a situation or the way life turned out. When people are invested in what they believe in with regard to how their life should turn out, they reserve their most vitriolic strain of feeling for those closest to them.

Winslow wanted to walk upstairs, but his feet were stuck. They were trapped in years of emotions that had melted the ground underneath him and left him unable to move at times. And this was one of those times. But his head said that he could not live like this and really love Alan. He needed to put to bed the feeling that his life was controlled by an inability to act, to act when it counted most, to move when the movement was called for and not be gripped by a feeling as well as not paralyzed.

J.H., his father, had disempowered him; had not given him the keys to his manhood, but rather took them away. All because Alan did not fit his definition of manhood. J.H. had with looks and words did things that sticks and bruises could not do to him. He could walk upstairs and tell him that. J.H. was weak now. He could not act on the threat his body made so many times, so he did not fear him in that way.

He lifted his left leg first, thinking, "My God, it moved," as if he truly expected it to be rooted and incapable of motion. Then his right leg and the stairs began to walk down him, or at least that's the way he felt when he had made it to the top. Winslow could feel his heart racing; he could hear voices down the hall and they were familiar voices, voices standing in front of the dark room, jumping in and out in an almost childlike manner. He could see images of them from years ago laughing by the room and yet he knew that could not be them.

Winslow quietly knocked on the door. His hand moved so slowly that he felt the cold steel of the door on the skin of his forefingers. For a moment Winslow thought to step back and simply walk away, but the time for walking had passed some seven years ago. Feeling resolute, bolstered from the years of love he shared with Alan, Winslow paused, took a deep breath half out of anxiousness and half out of anticipation, and then stepped through the door. There was the woman Gertrude that called herself his mother.

There was the woman who checked him for fevers and decorated Christmas trees with things that she'd picked out herself that she thought he might like while walking through malls. Gertrude had not done enough to stand up to J.H. in those years, but she was a victim in her own way, too. He ignored her and spoke to the dog instead of her as if Bear could actually tell her what he was trying to say. It wouldn't have mattered if Bear could talk anyway; she was never less than three feet from J.H. during their conversations. Or maybe he was really expecting Bear to translate for him, not what he was saying, but what he wanted to say.

There was something about the lilt in J.H.'s voice when J.H. called out "Winslow!" that seemed to instantly melt away years of anguish caused. He was so ready for his life to be different that he was open to any form of hope that the universe provided. He thought for a second about that notion. Had the universe/God answered his prayer? Was this how it happened? Do people always almost miss it like he almost did, or was he just so desperate to feel anything but the feeling that he was waiting for his real life to begin, that he had put the lightness in the sound of J.H.'s voice. "Winny?" Gertrude's voice snapped him back to reality. "Winny, I'm so glad you're here. Are you okay? Are you really okay?"

CHAPTER EIGHTY-EIGHT
The Following Morning – Paul Meets the Local Police

Paul drove into town and quickly located the local police station around 7 a.m. It was a quaint rustic building reminiscent of municipal buildings from back in the 1940s if not earlier. When Paul walked into the building, he thought to himself that indeed it might be listed on a historic registry, for even the furniture and telephones seemed to be just as dated as the building itself. A portly man in his 40s with thinning grey-streaked hair sat at an oak desk from the period, looked up with a deterministic glance and then stated, "You must be Detective Johnson."

"I am, and you must be Officer Liam."

"You found the place alright? No troubles?"

"It was not a problem at all."

"Glad to hear it. Have you had breakfast yet? Coffee?"

"No, I have not. I just drove in and didn't want to keep you waiting."

"Well good, we can grab a bit of breakfast at the diner before driving out to the lake where the suspect is always at on a Sunday morning."

"Always, huh... that predictable?"

"Yes, in such a small town like this, people get comfortable in their set patterns. It's a simple life, not too much excitement around here, and this is how we like to keep it. No reason to rock the boat of something that works to keep everyone content."

Was contentment the primary goal of most people, Paul wondered. Is that all that really mattered or all that could be hoped for? Or was there a possibility and perhaps a greater need to live and strive for more than contentment, to strive for happiness that extends the boundaries of being content.

The diner itself was just across the street and convenient to the police station. "Hello, Officers!" greeted a woman in her late thirties plucked out of "Mel's Diner" with an incredible likelihood to Flo with her bleached blonde hair tied up in the back with a white ribbon and pink mid-thigh waitress uniform adorned with white cuffs and neckline. Liam didn't wait to be seated and led Paul to a corner booth with a direct view of the police station and the whole of the diner. "So who is this new one you have here, Liam? He looks as delicious as our apple pie!"

"Now, now Carly, let's not scare him away yet. He is an old friend just in town for the day." The waitress was looking at Paul appraisingly and taking note of his badge.

"Well, Officer Johnson, speaking of apple pie, you must have some. I bet you never could get a pie as delicious back in San Fran."

Paul chuckled and felt he had to follow suit by matching the small town charm "I'd be much obliged."

"Sugar and cream?"

"On top of my pie?"

"No, no, silly boy, for your coffee. You are going to have some coffee with your pie, right?"

"Oh…" Paul smiled a little embarrassed "Yes, of course, is the sugar and cream on the side?"

"Anything you want, darling. And Liam, you will, of course, have your usual?"

"Oh, of course, Carly. Your apple pie is what makes my morning!"

Carly was beaming with a smile that was wider than her face. "Ain't you the sweetest thang!"

265

"Should we talk more about…" Paul started off asking Liam to get down to business after Carly left the table.

"Shhh. Now, now… there's no need to talk further on that here. We have already said all that needs to be said. The rest is up to you. Just keep things on the down low is all I ask."

After that Liam and Johnson sat mostly in silence, eating their pie and drinking their coffee, which always seemed to be full. Every once in a while, Liam would insert a comment about some of the townsfolk and their simple ways, and Paul would respond with a smile and a polite nod.

Finished eating, Paul took out his wallet. "Officer Johnson, don't you worry about that. Carly just put his ticket on my account."

"Sure thing, sweetie. Come back and visit anytime, Johnson. Now will you have a coffee to go as well?"

"Why, thank you kindly." With his coffee mug filled with fresh coffee, Liam walked Paul out of the diner.

"So, Johnson, the lake is really simple to get to. It's just a few miles down the road. You'll see a dirt road to the left with a sign 'Maramount Lake.' Take that road for like three miles. If you veer to the left of the fork in the road at that point, you'll have a good lookout view of the lake where Ordin fishes every Sunday. If you veer right, you'll go right to the dock where he docks his boat."

"I thank you again for your hospitality. Be assured I will keep this quiet so as to not disrupt the flow of things in your town."

"Much appreciated I'm glad you understand." With that, Paul drove off towards the lake, towards a future as yet undecided.

266

CHAPTER EIGHTY-NINE
Next Morning - Ordin and His Lake

Friday was the evening when he did the impromptu cell to cell "mock" call-in radio show entitled 'Late Night Radio.' To the south, the souls were lined up and being warehoused in the same row as he. Ordin could start with an opening commentary that spoke of a topic or a notion that he knew would resonate with the masses. This was his way of moving them to speak up and out, urging them from their bunks where they usually sat in either despair, plotting, or hoping. Usually after Ordin's orations, he would hear his words mimicked throughout the week as a sign of respect and appreciation. "Hey, O' you going t' do the show this Friday?" they would say and then, "Go ahead, caller, you're on."

The inmates were encouraged to first identify their cell number or name, should they choose, or they could remain anonymous. Ordin would then respond by saying, "Okay cell... cell number 12, go ahead, caller, you're on." This was how each call would go. As the caller finished his rant, the clapping began. Ordin stood there with a smile, lightly chuckling at the last caller, but his eyes started to become bleary, and his head began spinning. His cellmates' faces began to sway and melt.

Ordin could still hear the clapping of the hands, but they began to sound more like the lapping of waves against a boat. The more the lapping sound came into his consciousness, the more Ordin began to realize that he was not in his cell on a Friday, but on a boat, with a pole, drink, some bait, some music, and silence. No sound. No thoughts. Just silence. To the right there were some spruce trees, standing like giant sentries, guards of a private sanctuary for hundreds of years, dark green, brown undertones, limbs like muscular arms. To his left, there was a weeping willow which was not naturally grown in the region, seemingly placed there with the feeling that there is a need for tears here as if someone thought this place was so beautiful they could cry. Pink and blue hues decorated the landscape of the lake. His lake. Here on his lake.

Ordin had been through so much in the last seventy-two hours. His daymares had reached a fever pitch, his son had contacted him via a letter to which he had responded, he had seen the picture and even spoken to the man that played a coincidental part in changing his whole life, and Ordin even spoke to his son over the phone. He needed to hear from God right now. The shaking of his hands made the oars that he had in his hands fall into the water. He was standing. How and why he did not know. His heart beat so hard that the shiny lure that was in his breast pocket leaped up and out of his pocket into the water and rocked slowly as it sank deeper down toward the lake's bottom. Ordin's hope sank as well. He fell to his knees, riveted by being transported back to his senses.

"Why won't you speak to me? Give me you! Say you love me. Show Up!" In his heart, Ordin knew he was there for he had memorized the words, "For he will never leave you nor forsake you," and Ordin knew that God never had. "But why won't you speak to me?" Ordin was crying now, streaming more than tears. He was streaming regret, anger, and a flood of other emotions that had held him in suspended animation for years. He needed a release; he needed to exhale and move on. Let it all go. He also knew he needed to hear from his God before he could let it go. He needed to feel redemption. Hadn't he paid? Hadn't he given?

The voices rang out loud and clear, in unison, in harmony, filled with hope. Hope that a mere moment of joy could transform an experience. Changing one experience into another. Changing an experience meant for pain, into one with the sublime gift of peace experienced with the choice of letting go, letting the past be the past rather than in the present, and moving forward, a choice of self-empowerment that most call forgiveness. This choice brings with it the power to cause one to forget. To forget where he left his heart, forget where he left his last joyful moment where his state of hurt began.

Ordin knew that the promise of salvation did not mean that there would be no consequences. He also knew he was not guilty of what he had been accused. It was this fact that broke him at times. All of these years, all of his anguish had not been that of a guilty man getting what he deserved, but rather that of a man deserving what he felt guilty for.

He felt that he had abandoned his child, been a coward in his relationship with his wife. He felt that he had let his pride get the better of him when he reached for the shotgun that turned out to be the instance where three men, two women and four children had lost their lives. He had spoken to one of those men just a few hours ago, a man that had taken a picture that told a story that shaped his narrative. Ordin could not get himself to see again the three children that would never see their father walk through their front door again, never be held again by him. Nor could Ordin handle seeing the world of hurt and grief of Peter's wife that yearned to look into the eyes of her mate and friend. It was for these people, for their situations and their struggles that Ordin felt guilty about.

For Ordin, each one of the lives was a life he was connected to by the chord of The Accident. Each time one of those lives shook from the pain as a result of the accident the chord strengthened. Each time one of those lives blamed his God for their loss, or asked, "How could you let this happen?" The chord was infected. And the infection had festered in him and rendered him weak and sick, and he knew that it was only God who could break the chord. Ordin knew God could free him with one word, one sound. Ordin

269

felt no wind and heard no sound. It was so quiet that he could hear the blood coursing through each vein, he could hear each hair as it stood on edge. And then a still, quiet voice said, "I'm here."

Ordin shook. His eyes grew wide, and he tried to will himself to stop shaking. Did he hear what he thought he did? Did he hear what he had been waiting and praying for so long? Or was it supposed to come like thunder in the distance when He spoke? A wave washed over him. He looked up and observed that a small pocket of clouds had formed in what seemed like grabbing distance, and a flash of lightning lit the cloud. Ordin blinked, and as fast as he thought the cloud appeared, it was gone. Had he seen it at all? Had he heard anything at all? Was it his own inner voice that he had heard?

Ordin sat in the boat steadying himself, half in a daze, half out. In the moment when Ordin calmed himself again, he heard the still, small voice again say, "I am here, and I have always been here."

This time, instead of questioning his sanity upon hearing the voice, Ordin decided to go with it and asked inaudibly to the still, small voice, "If you have always been here, why do I just hear you now?"

"I have always been here, the voice answered. "You have not always been listening, nor ready to listen so much because you were wallowing in your own sorrows and pity."

Ordin thought about this and had to admit, that he had spent all these years on the lake in this unknown town where he had sought to forget and be forgotten, he had also closed himself off from everyone and everything else, including his God. Today was the first time in all these years that he was actually open to more than just himself. This was evidenced in that he took the first steps just yesterday to seek forgiveness from his son, and to give forgiveness to Laurence, the photographer by acknowledging how he had wronged them.

"Yes," the inner voice confirmed, "in your choices to accept and take responsibility for your actions, you have opened up your heart and soul to listening beyond yourself. To listen in a way that you can now acknowledge and hear me and the true yearnings of your own soul, beyond the fears of your mind, where you have kept yourself imprisoned all these years."

Imprisoned. This was how Ordin had felt all these years. He may not have been in the horrible jail cell that pronounced his many dreams during the days and nights, but he felt alone and imprisoned all the same. Hoping to protect others, he had separated himself in vain, but in the truth, he was hiding and imprisoning himself in solitude, regret, shame, and guilt, yet never taking the courage to really take on the responsibility. He had run away like a coward, hoping to escape rather than face his troubles. Yesterday had been the first day he had experienced the full weight of the burden he believed had been placed on him by God, but in all reality, he had placed it upon himself.

"You now understand. Struggles and obstacles are not experienced as punishment by me, rather as natural occurrences most often by one's own hand or the hand of others in your life, or by the natural state of things and life put into motion."

Ordin now began to understand. He now felt that God may have created life, created the earth, but other than creating and setting things in motion, God allowed all to create their own course in life. He allowed for the natural evolution and consequences to follow from choices and a set period of time to exist for each element, animal, insect, and person. "But why was this so?"

"How else are you to grow and create yourself? Without free-will and the responsibility equal to that?"

271

"Then why do you answer me now, if free will is to not act for and on my behalf?"

"I am here to guide as you are ready for my guidance and for you to know you are not alone. Nothing more and nothing less. I am not here to decide for you, nor am I here to take away the responsibility of your choices. To do either would diminish free will, which would diminish your potential for growth and more fully actualized self."

Ordin now sat to ponder how he had felt yesterday when he had asked for and found forgiveness and relief from the weighted burden of guilt in those two lives. He was now anxious, a little afraid, but mostly excited and hopeful of going to see his son tomorrow, of getting the chance to get to know his son and to be a part of his life. It felt like a fresh start, a new life full of possibilities. What greater way to begin a new life than to have his only conversation with God in all these years as he understood him on his lake before he left this town and state of solitude. And yet, if he had decided earlier to reach out and seek forgiveness and to forgive, he may have had this sooner.

"It matters not when in the whole of things, just that you do at some point."

"But would not sooner be better?"

"Sooner would mean you had learned sooner, but since life is eternal, there is no specific time, rather just the chance for you to learn and grow must be given."

This was to be the last time Ordin would ever be on his lake, at least as far as he knew. And even if he were to revisit the lake, which had become his lake, it would never be the same, for he would not be the same. As foreign and unchartered this may be, Ordin felt a sense of jubilance in it. The hope for a tomorrow, which he had not had all these years, was now his again. He felt more the master of his own fate than he had ever had. He was free from his own imprisonment.

As Ordin rowed back to the shore to prepare for his journey back to his son, the weeping willow seemed to no longer be shedding tears of sorrow and loneliness, but rather the tears of joy as the sun sparkled on the edges of its leaves. "Thank you, God," Ordin spoke in a soft and humble whisper.

CHAPTER NINETY
Choices

Throughout life, we are always making decisions. At various points, these decisions become more conscious choices. Many choices affect nothing other than the experience at the time. Some choices are crossroad decisions, where the impact of the decision affects all other choices and the flow of our life thereafter, regardless of whether we acknowledge it at the time, realize later, or never fully realize it.

Where does choice come from? Why do we as humans possess it? And what does it mean to have a choice? A whole novel could be written on these questions alone. Herein, a short treatise on them is offered.

In the origin of choice, there is no absolute knowledge. We are aware of our ability to choose, and with that awareness, we have a choice. Even without our awareness, any self-made act, thought, or movement is itself a choice. There is no one person, entity, or thing pushing a lever to make our fingers move, or pushing a button to send an electronic pulse forcing any movement or thought.

There may be some purists of philosophy who might argue that we cannot prove there is not a person, entity, or thing pushing buttons and levers or any other form of direct act upon us. However, since we cannot prove there is either, let's just hold to our experience in awareness of self, our actions, thoughts, movements, etc. Let us hold onto our own autonomy of choice and assume, by others sharing their own experiences of autonomy of their self-directed acts, thoughts, and movements, a sense that we all indeed have choice.

Self-awareness is the foundation of sentience. Sentience is the foundation of self-determination that is the definition of free will. Free will is the foundation of choice, the ability to decide for oneself one's thoughts, actions, and movements. A person can be self-aware without being fully aware of all around or even within themselves.

Take for example a classroom of students. They all have the same textbook, teacher, and room in which they sit with the assumed intention to learn. Nonetheless, although all share these commonalities, they will not all have the same experience. They are all at different levels of awareness, understanding, attention, and alertness. And yet each is self-aware enough to know of their being in the same classroom, the same teacher, the same subject of study, and of being there themselves. Some may hear the bee buzzing outside the window, others the pencil tapping or the shuffling of feet of another in the classroom. Others may only be aware of the teacher talking and writing on the chalkboard. All of this is present, but the individual awareness of it all differs.

Much is the same with the awareness of choice. With all that is available to experience (and surely more is available than most if not all are aware of), what we choose to acknowledge (be aware of) or not, structures our experiences and knowledge. This becomes our framework for future choices, which then affects our future experiences. At any time one may choose to alter one's perception, one's framework, and one's awareness.

If you make the choice to pick up a green pen rather than a black pen, the only effect is that you are holding a green pen instead of a black pen. If you make a choice to drive faster than the speed limit, and thus by doing so, cannot stop in time to avoid hitting another, your choice affects both. Most choices are as benign with their effect on the choice between the green or black pen. However, some choices affect more than just self.

If you hike, you become aware that there are often points where the path provides you with a choice to veer left or right. Some of the side-paths eventually lead either back to the same main path or at least to the same destination. Some alternative path choices lead you to an entirely different set of paths and destinations. Most choices in life are like the side-paths that still lead you to the same destination, but provide you with a different experience along the way. The alternative paths that lead you to an entirely different set of paths and destination are the crossroad paths. Such is the nature of crossroad choices.

CHAPTER NINETY-ONE
Next Morning – Stakeout and an Answer

"Coffee tastes better cold," Paul thought. "Whoever thought of doughnuts as the default food for cops on stakeout?" It was more of an observation than a question. Paul had been sitting in the same place for about two hours wondering when he would see his target, Ordin, the entire reason for his trip, the reason for him leaving his little girl on their day. Ordin was the reason that Paul was questioning everything he had thought about the force for the past six years. Paul had occasionally had a passing thought that the police force had no small part in his family falling apart for the last four years, but never would conceive it until now. His wife was correct in her assessment that he had brought it home with him. The 'it' was all of the ugliness, all of the hatred, and all of the associated depression. It was everything he saw on the streets that caused him to question the purity of mankind, where he began to slip into the thinking that corrodes so many police officer minds eventually, that everyone was a perp in some manner and just most had not been caught.

It was that attitude that had Paul on the verge of losing his family, his daughter and his integrity. His mind returned to a day when he was sitting at an outside cafe with his daughter and waiting on his wife when he had noticed a tall, thin gentleman gazing in their direction. At first, he glanced and saw the man from the corner of his eye, then he glanced again and noticed the gentleman smiling in their direction. His instincts told him that the man was some sort of pervert looking at his little girl with twisted intent.

He heard his wife call out to them just as he had made up his mind that he would go over and let the man know that he was a "pease" officer and that if he didn't stop staring at his daughter he would run him in for a 647.6 which in his language was the penal code for annoying or molesting a minor.

It was at that moment that he was shoving the man over that he also heard a voice call out, "Oh, my God! Dad! Dad, what's going on?!" His wife had shrieked with humiliation as she ran up and began to admonish him. The man's daughter had come upon them as well and was now screaming at him as she began to pull her father up. He noticed a striking resemblance the woman had to his daughter, and it was as if she could have been his little girl's mother.

When the dust settled, and the explanations came out, it was told that the man was looking at Paul and his daughter. He had been looking at them because the girl and he reminded him of himself and his daughter at that age, and he had been waiting for his daughter to join him for their weekly lunch. It was at that time learned that it was a ritual they had carried on for fifteen years without fail at the same cafe and at the same time. Besides his story being entirely true, it was corroborated by the fact that the woman bared an almost uncanny resemblance to his daughter. It was then that he had begun to see how if he were the man and saw the little girl that he would have looked in almost astonishment and would have absolutely have smiled a broad smile at her.

It was at this moment that Paul began to question himself and come into some semblance of consciousness of what his wife had been saying to him for years, that he was not the same man that she had married. The ideals and principals he had fought for were gone and had been replaced by cynicism and suspicion. There was no glow of chivalry anymore; it had been replaced by stoicism and second guessing. He thought how each time he yelled at his wife or daughter that the anger came easier and easier. He was indeed becoming the men he saw and worked side by side with each day

278

that made the comments about the scum that they were scraping off the streets and how he said to himself, or under his breath, at any rate, God, I hope I never become that guy." But he had. He had become that guy, and now he was sitting in a cold car with cold coffee on a hill overlooking a lake.

The lake that was singularly beautiful. It had wonderful colors with pussy willow stalks around the edges, blue spruces, a weeping willow tree, and a small dock just big enough for one or maybe two boats to cast out into the lake to have a peaceful day of fishing. He could imagine two old friends casting off with a cooler carrying sandwiches and a few beers, some bait, and a piece of fruit or something. They would tell each other stories about when they were younger and stronger men, some of their triumphs, some embellished and some true, but mostly just memories of themselves when they were young.

This was the kind of thing he used to do with his father. But he wasn't there to fish or tell stories. He was there to apprehend a perp, a man who he had been told had murdered his own friend in cold blood during an argument over a contest involving bird hunting. This same man had received a break in the court system and somehow escaped justice. But thanks to a tip from a show called 'Cold Case Killers' and their 'Cold Case tipsters,' he was about to arrest the man and bring him in so the truth could come out, and justice prevail.

This was who he had become, and it was starting to sink in that he was the ugliness and the doubt that he feared. He did not see a kindly looking older man down there on the lake; he saw a perp. He saw only a perp. The realization ripped through him like a tsunami wave across a desert island in the middle of the sea and Paul began to sob. Paul's sobbing turned into weeping, and his weeping turned into to wailing. Paul's body and his head shook as he brought his emotions in check and simply stared, stared at the man sitting in the boat, who in turn was staring at the water.

Paul's thoughts returned to his own father, whom he could imagine seated in a boat, resting his eyes, daydreaming about his granddaughter. Paul knew how dear his father was to his little girl and if the man fishing was a father or grandfather and if he was, could Paul take him away from his family, his son, and his granddaughter? Paul began to feel butterflies in his stomach. His head was literally spinning, and his eyes were still swollen. Paul saw his office with his name: "Detective Paul Johnson." It was a vision of his name displayed on the frosted glass of the window. He would have a mahogany desk with embossments and gold accents. He would have a picture of his family in the middle of the desk, then one of his wife and daughter on either side.

The light reflected back from the glare on the lake Paul was looking down on. From his perspective on the top of the ridge, Paul could see the entire lake and was struck by how beautiful it all was. The tall weeping willow tree among all the serene blue spruces, the colorful blooms that covered the shoreline, and of the lake as well. It was so beautiful that Paul found himself daydreaming about fishing with his dad and daughter as had been the plan for that weekend. It was the weekend he had given up to drive half across the world chasing this perp, chasing his career, chasing down answers about his career, and chasing answers about himself.

Paul thought he saw a flicker in his peripheral vision. As he turned his head, the light grew brighter and brighter until it was a blinding light. Paul knew that he should be shielding his eyes to block the light from inflicting permanent damage to his naked retina, but he neither squinted or flinched. The light was expansive and cooling to his eyes, and within the light, Paul began to hear a small, still voice. "Believe in the light," the voice said. "Believe," the voice repeated and then became ever louder, "BELIEVE." The voice repeated the word over and over, the sound now booming so loud it was deafening.

The windows of Paul's car began to rattle. They seemed to pulsate, and even the road ahead of him appeared as a gray liquid. Paul clamped his hands over his ears and screamed as loud as he could, but no sound came out. And yet somehow he could still hear the voice saying, "Believe." Paul felt his eyes began to well with tears and then noticed his tears were blood. He looked in the rearview mirror and saw his forehead had been pierced in several places along his brow. There was a dull ache in his hands and feet that began to grow and intensify. The pain became unbearable, and Paul's hands were shaking. He looked down at them and what he saw brought his heart to a near standstill. There were small holes in his hands, right in the center. There were light streams of blood coming from them as well. His feet felt wet somehow. Paul was sure the pain in his feet was the same as in his hands, and the wetness was a stream of blood pouring into his shoes.

Paul was in full panic mode by this point. And then as suddenly as soon as it began, it stopped. All of it, the light, the sound, the pain, all of the visions all just stopped, and it seems as if had never occurred. There was no dull lingering ache underneath, such as like at the end of a migraine headache. There was nothing, nothing except the lingering word "believe," It was at the forefront of Paul's thoughts as if it had been burned into the front of his brain, and now his eye had to somehow look through that portion of his mind to see.

Paul did not know if what he had just experienced was real or rather a vivid dream brought on in part by the lack of good sleep from being on the road virtually non-stop since yesterday, and having had only four hours of sleep at that. And perhaps it was due in part to the self-questioning guilt the trip afforded him time to contemplate on. Regardless, Paul was visibly affected, shaken.

"My God?" Paul murmured. Believe. "Believe in what?" Paul thought. "Believe in the agency that I've been working on for all these years, the one that is sworn to serve and protect and has been twisted and perverted into some sort of close minded gang, with questionable ideals and morals? Should I believe in a marriage that just seems like a dead relationship full of blame and loss, believe in the honor of a man that wears a badge and uses it to persecute the son he wishes to admire him? And what about the man whose life I came to claim again, so that he may die again, unlike the man whose life he took? What shall I believe in?" Paul's voice rang of indignation.

Paul had stopped crying and now seemed angry. He was angry that his perception of God and the dream of God in this world had not been met. Paul wanted to rail against him, but his heart quieted, and peace came over him. Now he wept gently. He still felt like the presence was with him, but no longer manifested as an impression burnt on his brain. Now it was more like a soft whisper in the back of his mind.

Paul thought about how he had been missing. Was it physically or psychologically? Was it emotionally or spiritually? The truth was that it was all of them. The truth was that he had been missing in every way he could be, from his family and from himself.

Paul cleared his eyes and looked one last time at the lake. Looking down from the ridge, there was something about the scene that made Paul feel serene and decisive, all at the same time breathing deeper and deeper with every moment. The last two days had been long and heavy for him. Things had happened, and they had profoundly changed Paul's manner of thinking. They had altered his thinking about who he'd been, who he was at the moment, and who he wanted to be. He had gotten into a car and began a journey that was coming to an end, but not just this journey, every journey he had been on for the last 10 years. That included the journey from boy to man, from boyfriend to husband, from husband to father, from father to missing, from missing to found, and from found to aware.

It was this new awareness that contributed to Paul deciding that he would not disrupt the life he saw before him. Indeed, not the life of the man that sat in a boat on this lake, and certainly not the life of the child who was awaiting her father to give her more of the time that he had made seem so very precious every time they spent even a single moment together. Nor would he disrupt the life of the beautiful woman that had not only challenged him but whom nurtured and believed in him.

It was this expanded notion that had him looking down and seeing a man that would live his life beyond this day, just as he would live his life from this day forward. The man that was sitting there was still there. He had not moved. He had not stirred. He had been oblivious to the event Paul had just experienced, just as he was oblivious to Paul sitting there. He had no idea how close his life was to being altered, disrupted and broken again. Paul thought about all the responsibility he would be letting go of if he simply drove off. He also thought of his daughter and whom she needed in her life. Did she need a good detective, or just a good father? Paul made a decision, looked out upon the lake, started his car, looked ahead, and then promptly drove off.

Paul knew where he was headed. He was headed to his daughter, headed to his wife, and headed to redemption. Paul was heading home. He reasoned that if he was to believe, it would be in the still quiet voice in the back of his mind that now warmed his conscious, warmed his heart. As the miracle of Paul's epiphany warmed his soul, he could not imagine a more peaceful feeling, even if it had been him sitting out there on that lake. Paul could not imagine that he could feel any more peaceful, even if he had been fishing with God.

Paul picked up his phone, dialed his father first and left a message. "Dad, I'm just calling you to thank you for all you have taught me. I have decided to make a change in my life and alter my course from that of being a police officer. Please feel free to call me back when you can. Love you."

Next, Paul dialed and spoke to his wife and child. "Hello, Kristina. I'm coming home now. I am sorry I have not been around as much as I would have liked and as much as you and Willow deserve. I have not been the man and husband you deserve, and I have veered off the course of who I am. I'm going to make a change, though I'm not sure where it will lead. But I do know it begins with leaving the police force. This is something we need to talk about in person when I get back. Know that I love you, always have and always will. You and Willow are the best things in my life."

Kristina replied with surprise and yet elation. "I love you, too, Paul. Make it home safe."

The last call Paul made that morning was to his captain back in San Francisco. "Captain, I have not found what the syndicate "Cold Case Killers" is looking for. I am on my way back now. When I get back, I am handing in my badge. Being a police officer no longer fits what I want in life. Thank you for your support through the years I have been in your precinct."

After the Captain's "Okay," Paul hung up the phone. There was nothing more to be said over the phone, nor in reality even in person once he handed in his badge. For now, Paul would have the 14-hour drive back to ponder what would come next.

CHAPTER NINETY-TWO
Ties Re-tied

"Did it rise, Gerty?" J.H. asked. It was something that he used to say all the time, and he put the "Y" on the end of Gert, just like he used to do. He didn't think about it, he just said it. She could hear him in her sleep. She sprang up to a sitting position. She was smiling because when J.H. said that he was talking about the sun, he always asked if it rose as an indication that he was still trying to tell her that he was so happy that he thought he could have died and gone to heaven in his sleep. Gertrude never grew tired of hearing it.

Gertrude had learned long ago that peace and love were a gift of life. Even if he said it these days out of routine, it still sounded nice. The time and reconnection with Winslow would be a welcome addition to what looked like a reset of their family. It seemed that the human condition was fraught with the unpredictable. One day a person could be at the bottom of the pile, bills unpaid, the proverbial water rising to their neck and at the end of your rope. And yet the next day that same person could have the son that was judged, alienated and rejected walk back into your life and give you a chance to find redemption in his eyes.

To step back in time, through promises broken and achievements ignored by a father who would not could not acknowledge a boy struggling to understand his place in a world. A world that held that he must hide whom he chooses to love from their eyes. A world that purports that the God of all men, the God of love and redemption, cannot and will not love him because his choice of humans to love do not line up with the interpretation of the book that men wrote in that God's name.

285

The world was such that one may find themselves enjoying a hunting trip with a friend and the next day that the same friend may no longer exist, his body decimated by a weapon created by man's hand with but one purpose: to kill, and his existence that had been brought to an end by him. Then there was the fact that one's intention was doubted, the "motive" questioned, freedom was taken, one's esteem laid bare. One can walk into a jail cell as a man with a calm of presence and demeanor, and assured of his values. He could then leave that same cell with the psyche attacked and shattered. One could be made the center of the debate, between who should and should not own a gun and driven into solitary exile, unable to piece together the fragments of a relationship one thought would last forever.

In a world of infinite possibility and chance, it is plausible that a man, any given man, can wake one day, take his usual walk to class on his campus, all the while talking with friends about his ideals and goals. He may espouse his philosophy and attempt to dissuade his compatriots from their beliefs, and yet, amongst all his peers he may be little more than a blowhard who turns from his own beliefs to become the thing he disliked most about the society he wailed and moaned about. This man could find himself as an officer of the peace, duty bound and sworn to serve and protect. This could all occur even though one has almost attained their Master's degree. In such a world, a person could awaken one day and question all that they have been through over the past ten years and be compelled to embark on a spontaneous quest to attempt to answer the largest questions of their life, which would culminate in one decision to answer all their questions.

In a world where a young girl who looks upon her father as the shining sun and her mother as the adoring moon. In the universe of her family, she may see the sun set on her family as her father walks away from the mother she will come to regard more as a rival than a relative. She may develop her esteem based on this walk away and decide that her father; the only man she has known was now as all men will appear to her for the next 20 years of her life, as mere disappointments that have riddled her with lies, false hopes and walkways. It may be this perspective that drives this woman, who was once a girl, to decide that the prospect of her personal fifteen minutes of fame should supersede the so-called morally correct thing to do. It may be that this woman could rest the whole of her values in this world on the arm of a fictitious depiction of the exploitation of human frailty and agony. She could be so drawn in that the heart that sits in the seat of her souls, a heart crying out for love and acceptance, could be compromised by the lure of constant and astounding adoration by peers who have lives of mundane morbidity.

Amidst all of this living, there are ties that bind and ties that break. There are also ties that may be re-tied, and in this way, the expression of God can be a wash like a warm wave that flushes over the body that quiets the soul. It would be a quiet not unlike that which one would expect to feel if they were sitting on a lake fishing with God.

Perhaps it would be like walking on clouds, or crying underwater. To re-tie a tie is to attach a feeling that was once natural and now has become familiar. It's to open the heart to hurt and to hope. The internal motivation and instinct to protect and nurture that soul on the other side of the tie. The first compulsion must be to forgive, to forgive both the perpetrator and oneself, and then in some cases the God of all life.

There are those who believe that God should not allow or design humans with the propensity to inflict pain upon each other. Only after one has accepted and achieved all levels of forgiveness can one move on. For some, the prospect is too overwhelming, the notion too daunting of an emotional drain, to look back headlong into the pain. Still, there are some who would challenge the pain, whom still would not walk through it. And yet for some there is no other choice but to forgive, to prevail, to understand that pain happens, wounds heal, but scars remain. It is our individual choice, based on our unique combination, of nature versus nurture, to wear our scars as beauty marks or birth defects. Which do you choose?

CHAPTER NINETY-THREE
Next, Morning – Cold Case Killers Notified

If you've been here twelve hours, if you've looked at 200 hours of stock footage to find the three minutes of footage that was taken almost twenty years ago because you're working on your story, then when the call comes in, you take a second and think about it. At this point it's not about wanting, it's past needing. It's something that has a deep urge to exist which pushes out from you, pushing against the skin as if it has a pulse, so you look. You look out for someone looking back. You look back to see if someone is looking for you. It's like a long lost child looking for his or her father or mother. This is because you know that one call, that one look is going to change it all. Lift it off, let the light in all the time, but there's an action needed, and the action starts in a second. A decision half way around the world becomes a phone call, becomes an email, becomes a text, and then becomes a call. That call.

Brent thought, "It's not that show changes someone's life. It's that something worked out. The years of planning, the years of being on the verge of hitting a big one, which to some seems adolescent. It was just about feeling something good, something other than hope." Hope was not a bad thing to feel, he was just tired of feeling it. Some people struggle with hopelessness; Brent did not. Hope was linked to faith, which Brent had plenty of also. What he most wanted to feel now was a victory. He had felt it before, but in small doses, but never in an overwhelming way and right now he wanted to be overwhelmed.

There's a Colin Hay song that says, "I'm waiting for my real life to begin." The lyrics "any minute now, my ship is coming in, I'll keep checking the horizon. I'll keep checking my machine,

289

there's sure to be that call. It's going to happen soon, soon, oh so very soon; It's just that times are lean, and you say be still my love, open up your heart, let the light shine in. Don't you understand? I already have a plan. I'm waiting for my real life to begin. And you say, just be here now, forget about your past, your mask is wearing thin. Just let me roll one more die, I know that I can win, I'm waiting for my real life to begin."

These were more than just lyrics to Brent; they were religion. So the prospect of his story changing with a call steeled him. These days it was texting that were the preferred mode of instant communication.

A lion sounded, and a rustle of reeds was heard as if one were right next to him. This was the sound that was set as the notification that alerted Brent that someone was sending him a message. Brent snapped his head down, grabbed his phone and looked at the screen. His face lit up. It was about Ordin. The subject of his show was there, and it was only a matter of time before they were taping a spectacle. It would be a spectacle that spoke volumes about a society that had forgotten one of the greatest commandments ever given: "...to treat our brothers as we would treat ourselves." What Brent had planned for the 100th episode was beyond a spectacle; it was cold-hearted hurt meant to break a man and make sure it was on camera.

This was the America that Brent lived in. Brent didn't really criticize it. He understood why it had become to be this way. Still, like so many people, he did feel a deep appreciation for the love God showed us by letting us be born in America. Yet at the same time lamenting the fact that America could so much more and be much closer to a nation that truly fit the creed of the god most of its inhabitants professed to believe in.

His cameramen were to enflame the situation until it was at a fervor pitch and then leap out as the sheriff swooped in to make the arrest. And hopefully, there would be a modicum of violence as the crew set the scene for the moment that would finally mark a substantial victory for Brent.

He was lost in the memories of other times when he had been at the precipice of success. There had been the leap to New York right after college to make significant films, only to find the work dry up after six months. Then there had been the move to Los Angeles where he had worked his way up the crew ladder, yet never landed the big break, as each show he had worked on never went beyond the first season. Each time the feeling of hope took over with an anticipation of waiting for his "real life to begin," and then the crush of disappointment followed when things did not work out. And each time he had asked himself, and asked God, "What have I done so wrong to not be deserving of success?" Was he such a horrible person that he did not deserve to savor victory at least once?

This time felt different. There was nothing that could stand in the way of being able to move forward and grasp the next opportunity that would come once he completed this milestone episode. The stage was set for the spectacle.

"Mr. Simmons, phone call for you on line 2!"

"Brent Simmons here."

"Hello, Mr. Simmons? This is Detective Johnson from the San Francisco police department assigned to the case investigating Ordin Aire. I need to inform you that I have not found this man to be the man you are looking for. I'm sorry that I have nothing further to report or give you that would aid in your station's broadcast show. Thank you for being supportive of the S.F.P.D."

Brent Simmons held the phone in his hand without a word, even after Detective Johnson ended the call after realizing Brent was not going to give a reply other than the "uh, huh."

The stage was now dark, dulled from existence.

CHAPTER NINETY-FOUR
Next Morning – The Graves

When Winslow opened his eyes, he found himself wrapped like a taco on the small brown couch that sat off the far side of J.H.'s hospital room. Alan had apparently come in that night after Winslow had fallen asleep, during his portion of "The Watch." Winslow and Gert had decided to take turns watching J.H.

Alan had given J.H. a positive prognosis of recovery with the recognition that J.H. had really given everyone a real scare. J.H. liked the way Alan spoke; it was very concise and reminded him of his grandfather, which made him feel oddly comforted, even though J.P. Graves (J.H.'s stone face grandfather, County Sheriff for over 30 years) was not a very tender man. He had had a way of speaking that made even the most resolute perp relax and become strangely disarmed. Alan possessed this same quality. It was usually said that he had the best bedside manner that anyone had seen.

Alan had requested that J.H. be kept overnight for further observation. Winslow had decided that he would take the first overnight and if need be Gert, could take the second. Winslow was barely unwrapped from his taco shell when J.H. called him over to the bed. Winslow looked at him. "It was true," he thought, "people do look smaller when they're sick."

"Winslow, boy, come over and talk a bit," J.H. said. It was the softest he had ever spoken to him. "Winslow, I been thinking 'bout something while I've been lying here watching you sleep last night. Yeesh, you sure are a lousy watchman, heh heh. But that wasn't what I wanted to tell you. Boy. Whinni, well hell, I probably shouldn't have nicknamed you that. It's probably that that started you on the path to being soft like you are, but that's not what I was thinking. Winslow, I'm a lot like my grandfather. I'm mean, fair and straight to it. I used to think that was the best way to get things done, so like my grandfather, I became mean, straight, and up to now, well, up 'til now I thought I had been fair."

"I was lying in the still quietness of the night, and it seemed like everyone had left the hospital, and it was just me here. I mean, I didn't even see you lying there, not ten feet in front of me. And I tell you, it was so dark that I couldn't even see you. I thought I heard a voice whispering, "Indifference alone," as if it wanted me to turn away and let go. And I thought that my meds might be off, but no, that wasn't it, Winslow. No, that wasn't it at all."

J.H. continued solemnly. "See, there was cold in the air, and it didn't have no weather to it. It was like the darkness was a living thing that envelopes you and wraps you in it. I felt afraid of it, and it seemed to be forcing its way onto me. I could tell it felt it had dominion over me. It was in the fear of that moment, a fear that nothing I wanted would ever make it through the heaviness of that darkness. Then I saw a pinhole of light as if it was miles away, but I could see how small it was. Remarkable! Then it grew, Winslow, and amidst that cold, it grew and the voice that I thought I heard whispered, 'Indifference alone;' was saying 'in difference love,' not as if the -voice wanted me to turn away, but as if answering for me. How? How do I love? Love my wife, love myself, and how do I love my son?"

"The question rose in my heart, and the voice grew with the light until the room was bathed in a light that would have burned right through my best pair of road shades. But it was warming, and my eyes saw every ounce of light. As the light grew, so did the voice, and I thought that I should cry out "I did" and the voice said, "Go," and the darkness shrank. No effort was needed, no strength. No attempt to convince the darkness or wage war against it. It was like the simple command go was a sword. I started to cry and then it was gone, but not gone. It's still here in my head."

"So what I'm saying Winslow, is that I know you're different than I would have you. I know my idea of a man caused you a lot of pain, and it caused your mother more than pain. That woman loves you from a place that has to be so deep it could transcend the bonds of blood and go deeper to find a soul love. She said once that your soul in her presence made her life light. I thought she was just being a daffy woman. I can now see what she meant. I could have spent an eternity in the presence of that voice."

"Winslow, she loves you that much and I haven't done nothing but run you away from each other, because you were different in my own eyes. Now I have to do what my father, your grandfather, could not and would not ever do. I'm going to say I am sorry. I'm so sorry, Winslow. I'm sorry I never saw you as the son I wanted, only the boy I had. It occurred to me that when I needed someone to just be strong, you walked into this room and put away all the hurt and just gave strength. That is what my father, a man, would have done. At that moment I knew that who my boy loves has nothing to do with him being the man I want him to be. You are my son."

With that, Winslow, heart pounding, eyes tearing, a lifetime of waiting to be good enough to be J.H.'s son, found a resolution. Winslow bent over and kissed his father on the head. Gertrude was waking and saw her son draw back from placing the kiss on his father's head and assumed the worst, that J.H. had passed and that Winslow was being dutiful and saying good-bye. When she saw the wide, closed mouth smile, stretch across J.H.'s face she didn't seem to be able to make sense of it.

Alan came into the room just then to do his morning rounds. Gertrude, seeing Alan in the room with J.H. and Winslow, at first got a start but then flashed back to when she would make cookies for the boys in her kitchen. There was a bliss then that Gertrude had longed for. There was an ease in the room that said, in a subtle and private way, that whatever storm that had been there for all these years raining hurt and obscuring the sunshine of this family's potential with clouds had lifted. The clouds had parted, and the warm sun was filling the room. In her heart, there was a stillness, like casting off the dock in a small boat and enduring the rocking and rolling and finally getting to the stillness of being upon something floating effortlessly, like preparing to sit still and fish.

Alan spoke up and said, "Good news, gang. J.H., you're clear to go home. There is a slight stipulation, though. You'll need to be monitored thoroughly for a month or so, so Gert, Mrs. Graves, you and J.H. will have to talk through this pain chart and a few other tests I will teach you how to do. His glance at her was absolutely telling. It said that he had known, whether through sheer intuition or by Whini's telling of his parents' less than a beautiful relationship, it said, in this way, you will re-discover each other, and there will be moments of compromise and tenderness. Gert simply looked over J.H. and smiled. J.H. had a glint in his eye that said his heart was racing again for her after all these long years.

Winslow looked up at Alan. No words were really needed. Alan was glad to see that Winslow yearned to have the opportunity to re-bond with his father again. "Winslow, why don't you accompany your parents' home? Take the week off. I will contact your school and your internship for you to let them know you need one week away for family medical reasons."

Winslow looked towards Gert and J.H. and saw the most welcoming smile and assuring nod. "Yes, I think I will, as long as Mom and Dad can handle having me along for the ride," Winslow replied with a smile and joy in his voice.

J.H. jovially replied, "Well, why the hell not? The more, the merrier!"

Alan beckoned for Winslow to come over and pecked him on the cheek. Gert quickly looked over to see J.H.'s reaction, and much too her surprise, he gave only a curt smile and slight squint, then muttered to Gert, "What, it's not like I don't work in San Francisco," to which they all laughed. As Gert signed all the release papers, J.H. got dressed.

Alan wheeled J.H. outside to the curb while Gert retrieved the car. Gert got out of the car to get J.H., walking him to the car with her hand around J.H.'s waist and his around her waist. Winslow had lagged behind to say a proper goodbye to Alan.

When they reached the car, Winslow started to open the back door to get in when he was stopped by J.H. "Whini, I mean, Winslow, I need you to drive. Take the keys, son and get us home. Don't make it too bumpy by going too fast as it scares your mother."

These were the words that every boy that ever had hoped to identify as and become a man needed to hear. To complete their masculine journey, a boy needed to be referred to early on as a man by the primary male in his life in turning over the reins to a perceived masculine act. He needed to be told that he was good enough and strong enough to be trusted to be a man in this world. And just like that, Winslow's heart opened to the idea that he had a family, and the miracle whispered itself to life.

Sitting in the back seat with Gert, J.H. felt serene and let himself feel light and at ease. The warm hand on his shoulder, even her smell, felt good to him. The whirling of the air through the slightly cracked open window had a certain rhythm to it. It added to the peacefulness. He would still attempt to accomplish his goal of becoming the chief of police, but it would just have to wait for a while. For now, he just wanted to let himself be bathed in this peace, this feeling of serenity. It was the most comfortable normal feeling he'd had in years, as if he could be fishing with God and God had just taken the reigns and that all would be okay.

CHAPTER NINETY-FIVE
Next Morning – Karen Miller

It was seven in the morning and Karen had not slept, half because she had too much anxiety, and a half because she did not want the previous day to be over. This was because they had said they would be there, that day she would become somebody. This was to be the day that the longing stopped, that the hurting from a deep place would come to an end.

Meanwhile, no one saw her, or even seemingly cared about her. No one knew the lonely nights she stayed awake staring at her TV, then at her mirror, and all with a heart so heavy that it could have had its own gravity. Her house felt particularly vacant today like it did not even recognize Karen. Karen felt just as empty inside wanting something to happen, anything, imagining that someone, anyone, would show up for any reason and just walk up or in and say, "hello." How she would take them in, care for them, be anything that they needed just as long as they would not leave her there alone.

In this state, somewhere between mania and melancholia, over and over she wished, night after night she wanted, minute after a minute she waited and always there was nothing. Not a yes, not a no, not a sound.

Yet so many times a still small voice had spoken to her, in subtle ways, but she was not able to hear. She was too caught up in her life. Sometimes it was the shame she felt over such trivial things as her weight, or her hair. Sometimes it was just a simple song that was in her head that she could not get out of her mind, so she sang it until it became boring, tired, or was replaced by another.

Whatever the reasons were, day after day she was too full of inner noise to listen. She felt alone and abandoned as a result and yet still believing good things were hers to claim and to have. Karen had forgotten the most important part of the equation; the need to listen, to do, and take the responsibility of her life not holding another to do so.

She never really thought of herself as a spiritually empty person. Sure, she made some questionable decisions sometimes that were not the most ethical, such as her recent one to turn "Ordy" in. But she erroneously believed that life should just be handed to her, regardless of who got hurt in return. Ordy's world was to be destroyed so that she (Karen) could receive. It was her turn.

However, she was here, and it was seven in the morning the next day, and they had not come. No one had even called to say they were not coming. "Unfair!" she screamed out loud. "It's my turn!" she shouted over and over. The tears were flowing from her eyes soaking her cheeks and even shirt collar. These were born of disappointment and failed hope rolled up at the same time. Karen opened the curtains and let the sunlight in. How could this not break her? All she wanted was to finally be seen by somebody, everybody, anybody, and yet just like before there was nobody.

The phone rang, and Karen almost dove for it. She picked it up, dropped it, and picked it up again. "Yes, yes, it's me, Karen, I'm here."

On the other side was a familiar voice. "What is wrong with you dear? You're frantic again. Did another one of your boyfriends leave you again, or did the dog run away?" It was the voice of her mother. She shook with the kind of anger that one usually feels for the head of human resources at work when they call you into their office only to tell you that your annual review turned up a few questionable things.

"Oh, mother, what do you want? I'm waiting for a very important call and can't be bothered." Karen knew she could blast her mother for calling before 10:00 am, which was their agreement. In this way, neither of them had to face any hostility until they had had their morning cup of tea. But Karen would not take the low hanging fruit this time, not this morning. She was waiting for a very important call. What she could not know was that on the other side of town, a decision had been made, and two lives were changed. But not Karen's, her life would go on as it had before, just as dreary, without meaning, change, or growth. Her decisions made it so.

There would not be a triumph of the spirit or redemptive moment. For her, there would only be more disappointment. Her body screamed, "RESCUE ME," don't just leave me here to die, and yet no sound came. She would not be rescued. She would be hung out to dry. Here was Karen Miller, a thirty-something, a bit chubby, somewhat simple, definitely lonely standing there with the phone to her ear. "Mother, I've got to go."

"Okay, dear, but call me when you wake properly. And try and do your makeup today."

"Bye, mother."

"Bye, dear."

Karen looked up at the clock. It was 8:15. It had been an hour and fifteen minutes since she realized that it wasn't going to happen today, that maybe nothing was going to happen today. Invisible again. Someone once said something about comfort and the devil you know. This meant that there was a sort of peace in the most restless of situations so long as it was a situation that one was familiar with, that pain could be endured if a person had already experienced it before. In this sense, people cannot be broken by it, only hurt in a familiar way.

As a result, Karen became calm, walked over to her couch, sat down and attempted to let it all go again, just as she had done so many times before.

CHAPTER NINETY-SIX
Fishing with God

"I wonder if this is what it's like to go fishing and almost catch something, only to have to start all over again?" Karen could imagine herself fishing with her mother. She'd be sitting in a boat, listening to her droning on about marriage and grandchildren as if she really wanted them or maybe she just wanted someone else to criticize.

Karen could imagine what it would be like fishing with the women from her neighborhood association. They would never help her feel included or part of the group, even if this was her day. All of their judgments and prejudices would preclude them from doing so. They would make her throw the line back in, exclaiming, "If you would just throw it in the right way, Karen, we could catch something and stop wasting our time out here on this godforsaken lake."

She imagined what it would be like fishing with her father. He's been in his sweater and bath shoes as she remembered him, seething at her because the fish were biting and her shaking in fear spooked them off. "Karen, stop making things worse," he would say. At which she would just cave in further in her shell.

She could imagine what it would be like fishing with one of the many men that just walked out on her. "Karen, the fish, are just not biting for you, at least not here. I'm going to go someplace else and fish without you if you don't mind. You do understand, don't you Karen? I mean, if they were biting things would be different, but they're just not biting, and I don't have that much time to find a fish, you know? Okay, I'm glad you understand. I'll see you around, okay."

Karen could imagine what it was like fishing with Cynthia Rudd. "You call this a fish? This is bait for a real fish. Just focus and try harder. Haven't you ever fished before? You have to be gentle. You're just like the fish. What would you like? What would make you take the bait? Think, Karen, think like a fish for goodness sake. Okay, let's try again. Ow! You pinched me with the hook. Just stop, stop and go home. This has been the most awful experiment I've ever been a part of. Please leave."

Then Karen could imagine what it would be like to be fishing with God, how he would say, "My daughter, your hands are perfect, your sight is perfect for fishing. They grip the pole the right way. You make a perfect fisherman. He would smile a broad smile at her, and she would feel warm and protected. She would feel loved, seen, heard, felt. The embrace of his eyes would confirm her, the touch of his hand as he instructed her on how to cast the line would validate her, saying, "You're good enough. You're woman enough, and you're human enough to be here."

Karen wouldn't need anything else. She would be home here. She would belong, be accepted, nurtured, honored, cherished, and wanted in a way her mother, father, or anyone had never wanted her before. Karen would be fishing with God, and everything would be alright.

If in the end we only end up with who we are, then there we are. Lonely, happy, tired, or energized. We cannot in and of ourselves control the universe. It's all by chance and happenstance that we fall into our place. The place where we belong. That is what some people believe that God has a plan for all people that he sits in contemplative watch over us, all of us, all the time. He designs and orders our steps. We are powerless and helpless to change His plan.

Then there are many who believe that God, whatever form one assigns to him/her/it, is nothing more than the mere creation of a man who cannot or will not think beyond the box. Regardless of the source of our life and sentience there exists a very real truth that free will is all about the freedom and ability to make your own choices given any circumstance and the inherent responsibility of such where no one person or entity could be assigned any portion thereof.

Then there are those people that believe God does exist as well as free will. God lays out the framework, a series of pathways and possibilities. People, his children, through their choices experience life and challenges with choice, consequences, and responsibility are able then to learn and grow or not. Every choice affecting another, a string of decisions, playing in a cosmic existence of life, sentience, and possibility. The possibility, the learning, and growth that comes from free will and the inherent responsibility being the greatest gift a loving God could give.

Karen was one who believed in that God was the master holding the strings that would determine her life. She believed like so many that we truly cannot in and of ourselves control the universe, it is all by chance and happenstance that people fall into their respective place, the place where they belong. Believing that God has a plan for us, that he sits in contemplative watch over us all of us, all the time, designing and ordering our steps, leaving us powerless and helpless to change this. Karen hoped that her God wanted her to have good things and loved her, but she was powerless to change her life. She felt that she would be kept in a constant state of wanting, needing, asking, just the way she felt right now.

Who are you most like? In your loneliest moments when you bow your head or hope against hope for those things you believe God wants us to have, when you cry out "where are you?" Are you 'Fishing with God'?

About the Authors

Several years ago we met through a mutual friend. Within two hours of talking, we knew we both wanted to work together in writing this novel. Both of us were from different backgrounds and experiences, yet we shared the same basic philosophies in life that created an instant connection and friendship.

Our work on this fiction novel was very much enjoyed, and we hope you enjoy reading it. We also hope that the novel also encourages thought and contemplation regarding the basic philosophies that underlay the characters, their stories, and the story break chapters.

Chris Gordon was born in Babylon N.Y. the son of an Artist father and mother who was a gospel singer, Chris developed a love for artistic expression, listening to his mother sing and watching his father create. He remembers writing song lyrics as early as 10 years old. His love for written prose arose from a tenuous relationship with his 10th grade English teacher Mr. Stallman. I can freely admit that it was his insistence of phonetic understanding that he derived his current style of verbiage. He also accredits a large part of his literal style and understanding to Jacob Liptkin, the great American sculptor, who's works don the walkway of Harvard University and the Smithsonian, the time he spent in his tutelage shaped and impressed on him the art of storytelling. When he entered the professional world, he worked as a Stock Broker throughout the 90's, before becoming a Financial Consultant for Merrill Lynch and then serving as District Manager of Orange County for American Express Financial Advisors. Chris worked in high finance for several years, before he obtained his first job in film finance in, September of 2003. Today, he is a father and has become a seasoned feature film, documentary and television production and business development professional.

Shane Hutchison was born in Idaho Falls, Idaho at which he lived for a whole 10 weeks before moving on to Hartford, CT. From birth to present Shane has lived at over 90 addresses across 16 states including a short 6 months in France, proving to be a modern-day nomad with the drive to have as many life and people experiences as he can.

Shane was raised in "Mormon" (Church of Jesus Christ of Latter-Day Saints) religion where he gained the foundation of his own faith. A few years after serving an honorable gospel preaching mission for the Mormon church, Shane found himself no longer finding continuous expansive growth for himself in any religion. Later, at the age of 28, Shane accepted his same-sex attractions.

Shane completed his undergraduate studies in Psychology and Finance. He worked in social services field during college and until three years after. After a short 6-month break from this field, he got his foot in the door in the Information Technology field where he has continued his career to this day.

Shane has always enjoyed reading and writing since early schooldays. A very patient instructor at Goucher College was instrumental in helping him hone his skills from writing to the 5% to writing for the greater population, expanding the potential reach of his voice.

89025347R00186

Made in the USA
Columbia, SC
16 February 2018